MISSION PROMISCUOUS

LALA MONTGOMERY

You're such a good
girl, Brandy!

Lala
Montgomery

Cover Design by 100 Covers
Edited by Truly Trendy PR
Formatted by Vicki Nicolson Branding

I want to dedicate this book to me! Seriously, thank you for following your dreams and going for it.
No matter what, you did it! Good girl.
Also, to the little boy that said, 'eww' when I read aloud my first ever short story, Blood Warriors, thank you! I love horror, but romance is where it's at.
And, to Jason Momoa, thank you for being you.

CHAPTER ONE

GEMMA

Goodness. My eyes greedily scan a set of sculpted shoulders and tan skin. Seeing him like this is my favorite part of the day. I slide my sunglasses on so I can ogle him in peace. He's already worked up a sheen of perspiration from jogging down the beach, and his golden skin is glistening deliciously. It's like he's moving in slow motion to allow me time to see and memorize every muscle, every ripple of his body. What's that old show called? Oh yeah. I'm having my very own Baywatch moment. My eyes wander over his body from top to bottom. His dark wavy hair is slightly too long and flops and blows in the wind. He's tall, with a broad chest, which I've recently discovered I'm really into. He's, of course, not wearing a shirt. He must have heard my silent pleas to take it off, and I can see his muscles coil with his every movement. As he turns toward me, I study his chest and his glorious abs. Is that an 8-pack? I follow the taper of his waist, and I see that delicious 'V' as it disappears into his low-riding swim trunks. If he really could hear my pleas to take it off, now would be a good time.

He grabs his water bottle, and I watch him lick his full lips and take a drink. I sigh as I imagine those lips on me. I'd do anything to feel the soft caress of his lips against mine, his tongue sweeping through my mouth.

He looks up in my direction and thank goodness for my sunglasses. It's like he can feel the heat of my pervy gaze, so I hold my breath and pretend to read my book. I look up again, peeking over the top of my sunglasses, and exhale as I see him running into the water. If I thought his body looked good, slick with sweat, I can't even describe how delectable he looks soaking wet. He trudges out of the ocean, pushing his hair back as rivulets of water trail tantalizingly down his chest and abs, his blue shorts plastered to his body. I inhale sharply. It's like I can see the entire outline of his di-

I'm snapped out of my delightful stroll down memory lane by my vibrating phone. I flip it over to check the screen, and I see a picture of the gorgeous face of one of my best friends, Mia. She demanded I use this pic to show guys I meet that I think she may be interested in. I'm linking up with her and our other bestie, Sasha, for some retail therapy in about an hour.

"Hey, doll!" I sing-song as I answer. "I'm deciding

what to wear, and I'm leaving in 30 minutes. I'm right on schedule. I promise." Sadly, I'm that annoying friend who is always late. In my mind, everything takes just five minutes, and too often, I'm wrong.

She laughs. "Of course you are. I'm ready to go, but I thought I'd have a cocktail first." She takes a big, noisy drink of what I'm sure is a margarita. I blanch. I've had a few bad experiences with tequila, usually involving dancing on and falling off bars, stained clothing, and random bruises, so I try to avoid the stuff. Mia is the opposite; she loves it and can drink it from day to night.

"Wow, you couldn't even wait for us?"

"You'll just have to catch up."

"I'll try my best. After the week I've had, a little debauchery is very necessary."

"Perfect! I'll see you soon. Bye, doll!" and she ends the call.

I quickly dress in my favorite sundress, put my long, dark curly hair up, grab my jacket and purse and head out to meet the girls.

My friends, Mia and Sasha, are my very own devil and angel on my shoulders. They are both sweet as pie, but Mia has always been that friend who tells you to take that extra shot or go home with that hot guy. Meanwhile, Sasha reminds me to drink more water and to send her pics of the IDs from any guys that I meet. They are my soul mates, and I couldn't imagine my life without them. We've been best friends since birth, and I don't think I'd be who I am today without them. I walk into one of our favorite shops and see Sasha and Mia are already browsing. "Hi, friends! Find anything for tonight?"

Sasha gives me a big smile as she tugs me into an embrace. Mia holds up a little black dress "Um, is that a shirt? That won't even cover my ass." Mia laughs and says, "That's why we get lasered and wear pretty panties...or no panties at all."

Sasha and I burst out laughing. That's our Mia. "Yes, I suffered through lasering away all my hair so that I could confidently wear a shirt as a dress. I made such a sound investment."

Mia winks at me. "Exactly!"

Sasha pulls me over to look at another rack of dresses. "These are more your style." I shoot her a grateful smile and start flipping through the rack of A-line dresses and patterned skirts.

An hour later, we're all trying on our finds and come out of the dressing room for everyone's opinion. Both my friends are gorgeous. Mia is tall, with cascading blond hair, while Sasha is the shortest of the three of us and a striking brunette. Our styles could not be more different; Mia is always on trend and can be a bit edgy, while Sasha has a demure style that is enviable. I like to dress more for my mood, and I love the Chicago street style. I'm sometimes sexy, sometimes sweet, and I can't say no to patterns or polka dots.

Mia struts out in a sexy red dress that's low-cut in the front and backless. I try to give her a little wolf whistle, but nothing comes out. Thankfully, she gets the drift.

Sasha asks, "So when would you wear that? For date night or girls' night?" Mia is a stylist and beauty and fashion blogger, and she prides herself on picking just the right look for any occasion. Mia considers her question. "This is a vacation look. It could be worn on a night out with friends or with bae." I nod in agreement. "Yes, I can see it working in Miami, for sure."

Next, they critique my look. I've found a gorgeous yellow halter dress. It has a bit of a baby doll look to it, but it has a deep neckline and stops mid-thigh. So sexy and cute. I love it because it showcases my toned arms, but it hides any possible problem areas around my stomach and butt. They both ooh and ahh and give me a thumbs up. This baby is coming home with me; I love it. I feel pretty, and the bright color looks amazing against my brown skin.

Sasha has found some gorgeous gold metallic shorts and a sexy sheer black top. "I love those shorts. You have to buy them so I can borrow them," I tell her. "Same," Mia adds, "but we won't look as good as you do in them."

After changing back into our own clothes, we head to the register with our goodies. This was an expensive shopping trip, but we work hard, and I think we deserve it. We head out for a late lunch and to game plan for tonight. We find a restaurant with a cute patio, and as soon as we're seated, I order a bottle of champagne.

Sasha raises her eyebrows. "A bottle for lunch?"

Mia is all for it. "Don't question her; just enjoy it."

I laugh. "I've been in a mood lately. Today I'm all about treating myself," I say, moving my neck back and forth with attitude. They nod in agreement.

My boyfriend and I broke up six months ago, and although I know it was for the best, I have not been able to pull myself out of this funk. We were together for two years after being friends throughout college. It was an easy relationship we just kind of fell into. We liked the same things, laughed at each other's jokes, and were comfortable together.

"Ok." Mia claps her hands. "That's it; tonight's the night we are getting you back on that horse."

Sasha adds, "I hate to agree with her, what with that gross imagery, but I think it's time. And I don't mean sex..."

Mia jumps in. "*I* do! I want you to fuck the shit out of some hot guy...or girl, tonight. I think it'll be a nice palate cleanser. Then you can be ready to find your Mr. Right. Even though I really think you should be looking for a few Mr. Right Nows."

I take all of this in and nod. "Ok, I can't say I'm going to fuck the shit out of some guy or girl, but I'm definitely going to make out with a few guys and see what happens."

"We'll take it," Mia says. We clink our glasses of champagne together, excited for the new plan for tonight.

Later, we end up at our usual Saturday nightspot,

Vinyl. We've loved this place since the first time we walked in years ago. It's a nice sized multilevel club with dark hardwood floors and booths lining the walls. I consider it more of a music venue, with its huge stage front and center and a DJ booth on a raised platform. A few stairs lead you down to the dancefloor and stage area. We've attended some epic concerts here. Some of my favorite memories are of us swaying with the crowd, singing along to whoever's on stage.

We slowly weave through the crowd to get to the bar. I've lost my buzz from lunch, so copious amounts of alcohol are very necessary right now. Our favorite bartender, Scottie, is working the bar, and he knows our drinks of choice. Sasha's vodka gimlet, Mia's margarita on the rocks, and my prosecco. Mia leans in to request three melon ball shots as well. We shoot those quickly before we take our drinks and do a lap around the club.

As we walk around, several guys pique my interest. I can't tell if I'm horny, my buzz is back, or if they really are as appealing as I think. I've always considered myself a sexual person, or at least I've always wanted to be. I've only had three serious boyfriends in my life, and for the most part, I have not really ventured outside of those relationships for sex. I meet a guy, I'm initially attracted to him, but for me, it is all about that first kiss. If the first kiss doesn't make me swoony and wet, then I know we won't be going any further. What's the point? If we don't have chemistry during a kiss, I can guess how the sex will be.

Maybe I grew up reading too many romance novels and my expectations are too high. I don't know.

The one time I went against my kissing rule, proved me right. There was this hot guy my sophomore year of college. We flirted for weeks, and he was what you would consider a catch. Everyone told me to hit that, or they would. After hanging out one night, we went to say goodbye, and he finally kissed me. I remember being extremely nervous and deciding to just go with it and unfortunately...it was dry...the kiss and my pussy. I chalked it all up to nerves and Mia and Sasha talked me into giving him another chance. Ok, they really didn't have to talk me into it because he was funny, sweet, so handsome, and tall – all of my favorite things.

A few days later, I'd worked myself up to going to his place 'to watch a movie.' We're in his bedroom, and we started kissing and again, nothing. It was like a desert down there. Tumbleweeds were aplenty. We're kissing and kissing, and I felt his erection start to dig into my hip. I will say I was impressed. It was large, throbbing, and so hard that I finally started to feel some arousal. I laughed to myself, giddy, as I thought, *I'm finally going to get dicked down, and the bonus is the guy is super hot.*

Feeling confident, I stroked his dick through his sweatpants. He moaned and thrust into my hand. I kissed him again as he started to take off his clothes. I did the same as I was so proud to show off my completely waxed vagina for the first time.

Completely naked, we lay there, kissing for several minutes. When he began kissing down my neck, it made me recoil a little. Again, at the time, I chalked it up as nerves and tried to stay in the moment. I thought I really wanted it. He continued to kiss down my neck to my breasts, leaving a trail of saliva, and I was immediately grossed out. I continued to lie there as he kissed and licked down my body until I couldn't take it anymore; I blurted, "I'm so hot. Would you get me some water?" And that was the end of that. Now, I know to listen to my body. Lesson learned.

Today I stand by my kissing rule. This is why my friends call me a kissing slut, but I'm not mad at them. You must kiss a lot of frogs to find your forever, or whatever the saying is. Drunk kissing is my favorite; I love feeling like the room is spinning and I'm being swept away. I'm on the hunt for that feeling tonight, so let's have some fun.

A Nelly Furtado throwback starts to play, and I look at my friends, "Ladies, this is a sign. I'm ready to be a promiscuous girl!" They squeal and laugh.

"Fucking finally," Mia says.

We chug our drinks before Sasha leads us onto the dance floor. We laugh and yell-sing as we dance together. Our energy appears to pull people to the dance floor because before we know it, men are circling us like sharks. Well, this is it. I eyeball the one closest to me. He's cute, a little short for my taste, but he'll do. I don't move away as he presses into my body. His hands immediately go to my waist, before trailing over my hips and down my thighs, and I sigh. Yes, this is just what I needed.

Elijah

I chuckle to myself as I shake my head. The airport demons came out to play today. That was the flight from hell. Everything that could go wrong did. Delayed flight. *Check.* A second delay. *Check.* Overbooked flight. *Check.* Ruined suit due to some snot-nosed kid. *Check.* Turbulence. *Check.* Lost luggage. *Check fucking mate.*

It's all so terrible; I have to suppress another chuckle. I have no energy to argue or complain, so I readily fill out forms and sign what I need to so I can get home to my own bed. I've been traveling for the last week, and I could use some downtime. I feel the gaze of the airline staff member sweep over me again and sigh. When I glance up, she licks her lips in invitation. *No thanks.*

I thank her for her help and take long strides through the airport to the exit, and I spot my driver immediately. A driver is one of the few luxuries I allow myself to enjoy. Chicago traffic, the cars, bikes, buses, and pedestrians, can be too much. Having a driver lets me relax, get some work done, and not stress about hitting people that are too stupid to obey walk, don't walk signs.

"Thanks for picking me up, Thomas."

He nods as I jump in the back of the SUV. I place

my carry-on and laptop bag beside me and lay my head back against the headrest. Exhaustion is nipping at my heels but also a bone-deep weariness. Don't get me wrong; I'm happy to be home. But what did I come home to? I'm going to walk into my cold, empty place and do what? The stress, long days, later nights, and blood I've spilled to get here, to find such success with my real estate development company have been worth it. But that tinge of loneliness, of something missing, punching me in the gut from time to time.

I rub a harsh hand down my face. I need a distraction; a pick me up. I guess I could make a few calls, let everyone know I'm back in town. I wince, but I pull my phone out and scroll my contacts.

Gemma

It's been two weeks since I started Mission Promiscuous, aka Operation Summer Slut, and I've been on three dates and made out with four other guys. Not too shabby. The girls are proud of me, hell, I'm proud of me, but it is a lot. I haven't gotten to the real promiscuous part yet; the guys have all been handsome but no major sparks. My last two dates went well enough, but I guess I'm still trying to figure out what I like... well, I know what I like; I just can't find it. Each of the guys was cute, and we had fun, but I didn't make it to a second date or base with any of them. So tonight, we're trying a new place, and hopefully, we'll find some new meat.

11

As we ride the elevator up to Nevaeh, a new to us rooftop bar, I scan the city's skyline. I love Chicago. Growing up in Indiana, in my sheltered little suburb, the bustling of the city called my name. Well, the big city and the proximity to my family made Chicago ideal. A few hours away by car made Chicago a perfect getaway growing up. My parents brought us here often for shows, concerts, and deep-dish pizza. Moving here after college has been everything I hoped it would be. I love the mix of people and cultures, the delicious food, public transportation, and shopping. The winters are a lot harsher here than what I'm used to in Indiana, but it's worth it.

We arrive at the top floor and step out onto the rooftop. I feel a few butterflies in my stomach. I already have a feeling that tonight is going to be one for the books. I'm wearing a hot pink fit and flare dress that has thin straps of material crisscrossing my back, paired with a teal clutch and strappy heels. My long curly hair is loose and extra wild tonight, making me feel that much sexier. I scan the rooftop, and I'm impressed by the spectacle of the white-on-white decor; Nevaeh, heaven spelled backwards, makes sense now. I see two beautifully lit white bars at either end of the venue. There's a DJ and dance floor in the corner with strings of fairy lights overhead, and at the other end sits an array of white couches and tables. The real draw is the beautiful Chicago skyline twinkling all around us. This just may be my new favorite place. The DJ is already playing, people are dancing, and I can feel the bass in my body, but we immediately head to the bar. Mia promptly orders three shots of tequila. Sasha's eyes flick to me and then back to Mia. Mia just smiles innocently. Ok, it looks like it's going to be one of those nights. We grab our shots and limes, clink our glasses together, and down our shots. I cringe and shiver. Ugh, I hate tequila.

I try to sneak and order a glass of water between drinks, but both Mia and Sasha are watching me. I can do this. I take a deep breath, hold my nose, and take my third shot of tequila. It's so gross. "That's it for me. Cocktails only for the rest of the night." Sasha nods in agreement. Mia also agrees easily, and I'm immediately terrified. She turns to the bartender and orders three margaritas, with an extra shot of tequila.

I cackle. "Ok, bitch!"

We take our margs and begin to walk around. This place is clearly where the beautiful people hang out. The women are all tall and gorgeous. My head is on a swivel as I take in the equally handsome men. Why is this our first time here? My eyes bulge as a sexy group of men saunters by us. Their sexiness reminds my body just how long it has been since I've had sex; I won't even consider how long it's been since I've orgasmed in someone else's company. Tonight, I'm going to change that...maybe, I reconsider as we head out onto the dancefloor.

I need a break and make the sign for a drink to the girls. They nod and keep dancing. I head over to a quieter spot to take in the skyline, and I see flashes of lightning in the distance. I take a few deep breaths and let the breeze blow through my hair and cool my flushed skin. I freshen up my lip gloss and finally make my way to the bar to order another round of margaritas. I've officially been pulled to the dark side.

I walk back to the dance floor, but I don't see the girls. I keep scanning and spot them talking to a group of guys near the couches. I walk over to them, trying not to spill our drinks.

"Help," I laugh as I get closer to them. They immediately grab their drinks and wiggle their eyebrows at me. I turn to look at the three guys they are talking to and holy fuck balls, they are all smoking hot.

Sasha introduces me. "This is our friend, Gem." The men all say hello, and the sandy blond one offers me a seat on the couch, next to my girls. Sasha points to the guys. "This is Drew, Xander, and Ty." I smile at each of them and nod. I leave my beautiful friends alone for 10 minutes, and this is what they are up to? Up to their twats in hot guys.

Mia nods toward the guys. "Drew is a lawyer, Xander is an investment banker, and Ty is a real estate developer."

She gives me wide eyes. Yes, I see the unicorns in front of us.

Ty is the tallest, with gorgeous green eyes and skin that reminds me of warm caramel. Xander has mischievous dark eyes, messy black hair, and a few days of stubble on his face. And Drew is clean-cut with sandy blond hair and blue eyes.

These guys are all handsome, but none of them do it for me.

"Hey, guys," a fourth voice says from behind us. Something about his voice feels familiar; it's deep and warm, sensual, but I can't place it. I feel goosebumps rise on my skin.

Xander stands and says, "Ladies, this is our friend, Eli."

I watch him walk around the couch and he does the whole guy handshake hug thing, then turns towards us. Mia and Sasha both stand to give him a kiss on the cheek, but I'm rooted to my seat.

I feel like I can't breathe, and I have to remind myself to breathe in, breathe out. He finally makes his way down to me. I look up slowly, and his brilliant blue eyes meet my brown. We stare at each other for a few moments, and there's a flicker of something in his beautiful eyes. I take in his familiar dark hair, strong jaw, and full lips.

"Hi, Elijah."

Holy. Fucking. Shit.

CHAPTER TWO

ELIJAH

I try to hide my surprise as I stare into her liquid brown eyes. How does she know my name? She seems vaguely familiar, but I can't quite pinpoint where I know her from. My eyes roam over her, taking in her smooth, golden-brown skin, pouty lips, and the dark curls flowing down her back.

"Hi. And you are?" I ask as I hold out my hand for her to shake. She hesitates before placing her small hand in mine, and I instantly look down at our joined hands and frown. Something akin to a current of electricity flows between us. I look at her again and she stands but I don't step back.

"I'm Gemma."

Yes, a gem, perfectly precious. I look down at our hands again, still touching. Warmth swirls between us then, and I feel my cock twitch in appreciation. This woman is stunning, and I'm instantly glad I decided to come out tonight.

This is our usual Saturday night spot, same table, same bottles. We are creatures of habit, but you can't beat the vibe, the city views, or the women. But I've never seen her here before; I surely would have remembered.

I was in the mood to stay home for a quiet night, maybe get a workout in, but the guys weren't having it. Especially after I skipped dinner. If they weren't already a few drinks deep, I'm sure they would have come by my place to *make me* come out. Instead, they resorted to incessant calls and texts until I relented.

I pull her away from the others to speak to her privately. She seems nervous, so maybe this will help.

"So, Gemma. How is it that you know these guys?"

She exhales a deep breath and looks around. "Actually, I don't. We just met them tonight."

Again, I'm glad I came. We walk over to a high-top table, and she finally pulls her hand from mine.

I continue to stare at her, and she avoids my gaze. She looks to be a few years younger than me, which I'm typically not into, but there's something about her.

"Gemma, you feel familiar to me. Have we met before?"

She looks at me and hits me with a breathtaking smile. *Fuck.*

"Actually, we have met before, years ago. You know my older brother, Greyson. Greyson Davis."

"Wow, Greyson. Yeah, I haven't spoken to him in forever." I scan her face again. "Wait, I remember you!

You were always reading on the beach." Memories fly at me as I recall the vacation I met Greyson.

She laughs. "Yep, that was me. I always had my nose in a book."

"I can't believe I ran into you again, after so many years."

Ten years ago, to be exact. I was about seventeen during that trip, and I think Greyson mentioned she was thirteen or fourteen. I don't remember much about her, aside from her reading. Back then, I was too distracted by women, young or old, it didn't matter, to hang out with a kid. That trip and that summer were one of the best times of my life.

I look her up and down again. She has grown up. I'm absolutely going to catch up with my old buddy, Greyson.

We continue to stare at each other. There is chemistry here, but fuck, she's my friend's little sister. I shake that thought from my head.

"What are you doing here in Chicago? How do you like the big city life?"

She looks up at the stars and exclaims, "I love it here!" She giggles, and it just may be the sweetest sound I've ever heard.

"I moved here after college, and I have my dream job as a junior editor with a publishing company. Yes, my nose remains in books."

"You're doing what you love. Getting paid is just a bonus. At least that's how I feel anyway."

She nods and takes a long sip of her drink, averting

her gaze. She's still nervous, which is kind of cute. Her friends approach us, and their eyes are jumping back and forth between us. I take that as my cue to exit.

"It was nice to meet you both, and it was great seeing you again, Gemma."

I smile and head over to the guys. Fuck. I need a drink, and then I need to talk to Greyson and find out what the fuck is going on with his little sister.

Gemma

I drag the girls to the restroom. Of course, there's a line, but this gives me a chance to fill them in and chug our margaritas.

Once we're in line and the guys can't see us, Mia puts her hand on my shoulder. "Was that your Elijah? Your wet dream? The guy that you've creamed your panties over for years?"

I look down and take a deep breath to try to steady myself. I'm not sure if it's the tequila or my hormones doing me in right now. "Yep, that's him. Fucking gorgeous, right?"

"Hell yeah, he's beautiful. Did he remember you? Is he single?" Mia is so excited.

"I didn't have a chance to ask him, but he did remember me. Or he remembered that Greyson has a little sister."

Sasha hugs me and swoons. "You crushed on him for years, and you run into him tonight!"

"Yes, right when you're all mission promiscuous,

this is fucking fate!" Mia interrupts.

I cover my face with my hands. This seems too good to be true. Is this fate or is the universe fucking with me?

We finally make it to the restroom. I check my hair and makeup while I wait for the girls. I'm feeling a little jittery. I am shocked beyond belief that I randomly ran into Elijah tonight and he is still as blazing hot as I remember. I would guess he's about 6'3", and he has gorgeous olive skin, blue eyes, and dark hair. It's a little shorter than I remember, but it adds to his overall appeal. I remember him being lean and sculpted - a beautiful work of art to teenage me. Now, his shoulders are broader, chest chiseled. Even through his clothes, I can tell his body possesses that demigod-like perfection. I'm a sucker for hands. His were large and masculine, with a hint of roughness that I imagine would feel amazing as he stroked my body, my clit. Shit, my panties are wet. They have been since I heard his voice. This has never happened to me before. I've never been this affected by someone, and I feel unsteady, like I may hyperventilate.

The girls are finally ready, and we head out of the restroom. My girls know I'm freaking the fuck out and take me straight to the dance floor. A new song starts to play, and I scream and throw my arms in the air. *Closer*, by Nine Inch Nails. I have loved this song ever since I saw Joe Manganiello dance to it in *Magic Mike XXL*. He was so sexy, and since then, I've wanted to fuck to this song.

The tequila has hit, and I feel my inhibitions drift away, and I just dance; eyes closed and arms raised above my head. I feel myself getting wild, my inner dirty girl peeking out, ready to play. I open my eyes, and I find Elijah watching me. The heat of his stare almost drowns out the sound of the music and all the people around us. He's sitting with his friends, sipping a drink. He doesn't look away, he holds my gaze...and he has that look, you know the one. He cocks his head to the side, licks his lips, and raises his drink, giving me a little salute.

Fuck, is he for real? That gesture further ignites the fire in me, as I continue to dance. I close my eyes a few times, but I like watching him watch me. My dress starts to rise up my thighs. I can sense him taking notice right before he leans forward. My body can feel his heat all the way across this dance floor. The song takes me over and I whip my hair around, channeling a stripper and a porn star all wrapped up in one.

I can no longer control my body, and I turn around to give him a better view. I writhe, gliding my hands down the side of my breasts, down my hips, imagining they are his hands. I imagine his body grinding against mine. I look over my shoulder. He's still there, staring, and so are his friends.

Elijah

I don't care that she caught me staring. I'm mesmerized by this beautiful, wild woman.

I already texted Greyson, letting him know I just ran into her. Using that, what a small world, crap to try to get some information about her. He told me she had been in the city for a couple years and she's single. He said he was a little worried about her since he hadn't seen her in a while. Since I'm such a great guy, I volunteered my services to check on her for him and see how she's acclimated to the city. Of course, he was on board. Could this be any more perfect? I laugh at my Chandler Bing moment.

I continue to watch her, heat thrumming through my body. I feel my hand clench into a fist. I can almost feel her hair wrapped around my hand as I grip it, holding her head just where I want it. The guys finally notice my staring and pull me out of my dark fantasy.

"What do we have here? Is someone smitten?" Xander asks, slapping me hard on the back.

Drew snorts. "It certainly looks like it."

"Calm down, boys. She is the little sister of a friend. Do you remember my buddy, Greyson? We met about ten years ago when we were on vacation at the same resort. She was just a kid back then. Apparently, she moved to the city a couple years ago."

"Milk has definitely done her body good," Xander chimes in.

We all laugh. "Shut up, asshole." But I have to agree with him. She has such a soft feminine body, which I prefer. She's toned but soft and lush in all the right places. I get a flash of my hardness pressing into her softness. *Fuck.* I quickly blink that shit away.

The song changes to *Feel It* by Jacquees. She must love this song because she screams again, and I can see her singing the words. She throws her head back and starts to sway and wind her body to the sexy song, that sexy hair swaying back and forth, begging to be pulled.

"Her friends are smoking, too," Ty adds. We all nod as we watch them burn up the dance floor. They've drawn quite the crowd. I watch several guys working themselves up to try to dance with the girls, just circling them waiting for their chance. They are a striking trio, but she shines brightest.

"So, how did you meet them?" I ask.

"We heard the blond, Mia, talking about needing a shot of tequila as they were heading to the bar. So, of course, big mouth Xander offered them a drink." Drew gestures to our table and bottles of Don Julio, Tito's, and Dom Perignon.

"Your girl came over to join them right before you showed up," Ty adds.

"She's not my girl. Relax." They just ignore me.

"Imagine if you stayed home tonight and she went home with me!" Xander barks.

"Fuck off. No one is going home with anyone tonight." The thought of her going home with him leaves a bad taste in my mouth, and I immediately take another sip of my drink.

I watch as some fuckwad finally grows the balls to try to dance with her.

He just starts to grind on her ass and my jaw clenches.

She shakes her head no, removes his hands from her hips, steps away and continues to dance with her friends. He's still behind her, not taking the hint that she's not interested. Fuck this.

One second I'm on our couch and the next, I'm striding onto the dance floor. This fucking guy needs his ass kicked. He goes to press himself against her again and I step in.

"Fuck off." My voice is low, and I can't remember the last time I was this heated. He looks up at me and shrivels immediately.

"My bad, bro." And scurries off.

A smiling Gemma looks up at me and throws her arms around my neck, pulling me into a hug. "Thank you. I was just about to kick his ass, but you saved me the trouble." I laugh with her and close my eyes for a beat. Her warmth is so unexpected. Her hands drop to my chest. We've come to a standstill. We're not dancing, just staring. She's looking up at me, and I feel like she can see right through me. I feel my friends join us, and they break the spell.

She goes to remove her hands just as I hear, *Shine Bright Like a Diamond*. I love this song. How fitting to dance to *Diamonds* when I'm with this sparkling little gem.

I hold her hands to my chest. "Dance with me."

Gemma

Finding an angry Elijah behind me, scaring off

some tool, may have been the sexiest thing I've ever seen. He stepped in to protect me, all possessive like. Was he really jealous of some rando trying to dance with me? This has never happened to me before. Honestly, I think I like the whole jealous, possessive thing.

With all these things flying through my head, I just reach up and hug him. Big mistake. Huge. His big body is solid against mine. I feel his warmth, his fire, radiating through me. The cherry on top of this delicious beefcake...he smells amazing. I smell clean skin, the smallest hint of sandalwood, and his pheromones. Can you even smell pheromones? Doesn't matter, I'm now addicted to his smell. I just want to lick him.

I barely remember saying something idiotic. The feel of his hard body against mine, under my hands, is overwhelming. As our eyes lock, it feels like I forgot how to breathe. Over the bass of the music, I think I can hear the rapid beating of my heart.

Then he says, "Dance with me," my eyes go to our hands on his chest, and I nod.

He lifts my hands up around his neck, his hands go to my waist, pulling me into his body.

Holy fucking shit. I'm going to combust.

Elijah's mouthing the words as we dance. I try not to stare at his lips; I know they will be my downfall. Instead, I look up at the sky, at the stars.

Have you ever felt like you were having a moment, a moment that you *knew* was a moment you'd remember forever? This was it. Something we would tell our grandkids about. I shake my head at that thought. *Down, girl. And how many more times can you say "moment"?*

He impresses me with how well he dances. My dirty little mind imagines him naked and above me, behind me. I cannot stop myself, thank you, tequila, and I trail my hand down to his chest again, then back up. I skim the back of his neck, pushing my fingers through his hair. He gives a soft moan. His eyes closing at the contact. Hmm, I've found a sensitive spot.

As he opens his eyes, I see desire, and something else I can't name. I wonder what he sees in my eyes. As we continue to dance, I feel my body start to soften and seek his. I feel like a flower, and he is the sun.

His hands start to roam my body, leaving a trail of fire along their path, and warm wetness settling between my thighs. He pulls me even closer, bends, and kisses my naked shoulder. A sweet lingering kiss. His neck is right there, and I cannot resist. I nuzzle him, inhaling his scent. He stands and reaches up and smoothes the hair back from my face and I look up at him again; our bodies continue the sensual grind.

Like magnets, we're drawn together. His hand goes to my hair again and he tilts my head up. I lick my lips as my eyes flutter close in anticipation.

Only then do I hear the crash of thunder, before the heavens open, and we're drenched in the pouring rain.

CHAPTER THREE

GEMMA

*M*y alarm wakes me the next morning, and I can barely lift my head from my pillow. Ugh. Why did I drink so much tequila? I feel like I've gone a few rounds with Mike Tyson. My eyes close again as I smile, and I think about Elijah. I touch my lips. I'm certain we almost kissed last night. There was something between us and maybe if it hadn't started raining, I would have fulfilled my teenage fantasy of kissing his beautiful face. I was pretty tipsy, but I'm not sure how much he had to drink. Did I imagine it? I cover my face with my arm, heat creeping across my cheeks. We all ran out of there so quickly; I didn't have a chance to give him my phone number. I see my dream guy all these years later, and I don't even get his number. Idiot.

My phone beeps. I check it, and it's a text from Mia to our group chat.

Get up, bitches. Sunday Funday starts in an hour.

Sasha and I both text back with the thumbs-up emoji. She must be in as much pain as I am.

I get up and jump in the shower. Thankfully, I washed my hair last night, since it was drenched from my impromptu rain dance, so that will save me some time. I can't be late, or Mia will kill me.

I search my closet. I feel like crap, so I need something fun and bright to cheer me up. I grab my white sundress with little lemons all over it. I love this dress; it's cute yet sexy. It just makes me feel happy. It has an off-the-shoulder detail with spaghetti straps and a cut-out on the back, right below where it ties. I make sure to tie it tight for some extra support since I can't wear a bra. I put on a little makeup, fluff my hair, and I'm ready to go when the girls text me to come outside.

We're heading to our favorite boozy brunch spot, The Brunch Bar, which is within walking distance from my place here in Wrigleyville. I love this neighborhood. We can pretty much walk to everything from restaurants, bars, and shopping. There's always something going on in this neighborhood. I've come home from work at 5 pm and there are people drunk, stumbling down the street. Who knows if they started too early or if they are just getting home from a wild night. It makes it a great neighborhood to people watch.

Sasha, Mia, and I all live on the same street. Yes, we are co-dependent. I love them, and we spend a lot of time together. But I'm a light sleeper, so quiet, me-time is important. I always hated when my ex, Dustin, would visit. If we didn't fall asleep together, he would wake me whenever he came to bed, and it would take me forever to fall back to sleep. When I think about it, he never woke me up for kisses or cuddles. He just climbed into bed, woke me up, and went to sleep. On the Mondays after his visit, everyone thought I was tired because of all the wild sex I must have had all weekend. I would laugh and go along with it, but sadly, it wasn't true.

We begin to recap the night as we walk to brunch. "Elijah and his friends! Fuck me! It's not fair for them all to hang out together looking so good," Sasha exclaims.

Mia nods eagerly. "Yessss, they were like the Fab Four! No, the Fuckable Four!"

Sasha and I cackle. "The Four Fucksmen of the Ho-pocalypse!" Sasha is practically crying.

"How about Forty Cent since they're all dimes?" I say through giggles. We have to stop for a second to catch our breath. We continue on once we've pulled it together.

"So, how was it seeing him all these years later? Is he as hot as you remember?" Mia looks at me.

"Yes and no. He's still hot, sexier now as a man and he got a little caveman alpha when that guy tried to dance with me. I remember him always laughing or being up for anything when he hung out with Greyson. Last night was a different side to him."

"Did he remember you?" Sasha asks. Clearly, we all had too much to drink last night because we already had this conversation.

"Initially, he said I looked familiar; then I told him who I was. I don't think it was a turn-off for him, though."

"I can definitely say it was not. I saw him watching you dance and then when you guys were dancing together, it was like your panties were on fire," Mia says.

"Yes! I think the rain started because you guys were blazing. The universe did not want you to combust on the spot. You looked too cute last night for all of that," Sasha adds.

We fall into each other again in laughter. These girls are the best.

"It just sucks that we didn't exchange numbers or anything. Am I going to have to wait another ten years to run into him again?" I huff sadly.

We finally walk into our brunch spot. I could use a mimosa or twenty to get me through this mini hangover and my sour mood. Mia chats with the hostess, and she leads us out to our table on the patio. She turns to us and says, "The rest of your party has already arrived."

The rest of our party? Huh?

I look up and see the Four Fucksmen, aka Forty Cent, at a big round table. My eyes bulge and I look over to Mia and Sasha. Mia says, "I figured you didn't get his number, but you know I could not pass up all this man meat." She throws me a wink.

Ok, here we go. Round two.

Elijah

I watch Gemma approach the table. She hasn't seen me yet. She's busy talking and laughing with her friends. She's fucking gorgeous. Her long dark hair is loose, and she's wearing a sexy white dress that I want to fuck her in. I can't remember much about the girl from that vacation years ago, but I think that's a good thing. I just want to think of her as the woman she is today.

She finally looks up and sees me. She tries to cover her surprise before she looks at her friends in question. We all stand as they approach.

"Ladies, welcome. You all look ravishing." Xander holds his arms up as he greets the girls.

I quickly approach Gemma and pull her in for a hug. The smell of her hair reminds me of a day at the beach and sunshine. I smell citrus and some flowery scent I can't put my finger on. I look down at her. "I saved you the best seat in the house." It's not my lap, but it's the next best thing, right next to me. I greet the other girls with a smile and a nod. Gemma sits and she appears nervous again; she's a little fidgety. It's odd how quickly I can read her.

Drew rubs his hands together. "Alright. What are we drinking? Mia, tequila shots?" They start to discuss their drink orders, and I turn my attention to Gemma. "Gemma, what would you like to drink?" She doesn't even look at the menu.

"We always order the bottomless mimosas. I'm going to start with pomegranate. What about you?"

"Bloody Mary all the way."

She scrunches her face. "Ew. You like Bloody Marys? I'm going to have to deduct three points for that."

I laugh. Fuck, she's adorable. "Wow. That seems harsh. Please tell me what I have to do to earn those back."

She smiles shyly. "I'll let you know."

I smirk. I have a few ideas myself. My eyes roam her face, and I lean in, everyone else long forgotten. "Last night was fun. Too bad our party got rained out. I was looking forward to getting to know you a little better."

She smiles softly. "Actually, I want to apologize to you for last night." I frown at that statement.

"I had a few too many drinks and I was all over you. I'm sure your girlfriend wouldn't appreciate me grinding and groping you. I'm not usually like that. Tequila makes me bold, maybe even stupid. So, I'm sorry. Can we start over?" She holds her hand out for me to shake, almost forcing me to retreat.

What? I'm so confused. I reach for her hand slowly and we shake. But again, just like last night, I feel a pulse of heat between us as our hands touch. She looks at our joined hands, maybe she feels it too. She wets her lips and looks at me with those big beautiful brown eyes.

I caress her knuckles with my thumb. "Gemma, no need to apologize. I had fun last night." I feel a smile tugging at my lips. "Are you ready for another drink? How about tequila?" I wink.

Gemma

I sit back and watch Elijah interact with everyone else at the table. I don't want to monopolize his attention, but I'm feeling greedy. He didn't react to my girlfriend comment, and now I'm really curious. As I watch him laugh and joke, I can see the young man I met and crushed on for that week in the Bahamas. We obviously did not spend any time together. I was 14 and he was 17. He barely even looked at me, but I still remember the first time I saw him.

We had just arrived and were walking up to our villa. I was sulking, upset with Greyson for being Greyson, when he walked out of the villa next door with his parents. He was wearing black low strung swim trunks, a white towel around his neck, and aviators. My parents have never met a stranger and immediately started up a conversation with his parents. They had just arrived for their vacation as well. I stood there trying not to stare, but he was breathtakingly gorgeous. Dark hair, smooth skin, perfect lips. I couldn't see his eyes, and I really wanted to. He'd taken his towel off to reveal his chest and abs right as he introduced himself to Greyson then me. I don't think I spoke. I just gave a little squeak and a wave and turned away. I admit, at that time, I was already a little boy crazy, but Elijah upped that by several hundred notches.

I blink back to brunch. Everyone was starting to get a little rowdy. The DJ inside was playing a few of my favorite songs, the drinks were flowing, and I saw that someone had indeed ordered shots of tequila.

I danced in my seat a little and sipped my mimosa. I had moved on to peach, and it was giving me life. This weekend had shaped up to be everything I didn't know I needed. I exhale at this feeling of contentment.

I scan the table, and I see Mia and Drew chatting privately. I'm definitely picking up on their flirty vibes. They look good together, like our very own Barbie and Ken.

Sasha and I make eye contact and do wide eyes at each other. She's chatting with Ty and Xander, she looks like the meat in that sandwich. She looks nervous, but I know she loves it.

I glance back over to Elijah, and he's watching me with a hint of a smile. "So, Elijah, what have you been up to? I'm still shocked that we ran into each other after all these years. I want to know everything." I smile.

Elijah tilts his head as he looks at me. "You know, you're the only person besides my family that calls me Elijah. Everyone else calls me Eli or E."

"I'm sorry. Would you prefer me to call you Eli? I can't even imagine calling you E, though." I giggle.

"No, I like it. I like how it sounds. It reminds me of home."

I look down. *I remind him of home. Swoon.*

"What about you? I've heard your friends call you Gem, is that what you prefer? It fits. You are precious. Rare, even."

I feel my face heating. I look up into his eyes. Did he really just say that? I thought maybe I had been tipsy the night before and I had misread his interest, but now I'm not so sure. I watch his gaze sweep over me from head to toe. Oh yeah, he's curious, even interested.

"I don't have a preference. Either is fine."

He nods. "Ok, so you want to know more about me. Here are the cliff notes since the last time we saw each other. Ty and I have been best friends since elementary school. We went away to college, met these two fools, moved to Chicago after graduation, and Ty and I started our real estate development firm. We've been working like crazy the last six years, and we've grown faster than either one of us could have imagined. We've quickly become one of the top firms in Chicago and we're not done yet." I watch him as his eyes light up as he talks about his work.

"What about a girlfriend or wife?" I cross my fingers under the table.

He grins at me. I think he knows what I want to hear. "No, I work too much. I wouldn't have enough time to nurture a relationship how I would like. Besides, I haven't met anyone that makes me want to even try." He shrugs.

Interesting. "What kind of woman would make you want to try?"

"I don't know. I've never really thought about it," he says as I feel his eyes sweep over me again.

Our waitress saves me as she returns with our food. I'm going to revisit this discussion later.

I look over at Elijah. He has a mouthwatering plate of chicken and waffles drizzled in honey. I look down at my bacon, eggs, and hash browns and I'm sad and disappointed in myself. How did I miss the opportunity to order that?

Elijah catches my sad face and laughs. "Are you jealous?" He licks some honey from his fork, licks it from his lips.

"I was jealous of your food, now I'm jealous of that fork." It looks like mimosas are just as bad as tequila for my brain to mouth filter.

His eyes widen for a second, then I see awareness in his eyes. "I wouldn't want you to be jealous." He spears some food, swirls it in honey, and offers me the bite.

I lean forward and close my mouth over the fork. He watches me intently as I take the bite. Closing my eyes, I give a small moan as I chew.

"You like?" he asks darkly.

I bite my lip. "That is delicious."

"Do you always moan when something sweet hits your throat?"

What!? This man is frying my brain. I bite the inside of my cheek to stop myself from asking if he wants to find out. Instead, I take a sip of my mimosa.

He smirks as he takes in my discomfort, then he licks his fork. "You're right. Delicious."

Heat and awareness swirl between us. My brain can't catch up, so I take another sip of my mimosa and try to calm my breathing.

"You get away with things like that because of how you look," I tell him as I take a bite of my hash browns.

He raises an eyebrow. "And how do I look?"

"You know. You're practically the prototype for any woman's wet dream." I count on my fingers. "You're tall. You're gorgeous. You have the most beautiful blue eyes and a kissable mouth. From what I felt last night, I could grate cheese on your abs. You have broad shoulders. You smell amazing. I could go on and on with a honey-do-me list of all my favorite things. What size shoe do you wear?"

He's watching me with a hint of a smile, his piercing blues alight with mischief. "Wow, is that all I am to you? A piece of meat? Anything else about me you want to objectify?"

"Oh please, you asked! I'm not objectifying you; I'm giving you a compliment. If I could whistle, I would whistle at you every time you walked by. You also have big, beautiful hands and nice long fingers. Seriously, what size shoe do you wear?"

He shakes his head. "Nope, I'm not telling," he pauses, "so my attributes are all of your favorite things?"

"Are you kidding me?! When I say you are every woman's wet dream, I mean me. I'm every woman, and I'm the first in line. You were my first real crush."

He looks at me, genuinely shocked. "What? I had no idea."

"Of course not. I was just some geeky kid when we met. You...you were this beautiful creature that took my breath away. When I used to watch you running on the beach or surfing, you made my body feel things it had never felt before." I can't read his face, but I know he doesn't remember the memories I'm spilling.

I put him out of his misery. "Breathe. You look like you're about to faint." I hand him his Bloody Mary. "Take a drink. You look like you need it."

Elijah

Shocked is an understatement. She's right, I don't really remember anything about her. She was just Greyson's little sister. Always around, always in the peripheral, with her book and cloud of curly hair.

I accept my drink and take a long swig. Fuck. I'm thrown.

"Whoa. I have no idea how I should feel about this. Is it creepy that I'm turned on? We're both adults now, so I shouldn't feel weird, right?"

Gemma puts her hand on my shoulder and leans

in. "Absolutely not. I don't. I'm looking forward to getting to know you now and seeing if you compare to the fantasy I've built up of you over the years."

"Fantasy? Your wish is my command. Satisfaction guaranteed," I whisper back.

She laughs softly and shakes her head at me. It's such a beautiful sound, and it's yet another thing that's pulling me to her.

"I'm going to need a few more drinks before I get into that."

She turns to her friends and asks if they want to head to the bar. They head off, and I exhale a deep breath.

All the guys lean in and look at me.

"How's that going? I feel like you guys aren't even here," Ty says.

"Yeah, but you guys look good together," Drew adds.

I nod. "She's gorgeous. I can't deny that. We'll see what happens." I murmur as I look over at the bar. They follow my gaze.

She's leaning against the bar, talking to her friends. My eyes roam up and down her body. Her body is so lush. Her thick hair is a little wild, and I watch her put it behind her ear. Sasha says something, and they all burst out laughing. Her bright smile and those pouty lips, the light in her eyes. All of it captivates me.

The song changes to something she obviously likes, and she starts moving her hips to the beat, and I feel it in my dick. *Fuck.*

She looks at me over her shoulder and gives me a mischievous smile.

I blink back to the guys.

"I don't know how to play this. She's my buddy's little sister, and she's a few years younger. I don't know if the hassle is worth it." I shake my head.

"For fucks sake, are you in love already? Are you going to marry her? Hold on, don't answer until after I braid your fucking hair!" Xander jokes.

The guys all laugh, and I scowl. "Shut up, dick."

Yep, I'm thinking too hard about this. I just want to get to know her and have a little fun. Love isn't on the menu.

I watch as some guy approaches her, and he puts his hands on her hips from behind. I feel my body tense. Not this shit again. Thankfully, she turns and brushes his hands off her.

Good girl.

He leans in and says something in her ear. She shakes her head, then turns and points to me. He turns, following her gesture, and looks me over. She then gives me a cute little wave and blows me a kiss. I smile and shoot her a wink. She says something to him, before he appears to grumble a reply and walks away.

The guys all hoot and holler and everyone turns to look at us.

I have a huge smile plastered on my face. I don't know if I've just been claimed or if she just told everyone, she's mine.

Either way, I like it. I like it a lot.

. . .

Gemma

I don't know what made me blow him a kiss, in front of *everyone,* but based on his reaction, he liked it.

I head to the restroom. I check my hair and makeup before I pop a mint. I open the door to head back to our table, when I run into a solid wall of beautiful man. *Elijah.*

He reaches out to steady me. "Sorry, lovely."

My heart flips at the endearment, and my hands go to his chest again.

"Are you? I'm not."

"You're right. You feel too good against me for me to be sorry." He takes my hand and leads me down the hall, away from the bar. "Now, back to these fantasies," he tilts his head as he waits for me to start talking.

I feel my face heat again. I never got that drink, and this is so embarrassing. I stare straight ahead at his chest; I can't even make eye contact with him.

"Back then, I really wanted you to be my first kiss. I had a fantasy that you had just finished surfing, you walked out of the water toward me on the beach, and lifted me up, wrapped my legs around you, and you kissed me. You were only surfing for a few minutes, but you kissed me like you missed me." I finally look up into his eyes.

He stares at me for a second, then gives me a slow sexy smile. "Your wish..." he trails off. He reaches down and lifts me up, my legs go around his waist. His eyes are locked on mine as he slowly lowers his head. His tongue sweeps through my open mouth, once, twice, then he sucks my bottom lip before he kisses me with those perfect lips. I can't believe this is happening. My body heats and hums, happy to finally feel alive. I whimper at the first taste of him, and my hand goes to his hair, giving it a tug. He grunts into my mouth, and I gobble it up as he pushes me up against the wall. Our kiss turns savage as I bite his lip. I can't get enough. I feel wild with need as I grasp and pull him closer. I'm so wet, and I feel like my heart is going to pound out of my chest. *This. This is how to sweep a girl off her feet with just a kiss.*

He has me pinned against the wall now, and I can feel his rock-hard cock in between my thighs. He begins a sensual grind into me and he's found the perfect spot. I could easily come just from this. His hand comes up to my hair, and he pulls my head to the side to expose my neck. Kissing and nibbling along my jawline and down to my neck, I shiver against his lips. He bites me right below my ear, sending goosebumps crawling over my overheated flesh. I moan as he brings his hand up to cup my breast, giving me a hard squeeze.

Someone drops a glass, and the sound shatters our arousal fog. He pulls back and looks at me with those beautiful blue eyes, a few shades darker now. Slowly he lowers my feet back to the floor. He takes a deep breath, bends, and kisses my shoulder. And that little move may just be my undoing.

He stands upright, and he readjusts my dress. I touch my swollen lips as I look up into his eyes. He gives me a sexy smile as he reaches down and puts my hair behind my ear.

"I think I like your fantasies," he murmurs as he adjusts his cock.

He hands me his card. "Call me when you're ready to make them a reality."

He bends down once more and licks my neck before he turns and walks away.

I sag into the wall. I'm breathing like I've run a marathon and if I were hit with a gust of wind right now, I'd come on the spot.

I grin. Holy fucking shit.

CHAPTER FOUR

ELIJAH

*I*t's late afternoon as I'm leaving a meeting in the West Loop. Taking out my phone to text my driver, I spot Gemma and her friend Sasha walking across the street. As I watch her, she begins to wave her hands around excitedly as Sasha laughs. Her actions make me smile, before I do a double take as I get a look at her outfit. She wore that to work? How did she make it through the day without getting bent over her desk? I was going to avoid her, but when she looks like that, I can't resist.

I cross the street and step into their path. Gemma's eyes widen as I look her up and down, as Sasha gives me a huge smile. She looks between us and says, "I'll give you two a moment," and she pretends to do some window shopping nearby. Gemma licks her lips as she takes me in. We have not seen each other since I fulfilled her kiss fantasy, and then I dry humped her against a wall - my body perks up, hungry for a repeat encounter.

I scan her body again. My dick twitches in approval before finally breaking the silence.

"Is this what you wore to work?"

She looks down, confused. "Uh, yeah."

I groan. "Fuck me. I would not have been able to get anything done if I worked with you. You are giving me naughty schoolgirl vibes." I sweep my gaze over her body again. She's wearing a navy pleated skirt with a sleeveless white ruffled shirt with navy polka dots, a red belt, and red oxfords. Her hair is tied up in a ponytail with a red ribbon. She is a gift I can't wait to unwrap.

She laughs, surprised. "Really? I thought I was cute but professional."

I rake my eyes over her body again. "You're cute but distracting." I pause before I reach out and wrap her ponytail around my hand and whisper in her ear, "I promised satisfaction guaranteed, so why haven't you called and taken me up on my offer?" I curse myself internally for asking. I don't know where that came from. I hate how desperate I feel.

"Sorry, I've been busy with work." I see the uneasiness in her eyes, and I immediately release her as she looks away.

I frown. That's usually my line.

She looks at her watch. "I have to get going, Sasha and I have kickboxing in 15 minutes."

She stretches up, and I bend a little for her to kiss

me on the cheek. She lingers for a moment as we breathe each other in, before she walks away. I hear them giggle as they continue to their gym.

After that intense kiss we shared, I expected her to call me asap so we could pick up where we left off. Her demeanor today has me pumping the brakes on that.

What the fuck just happened?

Gemma

The delivery guy has just dropped off our Chinese food. I walk back into my living room and hold up the large bag. "Prepare to feast!"

The girls are over for our viewing party. We meet a few nights a week to watch our favorite shows. Tonight we're watching *Bachelor in Paradise.* I can't even call this show a guilty pleasure anymore because I happily watch this trash. I'm in multiple Bachelor groups and brackets each season. I'm not even going to complain about the number of nights I have devoted to this show and all the other spinoffs.

I set the cartons on the table and sit on the floor. Mia brings in plates, and Sasha grabs a bottle of wine. We start to dig in. The show starts in thirty minutes, so we have some time to catch up.

"Sasha told me you saw Eli today. What the fuck? How was that?" Mia asks.

I think back to his hot body in that sexy gray suit.

"Oh my gosh, he looked edible today, and I just

stood there like an idiot." I shove more food into my mouth. Fried rice always makes me feel better.

Sasha agrees, "He looked hot, and he looked like he was ready to eat you. Have you spoken to him since he practically fucked you in the hallway?"

I feel my face flame as I lean my head back on the couch. "No, I've been too afraid to call him. He's so damn hot. One call is going to lead to going out and then I'm going to end up on my back." I groan.

"Or your knees, Summer Slut," Mia laughs.

"Yes, or that. I'll admit I was flirty with him, but I didn't think it was going anywhere. I certainly wasn't expecting him to kiss me and for that kiss to set my panties on fire. I was so caught up in him. I would have gladly fucked him in that hallway. He's too dangerous for me."

The girls are looking at me like I'm crazy.

"Haven't you always wanted to be swept up in a kiss? That's your whole thing. It has finally happened. Why are you running from it?" Sasha reaches out and grasps my hand.

"I guess I'm just scared. I've had this crush on him for years, so all my teenage feelings are mixed up in there. And based on that kiss, I know he's experienced. Besides the fact that he'll probably dickmatize me, how am I going to compare to the women he's used to? I'm freaking out just thinking about it."

Mia continues looking at me like I've grown a third boob. "If anyone deserves to be dickmatized, it's you. Hello, you're in Mission Promiscuous mode. Have fun and let that bastard blow your mind. You're right. You don't compare to those other women, because you're you and you are incomparable."

Have I mentioned how much I love my friends?

I exhale a deep breath. "Ok, it's now or never. He wanted me to call him, but I'm just going to text him. What should I say?"

Mia raises her hand. "Send a tit pic!"

We laugh. "Gross, no."

Sasha says, "Just call him and let him do all the work. Call him now so you have an excuse to get off the phone when the show starts."

I consider that. No, I would be too nervous. I'm going to text him. I begin to pace as I think about what to send.

Ok, here goes.

Hi, it's Gemma. I hit send before I lose my nerve.

I just wanted you to know you were looking really good in that suit today. Ugh, I sound like an imbecile. I bite my lip and watch my phone for a response.

The show starts, and I try to get into the drama unfolding, but I can't stop checking my phone. He still has not responded. Ok, don't freak out. Maybe he is busy or at the gym or doing any number of things, and he hasn't had a chance to check his messages. I grab my glass of wine and chug it. This waiting is nerve-wracking. I turn my phone on silent and put it under a pillow. I'm not checking it again. I'm going to enjoy this wine and watch this dumpster fire on tv.

I have more willpower than I thought. I make it through the episode and aftershow without checking my phone; I don't want to appear too eager and text him immediately after he texts me. This will teach him. I kiss the girls good night and tidy up my living room before I can't take it anymore. I grab my phone to check my messages...and there are none. Seriously? He ignores me after asking me to contact him? They say never meet your heroes because you'll be disappointed. I guess for me, it's never meet your fantasy boyfriend.

I've made it to Thursday, and this time, I'm heading to a boxing class. I haven't heard from Elijah since we ran into each other a few days ago and it is driving me crazy. Did I do something wrong? Is he mad at me? Is he with someone else?

I've slept poorly all week, so I really need to pound something in this class and maybe just exhaust myself enough to sleep well tonight. I was dragging ass all day. But as I walk to the gym, I imagine his face as my punching bag. I can already feel the rush of adrenaline flow through me. He may be the best pre-workout ever. I rush in to get changed. I wrap my wrists, throw on my gloves, and step up to my bag. The instructor takes us through our warm-up, and we finally move to striking the bag. I feel as if red steam is shooting out of my ears.

We start with a sixty second round of jabs. I punch the bag, picturing his face with each contact. *Who. Do. You. Think. You. Are?* I pace around during our rest period, hitting my fists together. What an asshole.

We move on to a sixty second round of hooks. Again, I see his handsome face as I pummel the bag. *You. Asked. Me. To. Contact. You. Then. You. Don't. Respond? Fuck. You.*

This goes on for the next fifty minutes. When I finally leave the gym, I feel like a weight has been lifted from my shoulders. I'm over him.

Elijah

It's Friday night, and I've had a shit week. Work has been all-consuming with new projects and a bid, so to say I'm stretched is an understatement. But that's all shit I can handle. Shit I love. The shit I can't deal with are the games.

My mind flashes to Gemma. There was definitely a connection between us. I think back to that kiss. That hot fucking kiss. That kiss pushed through my resistance. At that moment, she was just a beautiful woman I was attracted to. She wasn't my old friend's little sister. She wasn't a young girl who had a crush on me. To go from that high to the low of her not calling me or being cold when we ran into each other is exactly why I don't date younger women. My friends all seem to like the drama and the games, but to me, it is the biggest fucking turn-off.

So yes, my shit week has me in a shit mood. Thankfully, my guys are dragging Ty and me out to blow off some steam. We're checking out a new spot tonight, a new adult arcade. I've been promised games of pool, giant Connect Four maybe some karaoke, and tons of booze.

We arrive around 10 pm. The guys have reserved a large booth for us to sit at and people watch in between games. We immediately order bottles of vodka and tequila. We start with a round of tequila shots before we venture from our table.

I'm playing a game of Pac-Man when I see her. Gemma and her friends have just walked in and Drew immediately walks over to greet them. And at that moment, I know I've been set up. Fuck that. I'm not doing this tonight. I continue to play and try to ignore them all.

I feel the heat of her gaze, but I don't give in and look at her. They are over playing pool, so it is safe for me to return to our table. I pour myself a tequila and pineapple and take a seat. Unfortunately, I have a perfect view of the pool tables, and I cannot stop myself from glancing over.

Gemma is wearing a flowy yellow dress that tries and fails to hide her curves from our prying eyes. She is so naturally sexy and feminine. She's clearly enjoying Summertime Chi because she is beautifully sun-kissed and glowing. Her long dark hair is down, and she has one side pinned behind her ear, perfectly showcasing her slender neck.

I can feel the heat of arousal start to flow through my body as I watch her and hear her laugh. Her laugh is loud and infectious, and it makes me and everyone around her want to gravitate to her and find out what's so funny. She just sunk a ball and she screams and does a little happy dance. She's a terrible pool player, but she appears to be having a great time. Her energy, her smile, everything about her is captivating...and I watch as other guys take notice.

I take a sip of my drink. Good for her. Maybe she can play games with them. I'm not interested in her hot and cold act. If I'm honest, her rejection was surprising, especially after how flirty she was at brunch and after that kiss. I felt the pull to her immediately and her indifference surprisingly affected me. I smirk and shake my head. As I head back over to the arcade, I'm stopped by a gorgeous redhead.

Well, hello. Tonight, just got even more interesting.

Gemma

Our friends, together, as a group, are assholes. Introducing them was clearly a mistake since they are already plotting together behind our backs. I watch that handsome jerk from across the room. I fully intended to never see him again, but here we are. I hate to admit it, but he looks *goooood.* And before I can stop myself, I give him a little wave. He does not reciprocate. I exhale deeply. Alright, get me a drink, and make it a double.

I'm playing pool, or at least I'm trying to, when I glance over and see Elijah talking to a beautiful redhead. She's tall, willowy, and her face is flawless. Honestly, they look good together. She is obviously into him. I mean, who wouldn't be. I watch as she touches his arm and laughs at something he says. His back is to me, so I can't see his face, but I'm sure he's interested as well. She looks like what I imagine his type would be. I turn away before I get upset. Mia hands me a glass of wine and rubs my shoulder.

"I'm fine. Let's play." I smile. Mia, Sasha, and the guys smile back at me. Could this be any more awkward?

I've struggled through this game of pool, but I need a break. I excuse myself and head to the bar. Elijah catches my eye again, and this time he is chatting with a blond. Seriously? He's really starting to piss me off. He can't find the time to speak to me, but he can chat up all the other women here?

I turn to the bartender, but before I can get her attention, my very own blond invades my personal space. I blink up to his face. He's obviously a god, immediately reminding me of Thor.

He smiles. "What are we drinking, sweetheart?" Oh, and he's confident.

I smile at him. "I was just going to order some shots. Are you buying?"

He nods. "Anything for you, gorgeous."

"Perfect." I turn and wave Mia and Sasha over. "Ladies, this is..." I stop and look at him expectantly.

"Jake," he supplies.

"Ladies, Jake has offered to buy us shots. What do you want?"

Jake hesitates but is a good sport as we order two rounds of shots.

Jake seems nice enough, but I'm into tall, dark, and handsome types, so I try to pass him off to Mia or Sasha. Looking up, I catch Elijah glaring at me. Crap, if looks could kill. He must think I'm into this guy. This is the last thing I want. I'm into you, silly. I shake my head and excuse myself from our little group at the bar to head back to our pool table. Ty watches me approach and gestures for me to come over to him.

"How do you know Jake Dalton?" he asks me.

"I don't. I just met him at the bar. You know him?"

He nods and then I see that his jaw is clenched. "Yes, he works for a rival development firm. Eli hates his guts, but I'm fairly sure it's mutual."

"Looks like you hate his guts too."

Ty shakes his head no. "I'm more concerned about Eli. Not only does he hate him, but he saw him flirting with you. Eli has had a rough week, cut him a little slack."

"Me? I should cut *him* some slack? He's not talking to *me*. What do you know about that?"

Ty sighs. "You didn't hear this from me, but Eli likes you, and he was a little upset when you didn't call him after brunch. He thought maybe he had misread your interactions, and you just wanted to be friends, but he knows he's incapable of being just your friend."

My hand flies to my mouth, "Oh, gosh. Ty, I like him too. I was trying to play it cool. I was just so nervous to call because I didn't want to blow it." I let out a deep breath. "How do I fix this?"

Ty puts his hands on my shoulders. "Just be honest. He'll appreciate that." He looks over at Elijah as he heads down the hallway to the restroom. I follow his gaze. He turns me around and gives me a nudge in that direction and says, "There's no time like the present."

I look back at him and give him an exaggerated scared face. He mouths, "you got this," and winks. I've got this. I square my shoulders. What a turn of events this is. I started the night hating his guts, and now I'm about to apologize to him for his overreaction. But I need answers, so I'm going to suck it up.

I wait creepily outside the restroom for him, I guess this is our thing now, and I accost him as soon as he walks out.

"Hi, handsome," I smile.

He nods at me impassively.

I take a deep breath and let loose, "I wanted to come chat with you and apologize for being flaky this week. That's completely out of character for me, but that's sort of how you make me feel." I look down at my fingers. "That kiss, that kiss shook me, and I panicked. I was freaked out about what would or wouldn't happen between us."

I finally look up to meet his beautiful blues. "So again, I apologize, and I would like to start over." I stick my hand out for him to shake, "Hi, my name is Gemma, and I think you're really hot. Can I take you out sometime?"

Elijah laughs and accepts my hand, and there it is. I feel an instant reaction, a pull between us.

"Is it my turn to speak?" I nod in agreement. "I accept your apology. I also want to explain my side of things and apologize for my behavior. That kiss wrecked me a bit too. That kiss pushed through my reservations about my relationship with your brother, and your reaction made me second guess that decision. I overreacted and I apologize for being an ass."

He brings my hand to his lips and kisses the back of it. He smiles sexily. "I'm Elijah and I hear you like guys in suits?"

CHAPTER FIVE

GEMMA

*T*oday is the day I get Elijah all to myself. Last night, after our dual apologies, I promised I would call him the next day. If followed through, he had to agree to let me take him out on a date. He protested, quite a bit, saying he wanted to take me out for our first date, which was kind of cute. But I persisted and here we are. At precisely noon, I call him. I pace my living room and shake my hands out to get rid of my nerves.

He picks up on the first ring. "Good afternoon, Ms. Davis," he purrs.

"Well, hello, Mr. Adler. I'm calling to request the pleasure of your company today."

I can hear his smile through the phone. "I happily accept your request."

I laugh. "Perfect, I will text you the details. I'll see you soon. Bye, handsome."

"See you soon, love."

Hours later, I'm standing near an entrance to Oz Park. I'm laden down with bags of supplies and a large picnic basket. I watch Elijah stride confidently toward me. He stands tall above the crowd. He's wearing a slim-fit white V-neck tee, navy shorts, and some fancy low-cut sneakers. His hair is perfectly tousled, and he is wearing a pair of aviator sunglasses. I feel a flutter in my stomach. Damn, he looks good.

Elijah walks right up to me. "Hi, lovely." He bends and kisses my cheek before taking the bags and basket from me. I feel a buzz of excitement run through me. I never thought that this man would look at me the way he's looking at me right now.

He looks around. "It looks like we're having a picnic in the park." His blue eyes meet mine as he removes his shades.

"Yep! Follow me." I lead him into the park. I can feel his warm gaze all over my body, so I add a little extra sway to my hips. I take him to my favorite spot near a big tree that will provide us with some much needed shade. He sets the bags down and helps me spread out the blanket. I also have a few small pillows and an extra blanket.

He lies down quickly, and I join him. He looks over at me and with mischief in his eyes says, "I can't believe I got you on your back already."

I laugh and say, "Well, maybe I brought you here to get you on your back!"

"You wouldn't have had to work this hard. You can't even imagine how easy I am."

He turns and raises himself up on one elbow, and I turn my head to meet his gaze.

"I'm glad we are doing this. I'm looking forward to getting to know you," he says with a grin.

I smile, suddenly shy. "Me too." Holy fuck. I feel like all of my wet dreams are coming true and the butterflies in my stomach have just grown ten sizes.

I must be looking at him with lust in my eyes because I see his blue eyes darken as he scans my face. He cups my cheek and holds me just right as he brings his lips to mine. His tongue sweeps through my mouth and I whimper softly, before he deepens the kiss. Our tongues are dancing together perfectly as if we've kissed a million times. My hand comes up and I fist his hair. He groans into my mouth; then he's kissing my neck, nibbling my ear, before he returns to ravage my mouth. I kiss him back just as greedily. No one has ever made me feel like this before. I can hear my blood pumping, my heart racing. He is now fully laying on top of me, and he grinds into me, his cock hard and hot against me. I can only imagine what we look like, but he doesn't seem to care.

He gives me one last lingering kiss before he pulls away. He brushes my hair back from my face, looks me in the eyes, and says, "Whoa." And we both crack up.

Whoa indeed. When I imagined being swept away by a kiss, of feeling as if my world was spinning out of control, with my heart racing wildly, this is what I meant. There's such an amazing thrill to have that reaction just from a kiss.

I whisper to him, "It looks like we're having sex over here."

"I fully intend to fuck you outside one day, and on that day, there won't be any questions about what we're doing."

My brain splutters and all I can do is nod. He kisses me once more before sliding off me and returning to his elbow. "A picnic in the park. What a lovely idea, sweet Gemma."

Elijah

This woman is blowing my mind. I don't think I've ever been this physically attracted to someone in my life. Actually, I know I haven't. Gemma is so unexpected. She's the perfect combination of sweet and sexy. And the way she makes me feel when she looks at me with those big brown eyes, that open and expressive face, it's like I can do anything. That look makes me want to do anything, be everything, for her.

I watch her as she starts to empty the picnic basket. Today has been perfect so far. We've talked about our families. Apparently, Greyson is getting married this summer, and sadly I had no idea. We've talked about work, hers seems more interesting than mine, and we've moved on to travel. I've been so busy working the last few years that I have not had a chance to travel for pleasure. But hearing Gemma talk about all the places she plans to see makes me want to be the one to take her. I haven't had a true vacation in years.

I continue to watch her as she sits on her knees and empties out the picnic basket. We've already finished off a bottle of champagne, and I'm curious about what else she has. She's talking to herself as she pulls out a feast of meats, cheeses, fruits, crackers, nuts, and a baguette. She also has chicken salad and a pasta salad. She certainly knows the way to my heart.

She busies herself setting everything up, and I must admit, I like being fussed over. I haven't had this in a long time. My gaze drops hungrily over her body. I've had a hard dick since I got here. Her hot little body and her cute little toes are driving me crazy.

She's wearing a long polka dot skirt and a little white top that exposes a small sliver of skin around her waist. Her long dark hair is loose, and I just want to run my hands through it.

She arranges everything and then she asks me what I would like before she starts preparing a plate for me. I feel a rush of appreciation and warmth flow through me. Fuck, I've forgotten what it feels like to be taken care of. I can appreciate that she's not trying to impress me, this is just who she is, and it means a lot. She hands me my plate, and I set it down to wait to start eating when she's ready. She puts a few things on her plate before we both settle in and start eating.

I look over at her. "If you could go anywhere in the world, right now, where would you go?

She doesn't hesitate. "Would you be coming with me?" Surprised, I nod.

"Good, because if not, I would want to be right here with you. But if we could go anywhere right now, I think I would choose Iceland."

My eyes widened, surprised. "Really? I thought you would have chosen something tropical."

"Well, a close second would be the Amalfi Coast. I would love to explore either with you. What's wrong with Iceland?"

I shake my head. "Nothing at all. I hear people talk about their tropical vacations all the time. I've forgotten there are other beautiful destinations to choose from."

I imagine her beautiful body oiled up lying next to me in a colorful bikini. I shake my head to rid myself of the image. I sit back and begin to plot how I can get her alone and with little to no clothing.

"Ok, Judgey McJudgerson, where would you go?"

"Right now, with you? I'd say the Maldives. I've never been, and it would be the perfect place to take you and get that hot body in a teeny bikini."

Gemma

Elijah and I have spent hours at the park. We've kissed and laughed, and I've gotten to see a side of him I didn't know existed.

My back is against his front, and he leans down and kisses me on the shoulder. I feel the goosebumps prickle down my skin. So, things I've learned about Elijah today, he's loving and supremely affectionate. He must be touching me in some way, at all times. Whether it's touching my hair, stroking my hand, or even being a chair for me, he seeks out some form of physical contact. I've fallen in love with the shoulder kisses. They are a little bit sweet and a whole lot sexy. It speaks to a certain level of intimacy that is new for me. I never felt this connection with my past relationships.

I've also learned that I can spend hours with Elijah, talking about nothing and everything, and it's the most fun I've ever had. We both love our work and have a true passion for it. Talking to someone with a similar passion and love for their career is so sexy. I told him how things were getting hectic at work. Instead of trying to tell me what to do or how to solve my problems, Elijah just listened, stroked my hair, and offered some words of encouragement and support. He didn't try to make my job less important or change the topic to his job or things he felt were more important. Sadly, I never noticed this was a thing until it didn't happen today.

The biggest takeaway from these last few hours is that this man just exudes sex. I can practically taste it. It almost screams at me, satisfaction guaranteed, just like he promised. Each kiss, every touch, has my body aching for him. I've never been so wet in my life. He is so uninhibited when he wants to touch me or kiss me, he does it. I can't tell if he's just teasing me now or if he doesn't realize the effect he has on me.

He kisses my temple. I lean into it before I turn to look at him over my shoulder. "Let's go for a walk."

He agrees and helps me stand. He immediately pulls me into his arms and kisses my lips before taking my hand and leading me around the park.

I look down at my watch. We have about an hour or so. "I have one more surprise for you."

He looks at me with interest. "I love surprises," he says, smiling cheekily.

"Good, because it arrives at dusk."

He stops walking and pulls me to him again, his eyes searching mine. He pushes my hair back and puts it behind my ear. "Thank you. Today has already been amazing. I don't think you can top our picnic."

I put my hand on his chest, I can feel the racing of his heart and something snaps inside of me. I reach up and pull him down to me for a kiss, but I don't have to work too hard because he's already bending down to me. My hand goes to his hair, giving it a tug, and he groans. He grabs me and pushes me up against a nearby tree. The bark snags my hair and skirt, but I don't care as we continue to kiss desperately. He presses his hard dick into my stomach, and I can feel my pulse throb between my legs.

He releases my mouth and drops his head to kiss my shoulder before devouring my neck and nibbling my ear. I've never been a fan of ear nibbling, now it is my new favorite thing, and my body shivers in response. The things this man can do with his mouth, in public no less, are mind-blowing. We kiss and grind into each other for several more minutes before I remember his surprise.

I look up into his baby blues. "Let's head back to our picnic." He gives me another swift kiss and looks down at his dick.

He takes my hand and places it right in his dick. He gives it a firm squeeze with my hand, like I needed help with that. "Look at what you did. You are trouble, kissing me like that. And this mouth." He kisses me again.

I squeeze his cock again as it strains against his shorts.

I've never met anyone like him. Someone who made me feel sexy and beautiful. He makes me feel wanted. I want to hold on to this feeling, bottle it up.

"Alright, let's get you and that," I wave my hand gesturing to his dick, "back for your surprise."

He readjusts himself before he takes my hand, and we head back to our picnic site.

He looks around. People are streaming in from everywhere, walking around and lying on blankets in the park. We look over to the street where there are food trucks lined up.

Straight ahead, his surprise - a large movie screen is being set up.

I turn to him. "This is a two-part date. I'm taking you to the movies so we can hold hands and make out. Yes, before you ask, this is one of my fantasies." I do a little dance in my excitement. I told him it was a surprise for him, but I totally did this for me.

He grins. "I've never been to a movie in the park. This is so cool. Thank you." He kisses me again. And there's a little something different about this kiss, the passion flowing is always underneath, but this just feels tender and sweet.

"What are we watching?" he asks, as I lead him over to the food trucks.

"You'll have to wait and see.

We head back to our picnic blanket after we've ordered something yummy from each truck. Elijah wanted to pay for our first dinner, so he went a little overboard.

We eat quietly for a few moments before I catch Elijah staring at me. "What?" I ask.

He swallows before saying. "Why were you nervous or reluctant to call me? We have an obvious chemistry. Why did that scare you? Does it still scare you?" His words come out in a rush, so I know this has been on his mind.

My eyes meet his and I sigh, "I don't know. I think initially, I was nervous because I had this huge crush on you. I thought either moving past that would ruin all those fantasies I had of you or," I look down and laugh softly, "you would surpass my fantasies. I would fall in love with you, and then I would end up heartbroken when you moved on. I considered it too much of a risk."

He doesn't say anything, so I have to look up to his

face. He's smiling softly. "Wow, ok, I appreciate your honesty but let's just enjoy ourselves and get to know each other. We'll just start there, and we'll see what happens, yeah?"

I nod and he adds, "I had reservations initially, mainly my relationship with your brother and your age," I frown at that age comment, but he continues, "but every time I saw you, I couldn't wait to see you again. So, here we are. Let's just enjoy it. Let's enjoy getting to know each other, no strings." He shrugs.

I can't hide my smile. "Now, I appreciate your honesty."

He rubs his hands together. "It's agreed that we like spending time together, so let's make a deal. If that changes, we'll have an adult conversation about it. We won't just stop calling or texting or ignoring each other, but we end it respectfully."

I nod. "Casual, no ghosting, got it." I hold out my pinky finger.

He laughs and pushes it away. "I have other fingers in mind for you."

Then he leans over, and we share a messy kiss of cheese fries and nachos.

We laugh at our grossness. Ugh, and now I know I've got it bad; I would never kiss someone with food all over my face. This man.

Elijah

We clean up our blanket and freshen up at the

nearby restrooms. I lean against a tree as I wait for Gemma. She said the movie would start at dusk, so we're in no rush. She comes out of the restroom talking to two other women. I smile. She attracts people wherever she goes. Of course, that would include the restroom. She hasn't seen me yet, she's still chatting, so I have a chance to ogle her a little. I also notice I'm not the only one.

She has no idea the effect she has on men. My eyes run over her body and her face. Her lush body calls to me, and I want to worship at her altar. I don't think she's wearing makeup and she's naturally stunning. Her mouth is a sin, and her eyes draw you in, make you want to know everything. I love the way she dresses. Bright colors, polka dots, ruffles, it's all so her. Big, loud, in your face, sweetness. I cock my head. I would love to sample her sweetness tonight. I feel my cock throb as I imagine her creamy cunt spread open against my lips.

She says goodbye to the women she's speaking with and looks around for me. She spots me and heads over. I hold out my hand, she accepts it, and I pull her into my body as we walk back to our blanket. She fits perfectly under my arm and her body molds to mine.

We make it back to our blanket. She pulls out a citronella candle and a lighter. This woman has thought of everything. She lights it and pulls out pillows and lies down. I join her and she looks over at me.

"Why is my age a deterrent for you? I'm only a few years younger than you are."

I scratch my chin, wondering how much I should disclose. Fuck it, she wants honesty. "My company keeps me busy; I'm driven to succeed, so I try to limit my distractions. Which is why I usually prefer older women, single moms, or recently divorced women looking for fun and nothing else. They typically have their own things going on, they aren't expecting things from me or want a relationship, and it's easy to mutually satisfy each other when it fits into our schedules."

Her eyes bulge. "You're dating multiple women right now?"

"No, not dating. Do I have sex with them, when my schedule allows? Yes. I'm very upfront about what I'm looking for, and fortunately, I've found women who are receptive to what I'm able to offer."

She nods slowly. "So, what does that have to do with me being 24?"

"Well, younger women, or the women I've met, are actively looking for a relationship. Or they just want my time, time that I don't have or want to give. We can agree to keep it casual, but it never works out. So, I usually just avoid younger women altogether." I wince as I see the look on her face.

"Please don't look at me like that. I enjoy spending time with you. I'm happy that you came back into my life." I reach over and take her hand. "You've completely changed my mind about 24-year-olds. I've been missing out!"

She laughs and slaps my chest. "No, not 24-year-olds, *this* 24-year-old and I'm ready to blow your mind." She leans over and kisses me softly on the lips.

Well, shit.

Gemma

To say I'm shocked by Elijah's candor is an understatement. He purposefully dates, no scratch that, he fucks women whom he deems as unavailable, emotionally, or otherwise. Another piece of the Elijah puzzle slips into place. I'm not sure how I feel about all this yet.

I guess I can't judge. I just went on multiple dates and made out with random dudes, all in the name of Mission Promiscuous. Maybe I should ask him for some tips.

He raises up on his elbow and looks down at me. "Tell me about your dating life. When was your last relationship?"

I blow out a breath. "There's not much to tell. I'm not seriously dating anyone now. I've only had three boyfriends in my life, only two were serious. My last relationship, we dated for about two years, but we were friends before we got together. We broke up about six months ago."

"Why'd you break up?"

"The relationship just ran its course. We lacked

something. We were just too comfortable, and we reverted to being friends. I'll always love him, but we're not compatible."

"In what way? Sexually?" he raises a brow.

"I guess, and maybe it is just me, but I've never felt that intense passion for him or the other guy I slept with. I've never felt like I needed or wanted sex so bad I begged for it. So, we ended it, and hopefully, I'll find *it* with someone else. I'm not sure if it even exists or if I'm just not a passionate person."

His mouth drops open. "You are absolutely a passionate person, and I'm here to tell you wanting someone so badly you beg for it also exists. You've practically had me begging for it all day."

I smile as he reaches over and cups my face. My stomach flutters when he says things like that.

"You've only slept with two guys?"

I nod. "Before we ran into each other, I'd decided I wanted to be more sexually adventurous, or actually, a promiscuous girl, and then you walked back into my life." I bite my lip. I cannot believe I am telling him all of this. The words sound stupid when I say them aloud.

His blue eyes darken as he runs his thumb across my bottom lip. "You want to be more sexually adventurous?"

I lick where his thumb has touched my lip. "Yes," I whisper.

He begins to trace my entire mouth with his

thumb, and I kiss it. He inhales and slides his thumb slowly into my mouth.

I twirl my tongue and begin to suck on it, taking it deep.

He stares at my mouth for a few seconds then he meets my gaze.

He removes his thumb. "You want to be sexually adventurous with me?" His voice is low and gruff.

"Yes." I breathe. "You..."

Before I can finish my thought, he is on me and kissing me hungrily. He bites my bottom lip and pulls a bit before taking it into his mouth and sucking hard. I hear his groan as his hands run over my body.

Cheers from the crowd interrupt us. Pulled from our arousal fog, I note the movie has started on the big screen. But when I look at Elijah, I see the blaze in his eyes as he watches me.

Holy fucking shit. What did I just agree to?

CHAPTER SIX

GEMMA

I giggle. "The movie is starting." I stretch and kiss his chin.

Elijah composes himself and sits up to look at the screen. "I finally get to see the movie you want to share with me."

I continue to lay on my back. "Titanic is one of my favorite movies. I used to fantasize about us holding hands and making out while we watched."

"I'm here to fulfill your fantasies. Come here," he pulls me up. I sit between his legs, my back against his front. He cuddles me from behind. "I've actually never seen this movie. I'm glad my first time could be with you." He kisses my temple.

He just ramped up my fantasy. Boring, teenage me just imagined us kissing and holding hands. This, this is so much better. His strong arms around me, his solid body supporting me and molding to mine, and not to mention I can feel the hard press of his dick in my back. This is much better than my fantasy.

I lean back and look up over my shoulder and offer him my mouth for a kiss. "I'm glad I could be your first." He obliges with a deep kiss.

He stretches and blows out our candle before reaching over and grabbing the extra blanket and pillows. Putting the pillows behind his back, he then covers us with the blanket.

We sit like that for a while, his arms around me as he intermittently kisses my temple before he bends and kisses my neck. My eyes close and I lean my head to the side to give him better access. He kisses me just beneath my ear and goosebumps rise across my flesh. I feel his strong tongue lick my neck right before he bites my earlobe.

He turns my face toward him as he takes my mouth relentlessly. He holds me exactly where he wants me as his tongue starts to fuck my mouth. I gasp as Elijah reaches under the blanket and pulls my skirt up slowly. Running his hands up and down my thighs, I sigh as he spreads me open. "You're so soft here," He whispers.

God, I feel like I'm about to faint. I can't control my breathing. Holy fucking shit.

"Are you ready to be adventurous, lovely?" I can't speak, so I just nod. He uses his feet to widen my legs further and then holds them open.

He takes my mouth again as he pulls my panties to the side and I'm already quivering in anticipation. He inhales sharply. "Your panties are soaked," he whispers in my ear. "Is this all for me, love? Are you fucking soaking wet because you've been thinking about riding my dick all day? Taking my cock so deep down your throat, you gag on it?" He asks just as he swipes his fingers through my wet folds.

I shudder. "Yes," I whisper. I'd say yes to anything right now.

He palms me. "I wish I could taste this creamy cunt. I want to suck and lick you until you come all over my face." I called it; he's perfect. His words are frying my brain.

He circles my clit before he inserts a finger. He strokes my g-spot before inserting a second finger and twisting. Oh god, I feel like I'm floating above my body. I try to control my breathing as he slowly starts to pump me. I whimper as he slides his fingers in and out and massages my clit. As his hands work their magic, he continues to kiss me, swallowing up my moans and sighs. He scissors his fingers, stretching me. *Fuck.*

He inserts a third finger, and the stretch and burn are almost too much. I'm so close to exploding all over his hand. "You're so tight, love," he whispers into my mouth. "I need to feel you around my cock. I know you would take it all, take me so deep." He continues to hold my legs open, and I just have to take the mind scrambling pleasure he's giving me. I whimper, wishing we were alone so I could yell this place down.

My head falls back against his chest as his hand

drifts to my breast, tweaking and twisting my nipple. That's it, I can't take it anymore, and my legs start to quiver. His hand continues to drift up my body, pausing briefly to grip my neck as his other hand continues to pleasure me. His hand reaches my mouth and covers it just as the most delicious orgasm overtakes my body, and I have to bite my lips to help muffle my moans. I feel my eyes roll back as waves of pleasure run through my body. He releases my legs, and I feel my body desperately grinding onto his hand, seeking out every bit of ecstasy he's giving me.

He finally removes his hand from my mouth and withdraws his fingers, but he continues to gently stroke my clit, extending my pleasure as much as he can. Just as I can't take anymore, he stops stroking me and takes his hand from under the blanket. I turn and without taking his eyes off mine, he puts his fingers in his mouth, licking and sucking them hard. *Fuck.* He groans and closes his eyes for a few seconds. When he opens them, his eyes are darker, hungrier.

"Damn baby, you taste amazing," he growls.

I just stare at him in awe. I'm confident I just had the most intense orgasm of my life from just his fucking fingers! I've never enjoyed, let alone orgasmed, from someone merely touching me. I was right. He is going to wreck me.

I stretch up and kiss his mouth, tasting myself on his tongue. Hmm, I do taste good, or maybe it's just him.

He reaches down and readjusts my panties, then he picks me up and lays me down on the pillow next to him, before he pulls up the blanket, turning toward me. Our movie date is long forgotten. I smile at him and begin to pepper his face with little kisses. He just watches me, maybe waiting for me to freak out. I just got finger fucked, in public, where anyone could have seen us. I can see why he's concerned. I start to laugh at the audacity, and I have to cover my mouth before I draw attention to us.

He begins to laugh a little too and says, "Are you freaking out?"

I shake my head no. "No, that was amazing. You're amazing." I reach over and stroke the side of his face. He smiles, turns, and kisses the inside of my wrist. *Swoon, that little kiss.*

"Good. Fantasy fulfilled?"

I nod emphatically. "You fulfilled my fantasy and created new ones. So many firsts tonight. I've never enjoyed that before, and you've made it my new favorite thing. You may never get rid of me now," I say as I kiss him softly, "but now it's your turn."

I go to reach for the front of his shorts, but he stops me. "Tonight is all about you. I'm here to fulfill your fantasies." He pulls my hand up and kisses it.

I pout, and of course, he stares at my mouth. "But I want to give you something. Something to remember me by so you won't forget tonight."

"You gave me this thoughtful date today. And you

gave me you tonight. I'll have no problem remembering that and how hot and wet you were for me."

That's it. My smile is full of mischief as I have the perfect idea. I pull my skirt up and shimmy out of my black lace hanky panky's. These are a favorite of mine, I'm a little sad to see them go.

"Here, take these." I put my panties in his hand. "Remember me and tonight, always."

He stares at them for a moment before closing his hand. He looks at me again, and with his eyes locked on me, he holds them up to his nose and inhales deeply.

Holy fucking shit.

Elijah

I stare at the tiny scrap of black lace in my hand. *Fuck, she's blowing my mind.* Not only did she give me her panties, she gave me her *wet as fuck* panties. I can't stop myself from burying my face in them and inhaling deeply. She smells as good as she tastes.

I see her watching me, a little shocked. She has no idea that I'm a kinky bastard, oh, but she will learn. Very soon.

"Thank you. I think you just fulfilled *my* fantasy."

She giggles again. "You're so easy to please."

I kiss her pouty lips and place her panties in my pocket. She has no idea.

I remember nothing of this movie she wanted to

watch together. We continue to kiss and caress until the credits end and we reluctantly begin cleaning up our picnic. I carry the bags and basket out to the street looking for my driver. My black truck pulls up. I open the door and get her situated before putting everything else in the trunk. This beautiful girl really tried to talk me into her taking me home since she asked me on this date. I had to firmly tell her that was not happening, and I would ensure she got home safely.

I take her hand and place it on my lap and I begin to play with her hair. She's staring at me with a small smile on her face. "What?" I ask her.

She shakes her head. "Nothing, I'm just thinking about how much fun I had today. I'll have to surprise you with dates more often."

I smirk. "Yeah, you should. You're pretty good at it."

We pull up to her apartment building. I help her out, and she seems surprised when I ask the driver to wait.

She looks at me questioningly. "I thought you were coming in."

"I would love to... but not tonight. Next time."

She looks disappointed but nods.

I anxiously wait while she unlocks the door. I walk her to her apartment and place her items just inside the door. I only have so much self-control.

She stares up at me, and I put her hair behind her ear. "Thank you for an amazing date."

I kiss her quickly before she can say anything and get my ass out of there. I know she's not wearing panties and that's all my brain could focus on. She gets respectful tonight, but next time, she won't be so lucky.

Gemma

I walk into work Monday morning with a spring in my step and a huge smile across my face. I'd texted with Elijah Saturday night and throughout the day Sunday. He's quickly becoming one of my favorite people, and that's not just because he gave me a mind-blowing orgasm. Well, not completely.

I woke up Sunday to a text he'd sent late Saturday.

I can still taste you on my tongue.

My eyes bulged. My mind is blanking on how to respond to him. I put my fingers to my lips as I tried to think of a clever response.

You're welcome. I text before falling back into bed and giggling to myself.

I get to my desk, put my things away and jump right into work. I've worked at BHP Publishing Group for three years. I've always loved reading, and luckily, I landed my dream job here right after graduation. I've worked my way up in the last three years, and I was finally promoted this year.

To say I love my job is an understatement. I get to read and talk about books all day. I may discover the next voice of our generation one day or find my new favorite author. Right now, I'm sifting through a few too many BDSM or shifter stories. For some reason, the higher-ups think I'm the go-to person for these genres. I don't mind it, the guys are always hot in these books, but I would like to try my hand at historical romance.

I'm currently collaborating with the team on a book that's perfect for a CW television show. Think Gossip Girl but with snow and chalets. This keeps me busy all morning, and I barely look up from my work until lunch. I check my phone and there's a text from Sasha.

I walked by your desk, but you looked busy. I'll be back around one with lunch.

I check the time; she should be back in about ten minutes. This is one of the many reasons I love working with my best friend. Sasha and I started at the publishing house around the same time, but instead of editing, Sasha works in accounting. She's a whiz with numbers, and I can think of nothing more boring.

Twenty minutes later, we're happily chomping on our salad and sandwiches. I have not told Sasha or Mia the details of my date. I plan on doing that tonight during our tv night. As we're finishing up, a delivery guy arrives at my desk. "I have a delivery for Gemma Davis," he says.

I rush to my feet. "That's me." He hands me a beautiful bouquet of long-stemmed red roses and a white gift bag. I peek inside. There's a white box wrapped in a white satin bow.

Sasha seems just as excited as I am. "What the hell is that?" she whispers.

I shake my head. "I don't know." The roses smell heavenly.

I find the card and open it. It reads - *To Many More Fantasies, Elijah.*

Elijah. Oh gosh, he is the sweetest. Closing my eyes, I hold the card to my chest, remembering our sexy date.

Sasha grabs the card out of my hand. "Let me see, let me see."

She reads it and frowns. "To more fantasies? What is he talking about?"

I smile sweetly. "I'll tell you and Mia all about it tonight." I try to shoo her away.

"Wait, I want to see what's in the box."

"No, I want to open it alone. I have no idea what it could be."

She sticks her tongue out at me, grabs what's left of her lunch, and heads back to the accounting floor.

I look around to ensure no one is watching and take the gift box out of the bag. I stare at it for a second before noticing that it says La Perla. He didn't. I glance around again before I remove the ribbon and open the box. Inside, I find another note nestled in tissue paper. I put it on my desk, and discreetly pull out the black satin and lace thong.

I grab his note and it reads – *Surprise me. Elijah.*

Does he want me to wear these and surprise him by showing them to him? Is he going to be thinking about me wearing these every time he sees me? I shiver in anticipation. He's a cheeky bastard who just gave me some very cheeky panties.

Holy fuck.

* * *

Later that night, I'm sitting around my coffee table with Mia and Sasha for our TV night. Tonight, it's The Real Housewives.

"Wait, so he finger banged you, on your first date, surrounded by tons of people?!" Mia sounds impressed. "These are all the things I've always wanted for you."

Sasha shakes her head in exasperation at Mia. "How do you feel? I can't even wrap my head around this. Where do you go from here?"

I cuddle a pillow to my chest. "I don't know. It's weird to say, but it felt right, in the moment. We'd spent hours together, and the connection was off the charts. I don't regret it."

Sasha is still concerned. "What if someone had seen you? That would be my biggest fear. I would not have been able to enjoy it, no matter how gifted the fingers are." She wiggles her fingers at us.

Mia rolls her eyes. "Yes, you would, and please don't rain on Gem's happy pussy parade. She finally did something for her. Let her enjoy it."

I nod my head. See what I mean, my very own angel and devil and today, I am siding with the devil.

"It's not like it'll ever happen again, but I can now check semi-public sex off my list. But honestly, this has given me a few more ideas of what I would like him to do to my body." I shake my head to get rid of those distracting thoughts. "Anyway, today he sent me those beautiful flowers," I point at the arrangement across the room, "his sweetness turns me on." I cover my face with the pillow.

"Yes, we know about the flowers, obviously. Now tell us about the gift," Mia says.

I look to Sasha as she guiltily covers her face. "Well, you didn't open it in front of me. I needed someone to speculate about what it could be," she shrugs.

"So, what do you think he sent me? You both get one guess." They look at each other.

Mia jumps in immediately, "I have no idea, but I hope it's either handcuffs or a buttplug," she claps excitedly. We all laugh. Those would be interesting gifts.

Sasha thinks for a second. "I have so many guesses, but my top choice is lingerie. It's too soon for jewelry and lingerie is something you both can enjoy."

"Ding, ding, ding! Sasha for the win!"

"Oh my gosh, I was just throwing something out there! He's presumptuous or extremely cocky if he's already buying you lingerie," Sasha exclaims.

"Well, he did finger bang her at the movies, in a park, surrounded by people. I would go with he's a presumptuous bastard," Mia adds.

We all howl with laughter before they prompt me to show them the lingerie.

I take out the La Perla bag, and they are immediately impressed. La Perla is a definite statement.

"Let me start by saying this gift is sort of a retaliation."

"What do you mean?"

"After all of our fun Saturday, I took my panties off and gave them to him." I cover my face with my pillow.

"WHAT!" they both squeal. Mia looks like a proud mom.

I uncover my face and open the white box and pull out the thong. "I guess he got me these," I hold them up, "to replace the pair I gave him."

Mia takes the thong from my hands. "He's got great taste. It's gorgeous. I love the lace detail."

I nod. "There's more. There was also a note and it said, 'surprise me.'

Sasha looks at me with raised eyebrows. "What does that mean?"

I shrug. "My guess is he wants me to wear these or show him I'm wearing them somewhere unexpected."

"Yes, you have to tease him with them. Every time he sees you, he's going to wonder if you're wearing this gorgeous thong." Mia explains. "Don't wear it the next few times you see him to drive him crazy. I would casually run into him somewhere unexpected and then, bam, show him my ass."

I frown. "That sounds legit, but I don't know 'how hard to get' I can play when I know what his fingers are capable of. I can only imagine that he's good at everything else."

"No worries, we'll say a little prayer for you, a prayer asking for you to have the strength to keep your legs closed, just this once." Mia mimics prayer hands.

Please and thank you. Amen.

Elijah

I head to the court for my weekly game of basketball with the guys. Besides our Saturday night meet-ups, this is pretty much the only guaranteed time I have with all of them each week. I always look forward to it. It's a great time to catch up and unwind midweek since we're all busy with our high stress careers.

The guys are already on the court shooting around when I arrive. I have not had a chance to tell them about my date Saturday, so I prepare myself to be inundated with questions and shit talking.

"Hey, lover boy is here," Xander yells once he sees me.

I smirk. "Same thing your mom says every time I see her."

"Suzanne is going to kick your ass. You better watch it." Xander laughs. "She'll twist that ear right off your head."

And just like that, my mood has lifted. I'm ready to

play some ball. I join the guys on the court to stretch and warm-up before our game.

Drew looks over to me. "Mia told me you and Gem went out on a date Saturday. *You* went out on an actual date? I'm shocked."

Ty adds, "Yes, an actual date where you went out *in public* with her? You didn't just meet somewhere to fuck? This is remarkably interesting."

I shoot them a dark look. "Yes, pencil dicks. We went out *in public* together."

"Does she have a secret kid we don't know about? She's stunning, but we all know your type," Xander says.

"No, she doesn't have a fucking kid. Shut up. Listen, I like her, we went out, had a great time, and that's it. I don't need the extra commentary from you assholes. Let's shoot for teams." My little tirade doesn't shut them up. In fact, it makes it worse. I listen to their shit the entire game, and I think it was a strategy because I played like shit.

We walk off the court and head to the bleachers to grab our things. "Drew, since you've been talking to Mia so much, what's up with you two?"

He smiles. "She's a cool girl and a lot of fun. She actually wants to put together a beach day Saturday. I meant to tell you guys about it."

"Oh shit, you're planning a party with her? Both of you bastards are in love!" Xander laughs. "Fuck, we're not doing tea parties and shit."

We all laugh. "Nothing that you just said made any

sense. And on that note, I'm out of here." I point to Drew. "I'm in for Saturday. See you at the office, Ty."

I walk over to my waiting car, thinking about Saturday. Again, my mind flashes to images of Gemma and her luscious body all oiled up in a colorful bikini. Yep, I'll definitely be there Saturday.

CHAPTER SEVEN

GEMMA

I step into the shower letting the hot water rinse the sweat from my body and relax my muscles after a strenuous session at the gym. I've had a crazy week at work, so I missed a few workouts. I'm feeling that absence now. It never fails. I get into a rhythm and hit the gym consistently three to four times a week. As soon as I start to see some results, I get complacent, and I start to skip my workouts.

I close my eyes, wetting my hair, and tell myself that if you want to look good naked, you have to go to the gym. I mean, I guess I could eat better and cut back on all the alcohol and carbs, but that just seems excessive, I laugh to myself. Operation Look Good Naked is still a work in progress.

I step out of the shower, apply my body oil, and wrap myself in a towel. I think I'm going to put on a face mask tonight. I need to relax and recharge. It has been quite the week. I haven't spoken to Elijah since

Monday. I can only assume that he's busy with work. But you know what they say when you assume. Maybe he's not busy with work, but instead, he's busy with someone else.

I think back to what he said. He prefers to date women who are less likely to want a relationship or women who are otherwise preoccupied with other things going on in their lives. I want to fit into that category, so I haven't texted him to give off that vibe. I *have* been busy this week with work and my friends, and even though we haven't spoken in a few days, he's been on my mind.

I recall our movie date as I brush my teeth. He's a phenomenal kisser with magical hands, which makes me wonder, how much practice has he had? How many women has he been with? Loved? He's so affectionate. I can't imagine his relationships are as basic as he stated.

Still in my towel, I walk into my bedroom to find something comfy to put on. The girls may come over later for dinner and trash TV. Thankfully, I can be as ugly as I want to be with them. I'm rummaging through my drawer when I hear a knock on my door. That's odd. I should have had to buzz them in.

I throw open my front door and gasp at the sight of Elijah. He's looking delicious in a navy suit, bright white shirt, and red tie. His hair is perfectly tousled, and he has a sexy stubble adorning his face. I perv on him as if he can't see me as well.

He smiles knowingly. "Gemma, my eyes are up here." He gestures to his face.

"I know where your eyes are. What are you doing here?" I snap.

"That's no way to treat an old friend, a friend whose hand you came all over not too long ago," he holds his hand up, showing me those skillful fingers. "Honestly, I've had a crap day. I thought about what would help me improve it, and you popped into my head. So, to answer your question, I'm here to see your face."

My heart stutters as he scans my body. I'm still wrapped in a towel with my hair piled up on the top of my head. I'm sure I'm a complete mess.

"But now that I see you looking like this, I'm here to discuss our next fantasy." He reaches up and strokes my face. "May I come in?"

I turn my face into his hand. "Yes, I've given everyone enough of a peepshow." I step back and allow him to enter my apartment. He immediately overwhelms the space. Gah, I was not expecting this. I hope I don't have any bras lying around.

I close the door and he backs me up against it. He trails his finger from my lips down to my neck, gripping it briefly, before trailing his finger to the swell of my breasts where my towel is knotted.

"You would look amazing with a pearl necklace," he says, his voice sweet as honey.

I reach up to touch my neck. "I don't think I'm a pearls kind of girl."

"You will love my pearls. You won't want to take them off."

He kisses me briefly on the lips before turning and walking in to look around my apartment. My parents purchased this place for me as a graduation gift. Once they conceded that I wasn't moving back home after graduation, they wanted me to have a nice place to call home.

"Nice place. They did a great job on the updates without removing its vintage charm." He walks around, looking at different pictures I have displayed in my built-ins.

Of course, Mr. Real Estate Developer CEO would have an opinion. "Thanks. The first time I saw this place, I thought the same thing." I love my apartment and not just because of the location. The building was renovated a few years ago. There were four apartments on each of the three floors back then, but now, each floor houses two nice sized apartments. The huge windows overlooking my bustling street provide me with so much natural light and a place to sit and read. The large fireplace is perfect for Chicago winters, and the original hardwood floors are beautiful. Plus, it's so spacious, with two bedrooms and two baths, and open living spaces.

I straighten the pillows at my little window seat, and I squirm as I try to tidy up the small dining table.

"Nice couches." My yellow couches sit proudly in my bright, white living room, covered in a mix of black and white polka dot or striped throw pillows.

He finally turns his eyes back to me. Again, he scans up and down my body and the mood in the room changes from lighthearted to something sensual. The heat in his tells me he's done with the small talk.

"Like I said, I've had a crap day, maybe even a crap week. What are you going to do to make me forget all about it?" He starts to loosen his tie.

Uhhh. I have no words.

He takes off his suit jacket. "Don't be shy. I'm here to have my fantasy fulfilled."

I finally snap out of it. "You have a fantasy about *me?*" I squeak.

He nods slowly. "Absolutely. I have several, actually. But one in particular really needs your attention today. Thankfully you're dressed perfectly for what I have in mind."

I glance down at my towel, my brain still hasn't completely caught up to what's happening, but my body is responding. My breathing starts to quicken. I feel my nipples tighten into peaks, and my thighs start to feel slick with my desire.

He's still in his shirt and pants as he moves the coffee table aside and sits down on the couch. "Come here," he says firmly.

I immediately go to him and stand at his feet.

He looks up at me. "Let me tell you about my fantasy."

I swallow noisily as he readjusts his dick as it strains against his pants, begging for my attention.

The corner of his mouth tips up as he says, "I can't

stop thinking about your mouth. So much so, that I want it wrapped around my cock. And if you're a good girl, I'll give you a pearl necklace."

Confusion flashes across my face then my eyes widen in realization.

"Yes, exactly. Next, I want to fuck your tits, but we'll get to that later. Sweet, Gemma, are you ready to fulfill my fantasy?" He thrusts his hips.

I nod immediately and drop to my knees in front of him. My heart is pounding, my palms clammy, but I can't think of anything I've ever wanted more, and that includes a pony. He reaches up and roughly runs his thumb across my lips.

"You only have yourself to blame with these pouty lips. I need to see them stretched around me. I've thought about nothing else since we met." I kiss his thumb and my tongue darts out for a little taste. His eyes blaze at the contact. Oh, he liked that, he liked that a lot.

He reaches over, undoes the knot of my towel, and we watch it fall to the floor. I'm completely naked and open for him. He hisses in approval. "You're stunning." Again, he traces his fingers along my neck and collarbone, then down to my breasts before cupping them. My body arches into his hands as I feel a rush of wetness escape from my body. I've never been so turned on in my life, and he's still fully dressed.

I finally whisper, "Yes, I want to fulfill your fantasy." I meet his eyes, seeing triumph and something I can't describe.

He nods slowly. "Good, love, unbutton my shirt."

I reach up instantly, and with shaky hands, I start to unbutton his shirt. I try to calm myself with deep breaths as he watches me with hooded eyes.

He stills my hand and kisses it. "Why are you so nervous?"

I shrug. "This is new for me, for us." I lick my lips and meet his gaze. "Teach me. Teach me what you like, how to please you."

"You've never given head before? Your mouth was made for it." He shakes his head as if this is the most absurd thing he's ever heard.

"I have, but just like a little bit. Or I did it just enough to get it over with." My face heats.

He laughs. "I'll happily be your practice dick, but just know there isn't any 'little bit' or 'getting it over with.' You're going to take this dick deep down your throat and you're going to enjoy it just as much as I am."

My body heats at his words. He leans back on the couch with his shirt open and his bare chest exposed. *Fuck, he's gorgeous.* I open his shirt more so I can get a better look at his chiseled chest and firm abs. He still has that V that I love, that I need to taste. He continues to watch me as I explore his body with my hands and mouth. I lean in, press my breasts into him, and lick and suck his earlobe. He inhales sharply. I kiss down to his neck, inhaling his scent, and I continue down to his chest, licking a nipple as I go. I run my fingers through his dark treasure trail until I get to his waistband before I pause, looking up at him.

"Take my dick out."

I swallow and nod. *Holy hell, we're really doing this.* I undo his belt and unbutton his pants and gently pull the zipper down. The sound seems to echo through my apartment. It almost drowns out the sound of my wildly beating heart.

I expose his black boxer briefs. The sight of his hardness trying to escape makes my breath hitch. I look up at him again with a raised brow as I pull his shorts down just enough for him to spring free.

"Oh!" I lean back and just look at it, licking my lips unconsciously. I've obviously felt him through his clothes, but I did not expect this. He's long, much longer than anyone I've ever been intimate with, and so thick. This suddenly doesn't seem like a good idea. There's no way I can do this. I close my eyes briefly. When I open them, he's pulled his pants down further, and he's stroking himself with long, sure strokes. This is the most erotic thing I've ever seen. My eyes pore over his broad chest, taut abs, and I begin to salivate as I watch him.

"Tell me what to do," I whisper.

He doesn't respond, but he stops his movements and rests his hands on his thighs.

I lean up and kiss his abs, licking and biting down to his hip bones, and he bounces his dick once, twice, in response. I wrap my hand around the base of his cock, loving the weight of him in my hand. He groans as I stroke up and down his shaft a few times before I look up at him as I start to lower my head.

He reaches up and traces my lips with his finger. His voice is strained when he says, "you look so beautiful right now."

I give him a small smile, our eyes locked, and I take his wide head into my mouth.

"Fuck," he moans.

I work to calm myself and my breathing. I'm freaking out, but I can do this. I *want* to do this. I swirl my tongue around his head before taking him a little deeper. He continues to watch me, his brow furrowed, mouth open, forming a small O. I find a nice rhythm. I bob up and halfway down a few times before I feel his hands in my hair, gripping my bun. He takes over and guides me down and back up slowly. He continues with long slow pulls, and I suck harder and twirl my tongue. He guides me down and holds me there for a few moments.

Then he says, "teeth, I need your teeth." Oh, he likes a little pain.

I use my teeth to scrape up and down his length a few times, and I feel his hands tighten in my hair as he groans. That groan sends a shiver through my body.

"Balls, lick and play with my balls," he hisses. My body clenches at his words. I love this bossy side of him.

I stroke him with one hand, while cupping his balls in the other. I give them a squeeze and then a big lick before taking each one in my mouth and suck. He hisses again as he starts to fuck my hand. I take that as my cue to take him again deeply into my mouth as I continue to play with his balls.

Gone are the long slow pulls, as he guides my pace before he allows me to take control. He moans and his hips jerk, making me gag a little as I try to take him deeper. Seeing him lose control is the biggest turn on. I squeeze my legs together for some friction. I think I could come with the briefest of touches.

"You're perfect. You're making me feel so good. Open up for me, baby," he says this softly, and I shiver.

I relax my throat and take him as deeply as I can, over and over again, moaning at the taste of him.

I feel him start to swell as he pulls out of my mouth, pulls me back by my hair, and with the sexiest groan I've ever heard, comes across my neck and chest.

I look down with a whimper.

A pearl necklace.

Elijah

Holy fuck.

I lean back and try to calm my breathing as I loosen my hold on her hair. She immediately looks down at my cum on her chest.

"I was right. You look amazing. You're a fucking vision." I reach down and stroke her face.

She meets my eyes and then looks down at my dick, which is still partially hard. Without a word, she bends forward and takes me into her mouth again. She licks me clean before she softly kisses my tip and sits back on her heels.

Holy fuck. I like her kink.

"Did I fulfill your fantasy, sir?" She bats her eyelashes at me.

"You did indeed, but next time, you swallow." I reach over and cup a tit in each hand. "I'm in a giving mood and it's your turn." Just as I take her nipple in my mouth, I hear the door buzzer. Someone pushes it several times in some melody I can't place.

Her eyes fly to mine. "Shit, that's Mia and Sasha." She stands and grabs her towel. "Will you let them in while I wash off your lovely present?"

She doesn't wait for my response but runs over and hits the intercom. "Just a minute!" she yells before she takes off for the bathroom.

Slowly, I put my dick away.

Damn, this is not how I saw tonight going. I shake my head to get rid of the visions of her ankles around my ears.

Gemma

I race to my bathroom and smile goofily as I check out Elijah's handiwork in the mirror. Another first for us, and of course he's right, I look amazing! Swollen lips, flushed face, my eyes bright as I take it all in.

I get cleaned up, throw on some clothes, and head back out to my living room. I can hear my girls talking and laughing with Elijah. I like his laugh. It's deep and warm. He stands when I enter the room. He's giving me serious 'come sit on my face' face, but alas, not tonight. He turns and says goodbye to the girls, and I walk him to the door.

He kisses me tenderly. "You're always a pleasure."

I smile into his kiss. "I would say the pleasure was all mine, but I don't think that's true."

He bends and kisses my neck. "Thanks for blowing my mind...and my dick. I'll have to stop by with fantasies more often."

He kisses me once more and then he's gone. I hold my fingers to my lips and smile as I remember how he lost it and fucked my mouth not too long ago. Yes, we'll have to do that again soon.

I return to my living room, and my girls are looking at me expectantly.

Sasha says, "Soooo?"

I smile brilliantly. "I slobbed on his knob!" I sing. They help me finish the song as we dance around.

They burst into cheers as we all laugh.

Sasha asks, "You gave him a mouth hug?"

Mia squeals, "You smoked his pole?"

Sasha adds, "Her brain game is insane." They high five.

Mia laughs. "Let's cheers to this beej, you little head doctor!" She runs to the kitchen to check my fridge.

We follow her and she grabs a bottle of wine.

She pours us each a glass and says, "Not to take away from your moment, but I'm fairly sure that Drew told Eli about our beach day Saturday. After this, I take it you're alright with him coming along?"

I nod enthusiastically, "Oh yes, I'm all about seeing that body again, shirtless and sweaty." I imagine running my hands all over his broad chest and shoulders. Yes, I would not miss this for the world.

* * *

Saturday morning, the girls and I are unloading our Lyft with all our beach day stuff, and we are struggling.

Mia sighs. "Maybe I should have taken Drew up on his offer to pick us up and help with all of this crap."

We all nod, but we make the best of it. North Ave Beach is one of my favorite beaches. It is eternally lively; there are people everywhere, and they are always up for a good time. We grab a spot near a beachside restaurant because, duh, we need to be near the food and drinks.

An eclectic group of women, possibly in their mid-to-late fifties, begin to set up their spot nearby. They are already loud and rowdy. I overhear lots of laughter and F-bombs. They've gone all out with their setup. I look over their tent, fans, speakers, matching tables, bursting coolers, and loungers with envy.

I look over to Sasha and Mia and whisper, "Our mission today is to become friends with those women." I gesture with my chin.

They nod in agreement. "They are definitely goals," Sasha adds.

We lay out our blankets to cover a large area and set our chairs around in a semi-circle to claim our space. This beach gets packed, and people have no problem encroaching on your territory. Opening our cooler, I grab the bottle of our premixed mimosas. There's no alcohol allowed on this beach, so we had to be sneaky. Our 'orange juice' barely has any juice at all. I pour us each a cup and sit back in my chair.

"OMG, it is so hot already. You said the guys were bringing the umbrellas, right?" I ask Mia.

"Yep. They are also bringing more 'juice' since I told them we were bringing the snacks and chairs."

I'm about to respond when I suddenly hear a low whistle and a, "Would you look at that," from the ladies nearby. We turn and see the guys walking toward us. We burst out laughing.

Mia whispers, "The Fuckable Four have arrived."

We continue to watch them approach, along with all the ladies nearby, and I have to admit they are probably one of the hottest groups of guys I've ever seen. The blowing wind is a perfect addition to their stroll towards us. Hair's flying around, shirts are molded to their chests or blown open. It is definitely a sight to behold. My greedy eyes are on Elijah the entire way. I feel a little flutter in my stomach. I can't wait to get his shirt off. He's wearing a pair of Aviators, so I can't see his eyes, but I can feel the heat of his gaze on me. Once the guys get a little closer, we begin to catcall them. The ladies nearby join in.

Sasha leans in. "I told you, they are goals." We all laugh.

The guys finally make it to our blankets, and we go around and greet everyone, and I end up in front of Elijah. I'm suddenly shy as he stands before me. With his windblown hair, tan skin, and muscular body on display, I suddenly feel inadequate.

"Do you like what you see?" he asks.

I just stare at him dumbly. He is a little too much for me right now.

He senses my hesitation and leans down to whisper in my ear, "Come on, the last time you saw me, you had my dick in your mouth. Don't get shy now."

Shocked at not only his audacity but his ability to read me so well already, I laugh and punch him softly in the stomach.

"Well, maybe next time I'll be shy then too."

"Don't you dare," he growls.

I stretch up on my tiptoes to give him a hug. He's so much taller than I am without my shoes on. He pulls me into his body and wraps his arms around my waist. "That's better," he kisses my temple. A shiver runs through my body. I have never felt this attraction, this sexual magnetism toward anyone before. I feel as if his body is calling to mine. Can men be Sirens? I need to look into this. I feel another shiver run through me as I feel the heat and hardness of his body pressed against mine.

"Down boy," I whisper and step out of his embrace.

I busy myself helping the others get everything set

up. The boys brought several umbrellas that we desperately need. Setting them up is my first priority. We get their chairs arranged and get some music going. Now the fun can begin.

Elijah approaches me in what seems like slow motion and takes his shirt off in that sexy way guys do. My mouth gapes open. Holy fuck. He stands there for a minute and lets me gawk before handing me his sunscreen.

"Do you mind?" he winks.

I snatch it from him. Of course, I don't. I would slap anyone else who dared rub him down in front of me. I add the sunscreen to my hands and rub them together. "Turn around." I want to start with his back to give myself a minute to calm down. I take a few deep breaths and rub the sunscreen into his shoulders. His beautiful broad shoulders. His muscular back. I don't know what these muscles are called, but they are delightful. I feel a smile spread across my face. Ok, so rubbing sunscreen onto his back first didn't really help me calm down. "Turn around," I say huskily.

He obliges. Again, I start at his shoulders, working my way down to his chest. Pecs, I know what these are called, and he's got a great pair. I add more sunscreen to my hands and work my way down to his abs. Elijah inhales sharply. I look up, and he's watching me with hooded eyes. I continue to look at him as I spread the sunscreen across his abs and then down each of his strong arms.

I lean in to kiss his chest. "There you go, handsome."

He smiles. "Thank you. I truly have never felt more protected from the sun."

I giggle. "If you're going to do something, you might as well do it well."

"You could probably have a second career as a masseuse."

I burst out laughing. "No thanks."

He tilts his head. "What if I ask nicely?"

I lean in. "If you ask me very nicely, I would gladly be your personal masseuse. I'll even do house calls."

He licks his lips. "Now we're talking." He kisses me softly. "Ok, your turn."

He kneels and lays on my blanket.

"Look at that. I got you on *your* back already," I smirk, throwing his joke back at him from our first date.

He sits back and puts his hands behind his head. "If you don't know by now, I'm easy. Now, back to you. It's your turn."

I frown. "My turn for what?"

"Your turn to take it off, then I'm going to rub you down with sunscreen."

Oh.

I'm suddenly self-conscious. He saw me naked in my apartment, but he was hard and horny then. I knew I shouldn't have skipped those workouts this week. He looks like he lives in the gym. Ugh. I look down. I'm wearing a long white flowy cover-up. I knew I couldn't wear it all day, but I thought I had a little more time. I take a deep breath, reach down, and pull it off in one quick motion. I drop it to the ground next to him.

Elijah is watching me intently. I slowly kneel on my knees next to him.

He looks at me questioningly. "What's wrong?"

Again, he reads me like a book. I fidget and look down. "I don't know." I shrug.

He stills my hands and pulls me down to him. "Why were you so nervous?" He lifts my chin to look at him.

"It's silly. I missed a few workouts this week. Then I see all of this," I wave my hand around his body, "I got a little self-conscious. Obviously, you take care of yourself. I didn't want you to be disappointed."

"Are you serious? You could never disappoint me. I'm a big fan of yours, the biggest." He leans in and whispers, "Have you considered that you and your body may be all of my favorite things?" I stare at him dumbly, my hard-on for him growing several more inches. "I work out for my own personal reasons. Not to look good but to feel good. But I hope you love your body because I think it's incredible." He kisses my temple.

I cover my face with my hands for a second. Gah, I'm an idiot. Now he probably thinks so too. I don't know where that insecurity just came from, but I try to shake it off. I look up coyly, "I'm ready for my sunscreen, Mr. Adler."

He winks. "Happy to oblige, Ms. Davis."

He sits up as I lie down on my stomach. He

straddles me and grabs my sunscreen. My sunscreen is a spray, but he's not going to let that stop him.

I try to block out the howls of his friends as he undoes my bikini top. I shoot him a dark look over my shoulder, my face heating. He just smiles as he sprays my back and shoulders and begins to slowly rub it in. I close my eyes and exhale deeply. I knew he had magical hands, and this is bewitching. He continues to rub sunscreen into my back, and I can feel his erection laying perfectly in between my ass cheeks. He presses into me in rhythm with his strokes along my back. Again, there are people all around us, laughing and talking, but we're in our own little arousal bubble. He slides down my body. I feel his hands on my ass and look back at him.

"I don't think I need sunscreen on my butt."

"I never leave a job half done. Let me take care of you, woman."

I giggle and put my head back down.

He palms my ass with both of his hands before he slaps it, making me jump. I'm wearing a hot pink bikini with Brazilian cut bottoms that are super cheeky. He has an eyeful of my ass.

He rubs the sunscreen into my skin in a firm circular motion before he reaches around to grasps my hip bones. He holds me there for a second as I imagine him fucking me from behind, holding me exactly how he wants me. I look over my shoulder again. Based on the intense look on his face, I know he's thinking the same thing.

He finally snaps out of it, secures my bikini top, and in a husky voice says, "Roll over."

He lifts as I flip over onto my back, and he straddles me again. *Holy fuck, is this really happening?* Without breaking eye contact, Elijah sprays sunscreen into his hands and begins to rub it into my shoulders and chest. His hands glide under my bikini top as he massages my breasts briefly and squeezes my nipples. I try to suppress my moans; we're surrounded by people, for goodness sake.

His hands slide lower over my abdomen, my hips, and he continues to rub me sensually. Again, he focuses on my hip bones. He has me in a two-handed grip before his hands slide over my hips and then to my thighs. He finishes up my legs and lies down on top of me. "I love how you pretended to be shy with this hot fucking body. You're such a tease." He nips my ear and trails kisses along my neck.

Suddenly, he flips us over. I gaze down at him as I feel his hands roam up and down my body, squeezing my ass. He thrusts up into me as I moan quietly. I bend down and grab him by the hair and kiss him deeply.

Mia's loud voice breaks through my horny haze. "This is better than any porn I've ever seen."

CHAPTER EIGHT

GEMMA

*M*ia, Sasha, and I are lying on our blankets watching the guys throw a football around. Sasha shields her eyes with one hand and sits up on an elbow. She's watching someone intently.

"Alright, spill. Who are you gawking at?" I ask.

She looks around before responding. "Tell me everything you know about Tyson Ford."

Mia and I squeal. "Besides him being gorgeous?" I ask. We all turn our attention to the fine specimen running down the beach. "I don't know much. He and Elijah have been friends since they were kids. They started their real estate development company, like six or seven years ago, and they are extremely successful. I don't know his relationship status, but he seems like a catch, a definite sweetheart."

Mia nods. "He's hot, Sash. I would go for it."

Sasha continues to watch him. "We'll see."

We're quiet for a minute and then I ask, "Have you ever tasted your vagina? I recently read that women should be tasting their vaginas to ensure vaginal health."

Sasha looks intrigued. "I can't say that I have."

We both look at Mia, and you would think I just asked her about her favorite color. She smiles. "Of course, I have. Tell me, would you serve someone your famous brownies without tasting the batter first?" We shake our heads. "Why do you think I changed my diet?!"

We fall into each other as we howl with laughter. Of course.

Elijah

Gemma has been playing volleyball with some people she met on the beach. I must say, watching her jump around, bouncing in that bikini, is a fucking turn-on. I readjust my dick and grab a drink. Today has been a surprisingly good day. Our new little crew knows how to have fun.

I search for Gemma again. I spot her talking to a group of guys from her volleyball game. My eyes sweep over her body again. This woman shouldn't have an insecure bone in her body. She's naturally beautiful with curves in all the right places. I note she's not wearing makeup again today. Her innate beauty is so attractive and appeals to me in a way I can't explain.

I return to Gemma's blanket, lie down, and close

my eyes when I hear Sasha and Mia talking nearby. I don't turn to look at them, but I strain my ears to listen.

"Look at her flirting with those guys. They are all salivating at her feet." I think that's Sasha.

"Yes, Queen! She has them eating out of her hand."

"Operation Summer Slut is in full swing."

"Mission Promiscuous is live."

They walk away as I take a deep swig from my drink. The fuck? Jealousy washes over me, and I rub my hand over my face. Although I'm not looking for anything serious, the idea of her doing the things she's doing with me with someone else doesn't sit well with me. Uneasiness settles in my stomach. I feel the tension in my jaw as I head in Gemma's direction. She's just turning away from the group she was speaking to. She smiles instantly when she sees me. My anger eases a little at that small victory.

"Mission Promiscuous?" I say in a greeting.

Her eyes bulge and she pauses before saying, "Huh?"

"Operation Summer Slut?"

She shrugs. "I told you I'd just decided to be more adventurous or promiscuous when we ran into each other. Those are just the fun names we came up with for my dating life. I've been on a few dates and here we are."

"You're going on dates?"

"I've been on a few. Just checking off my list of Summer Slut fun."

"Am I on that list?" Fuck, where did that come from?

"You're number one, and there are five stars next to your name."

I lean in closer, inhaling the scent wafting off her warm skin, and put a few strands of her hair behind her ear. "Are there any perks for having a five-star dick?"

"So many perks. You have no idea," she says as she walks away.

I shake my head. What am I going to do with you, Gemma Davis?

Gemma

I finally make it home. I'm exhausted and still covered in sand. The day started off great, but I felt some tension with Elijah as the day progressed, and I'm not sure what to do about it. I jump in the shower and only then remove my coverup and bikini. I enjoy the beach, but I hate getting sand everywhere. I especially don't want it in my apartment. It's almost as bad as glitter; you can never get rid of it. As I wash my hair, my thoughts drift back to Elijah. The man is an Adonis. He's the perfect amount of brawn without being too bulky. I recall his smooth skin under my hands, and I melt. Everything about him turns me on. I picture his beautiful face, those blue eyes, that strong jaw covered in a few days' stubble, and his kissable mouth. I smile to myself. Hopefully, one day soon, I'll get to go on that ride. I step out of the shower just as my phone starts to ring. I'm not in the mood, so I ignore it, and I continue to pamper my skin. It needs it after today. I head into my room and grab some comfy pajamas as phones ring again. OMG, what?? Grabbing my phone, I shriek at the sight of Elijah's name across the screen. Holy fuck. I scramble to answer it. I take a deep breath.

"Hello, handsome."

I can hear his smile through the phone. "I could get used to that greeting. Good evening, lovely."

I feel my smile spread across my face. "Missing me already?"

"You have no idea. I know we just spent the day together, but I'm not ready for it to end."

Beyond shocked, I whisper, "Really?"

"Absolutely, so with that in mind, I would love to cook you dinner tonight at my place."

"Dinner? At your place? You're going to cook for me?" My brain simply can't compute what's happening.

"Is that a yes?"

I nod before saying, "Of course. I can't wait."

"Perfect, I'll send a car for you in an hour."

I mentally start planning a casual but sexy look for tonight. "I'll be ready. See you soon." I breathe.

"Oh, and Gemma, I'm in the mood to fulfill a few of your fantasies tonight. I hope you're ready." He hangs up before I can respond.

Well, holy fuck.

* * *

I'm dressed and ready in record time. I guess the promise of good things to come really motivates me to be on time. I went back and forth about what to wear. It was tough because I don't want to be too sexy or look like I'm trying too hard. I could have called Mia, but I know she's passed out from the hot sun and too much tequila.

I decide on a simple white maxi dress. It's flowy and casual and the spaghetti straps and a low cut back adds the perfect amount of sexiness. I feel a little like a Grecian goddess, and I'll take any extra boost of confidence I can get. My hair is in a long messy braid over my shoulder, and I've added a few gold accessories. I'd also considered wearing the thong he got me, but I will heed Mia's advice and make him sweat it out for a while.

My buzz has worn off, and the nerves have set in. A night alone with him. No interruptions. No people around. Holy hell.

I hear my door buzzer and head over to the intercom. "Yes?" and I wait for a response.

"Ma'am, this is Thomas, Mr. Adler's driver. I will be your transportation tonight."

Ma'am? So rude. "Yes, thank you, I'll be right down."

I grab my purse and head out to the waiting car. The driver opens the door to the black SUV, and I climb in.

Thomas has soft music playing as he drives through the city. I stare out the window, attempting to slow my breathing, willing myself to calm down. A night alone with Elijah is what fantasies are made of. We finally arrive at our destination. I take a deep breath as I step out. Taking a good look around, I'm surprised at the sight in front of me. I assumed he lived in some high rise overlooking the city or the water, but he lives on a beautiful tree-lined street in, what looks like, a family friendly neighborhood. Instead of a high rise, I take in the three-story brick home with an ornate fence and a beautiful vintage double door. Of course.

I smile a goodbye to Thomas and approach the door. I take a deep breath to calm my nerves and stop my shaky hands before knocking on the door. He answers the door with a kitchen towel thrown over his shoulder and a heart-stopping smile. I feel myself return his smile as my eyes roam over his face and body. He got some sun today. His olive skin is the perfect contrast to his fitted white shirt. My gaze lowers to his dark shorts and bare feet. This man is pure sex on legs.

He smiles knowingly and bends to kiss my cheek. "Hi, gorgeous girl."

I feel myself blush and my eyes close at the contact. The fire he ignites in me with just a smile and a soft kiss.

He steps back. "Please, come in. I've been waiting for you."

I shiver as I step inside. Surveying the space, my

eyes don't know where to look first. "Wow. Your place is amazing. Although, I didn't doubt that it would be."

He smiles proudly. "I bought this place and the lot next door a few years ago. It took quite a bit of time renovating everything to my specifications, but I'm finally satisfied with the overall look. It was built back in the 1890s. I wanted to keep some of that character, but my overall goal was to make it modern and open." He takes my hand. "Let's get you a drink and if you want, we can take a tour."

He leads me toward the kitchen, and I take in the hardwood floors, huge fireplace, and large windows. This place is amazing, and the kitchen is no exception. I imagine it would be a chef's dream. It is perfect for entertaining. I sit at the large island and Elijah fusses around for a minute.

His kitchen is bright and white, from the gleaming stainless-steel appliances and hood over the stove. It's a little intimidating to my inner wannabe chef. I run my hands over the cool countertop as I watch him check the oven and then I finally get a whiff of something that smells cheesy and delicious.

Elijah turns to me and asks if I would like wine or champagne. I choose champagne because I'm a bubbles girl and he grabs a bottle of Dom. This is my absolute favorite champagne, but I don't drink it too often since it can be expensive.

"How did you know this was my favorite?" I ask him after taking a sip.

His drink stops just before it reaches his lips. "I didn't. I just wanted to celebrate your first night here."

First night? Swoon.

"Why are you so sweet?" I ask him quietly.

He seems surprised by that. "Why wouldn't I be with you?"

I don't know what to do with that. Shaking my head, I change the subject. "I think I'm in for a treat tonight. Whatever is in that oven smells delicious. What are you making?"

He smiles and lets me change the subject. "You're in luck. Tonight, you get to enjoy my world-famous lasagna."

I cock a brow. "World-famous, huh?"

"Indeed. I guarantee it will be the best you've ever had," he says, his voice steeped in honey.

I no longer think we're talking about dinner and I feel the atmosphere change around us. Gone is fun and lighthearted as Elijah's blue eyes darken and I feel the zing of anticipation settle in my stomach. Elijah approaches me and plays with my braid. "You're glowing. I really like seeing this face," he says as he cups my cheek. I close my eyes and nuzzle into his touch. I feel the pull to him, and I lift my face and offer my lips to him. He bends to kiss me, and the oven timer goes off. We both jump and laugh.

He licks my lips and says against my ear, "Saved by the bell." I shiver as he kisses my bare shoulder before going to the oven.

I grab my flute and take a deep drink.

My eyes trail Elijah as he takes a pan of gooey cheesy goodness out of the oven. "I'll let this cool while I make a salad. Then I'll give you the tour after dinner."

I nod as he takes out everything he needs to prepare our meal. He is sexy and confident as he slices and dices the ingredients.

"You look pretty good in the kitchen, Mr. Adler."

He wipes his hands on a towel and brings over our salads. "Really?"

I nod. "Yes, this could be your next business. Women would pay beaucoup bucks to have a sexy man cook them dinner. Shirtless."

He sits next to me at the island. "Is that a hint for me to take off my shirt?"

I smile at him over my glass. "You certainly won't need a shirt for what I have in mind."

He smiles and continues to watch me.

"Well, if I recall, you barged into my place with a fantasy that needed to be fulfilled," I offer.

"Indeed. If *I* recall, you were more than happy to do so, and you did a marvelous job. I was willing to return the favor, but we got interrupted. Do you have something in mind tonight?"

I consider this before I stand and grab my purse. "How about that tour of the house?"

Elijah guides me through the house by the hand and shows me all the bells and whistles. I'm too distracted by lust and all the things I want him to do to me that I really can't pay attention. I just ohh and ahh when he points out different things. I'm surprised to hear this place has five bedrooms. Why would a bachelor need this much space?

We finally make it to his master suite, and I look around the massive space. There's a humongous bed against a dark gray wall, opposite a fireplace, with a high tufted headboard. The room is decorated in dark grays, white, and navy with chrome accents. There's a sitting area near the large far windows, and I imagine the doors along the walls are for the bathroom and closet. The overall vibe is dark and sexy. It's like you have to be bad just to hang out here. I inhale deeply, taking in his now familiar scent of sandalwood.

I stop and stand near the foot of the bed as I can feel Elijah's gaze on me. I sit on the bed, take off my shoes, and scoot toward the center before I meet his gaze.

"I do have a fantasy that needs to be fulfilled tonight."

He smiles sexily. "I'm here, always ready to serve."

He stands near the bed and I tell him, "Take off your shirt."

He obliges immediately, grabbing the back of his collar and pulling his shirt over his head.

I drink in his broad chest and defined abs. I know I just spent the day with him shirtless, but it doesn't matter. I make a mental note to go to the gym with him soon and watch him work out. I imagine it would be the best porn on the planet.

We continue to stare at each other, and I can feel

my desire wetting my panties. I squeeze my thighs together in anticipation.

He finally asks, "Is this going to be reciprocal?" I see his muscles flex. He's totally into this.

I shake my head no. "This is my fantasy. Just shut up and look pretty."

He laughs softly. "Watch it. That mouth of yours is going to get you into trouble."

"Promises, promises. Now, take your pants off, slowly."

He smirks and unbuttons his shorts and pushes them down his muscular thighs. He kicks them to the side as he stands there in tight black boxer briefs and a hard dick. I lick my lips as I feel my breathing quicken. We need to move this along.

I gesture with my finger, *come here.*

He kneels onto the bed and bends to kiss my inner ankle. His hands start to roam, and I shiver as he pushes my maxi dress up my body. I sit up and he lifts it above my head. I'm completely exposed except for my white lace panties.

His eyes roam my body as he inhales deeply. "You're beautiful."

He's still kneeling between my legs. I forget all about my original fantasy. So many more have come to mind now that I have him nearly naked in bed. I grab his head, pulling him to me. I fall back onto the bed and he follows me. Our mouths meet, we're kissing desperately, our tongues dueling. He sucks my lips and tongue before he sweeps through my open mouth again and again. I moan as I feel the full weight of his body atop mine. He finds my most intimate part and grinds his cock into me.

He kisses a trail to my neck, and he bites me hard, causing tremors to race through my body as I moan again. He continues to grind into me, and my body feverishly rises to meet his. His tongue trails to my neck and my ear before he bends and takes my nipple into his mouth. He bites me, and I keen, "Aah, so good."

"Baby," his voice gruff, "you feel so good. You've been teasing me all day jumping around in that tiny ass bikini, shaking your ass in my face." He grinds into me a little harder, in a steady rhythm. "Do you feel that? I've been hard all fucking day." If he keeps that up, I'm going to come.

I pull him back down to my lips. I bite his lip and pull his hair as I feel the start of my orgasm. "Oh, god. I'm going to come!"

"Yes, come for me, baby."

"I'm coming! I'm coming." I whisper as I feel an orgasm race through my body. I buck my hips and arch up to meet his. Elijah continues grinding, prolonging this feeling of euphoria.

He continues to kiss my neck before he makes his way back to my breasts. He squeezes them before biting into me and taking my nipple in his mouth. I feel so sensitive, I nearly jump from the bed.

He blows on my wet nipple. "Relax, baby. I'm going to take care of you."

I grab his hair again, pulling him closer, and lick his neck before meeting his gaze.

"Take my panties off."

He smiles. "Are we back to your fantasy?" he asks as he kisses down my stomach. He kisses my pussy through my panties, and I give him a small whimper. I hear him tsk tsk, "These are not the panties I bought you."

I snicker. "Doesn't matter. They are coming off anyway."

I hear him chuckle softly. "Fair point."

He begins to pull my panties off, and I see him close his eyes and sniff them deeply, which may be my new favorite thing to watch.

"I can't stop thinking about watching your pretty little face between my legs," I whisper.

His eyes rise to meet mine. "Same, I've been dreaming about how good you taste." He kisses the inside of my thigh, and I jump again as I feel his stubble scratch my sensitive skin. "You gave me such a small taste last time. Tonight, I want to drink you in. I'm going to make you feel so good, baby," he says, biting my inner thigh.

My nerves have flown away, and all I can think about is coming all over his beautiful face. I lean up on my elbows. "I can't get the image of your face between my legs out of my head. I've never really enjoyed oral sex before, but I want to do this with you."

He reaches up and takes my hand, giving it a squeeze, which melts me.

"For my fantasy, I want your face between my legs, sucking and licking me until I come, and I want to use this." I hold up my phone. "I want to take pictures, maybe even video."

He raises his brows. "Baby, have I told you I like your kink?"

I shake my head no. "Is that a yes?" I whisper.

"That's a hell yes," he says right before he bends and gives me a deep lick. I buck on a low moan and fall back onto the bed. He licks me deeply again and bites my clit. I moan as a sheen of perspiration covers my body. *Fuck.*

"Baby, watch me," his deep voice grumbles into me and I shudder. I lean back up on my elbows as I meet his gaze. He drags his mouth from side to side before sucking me deeply. I fall back again. Overwhelmed with the show he's putting on.

"Pictures," he growls. Oh right, I reach blindly for my phone, and with shaky hands, I pull up my camera. Elijah's eyes are closed. He looks like he's having the time of his life. I take a few pictures before I call his name, "Look at me."

His eyes open and they are now a deep, dark blue. I get several pictures of him looking into the camera, his eyes blazing, face covered in me. Our eyes are locked, and I can almost feel the tangible connection between us.

He inserts two fingers and begins to pump me aggressively as I cry out. I'm in sensory overload. "You're so tight. I can't wait to feel you around my cock." He continues to lick, suck, and pump me, now with three fingers. I take a few more pictures before throwing my phone aside. I close my eyes, allowing the pleasure to wash over me, through me.

My body starts to quiver as I feel my orgasm start to flow through my body. "Elijah!" He tongues me deeply. My body takes over and I fuck his face and hand as hard as I can. "Ohmygod, yes, YES!" My body convulses as I ride out a blinding orgasm that also steals my breath.

I vaguely hear the rustling of a condom wrapper over the sound of my blood rushing to my ears. I'm still floating in oblivion when I feel his cock stroke my sensitive clit and brush my entrance.

My eyes widen. Fuck, he's so big, this is going to hurt. I feel my body start to tense.

"I can't wait to be inside of you."

He must see the apprehension on my face because he immediately lowers his body and kisses me tenderly. I soak up the weight of his body covering mine and sigh at the glide of his lips against my own.

"Relax, baby. Open up for me."

I nod and open my legs wider. He watches as he feeds himself into me, slowly, inch by agonizing inch.

"Fuck, you're so tight. You're fucking phenomenal." He begins to massage my clit with his thumb, and I feel another burst of cream flow from me.

I can't respond. My mind and body are short-circuiting.

This is happening. *Holy. Fucking. Shit.*

. . .

Elijah

Fuck, this woman.

I can't describe the feeling of sliding into her tight pussy. I try not to think about how warm and wet it is, or this is going to be over too quickly. I continue to massage her clit. When I'm about halfway in, I thrust, driving in, sliding my cock in to the root.

She whimpers and I stop and give her a second to adjust. I'm not a small man, and she's in for a long hard ride tonight.

"Are you ok?" I ask her.

"Yes!" her voice is hoarse.

"I'm going to move, baby." Slowly, I slide out and re-enter her a few times. I swivel my hips to loosen her up. She's so tight. I groan at the feeling of her pussy milking me, sucking me in.

She grabs my ass and doesn't let me pull all the way out. Yeah, there she is. I quicken the pace, propelling my hips forward and we're both moaning. "Damn, baby."

I bend to kiss her as her hands go to my hair. I grunt at the feel of her nails scratching along my scalp. She gives a hard tug, and I close my eyes at the sting. Baring my teeth, I change the angle as I give her short, hard thrusts.

Fuck, the headboard is banging the wall, but it doesn't drown out her cries. I take her mouth aggressively, swallowing up her sounds, matching the movement of my tongue to the thrust of my hips.

I sit up, positioning her legs over my shoulders. I bite the inside of her ankle before licking her foot. Long, hard, deep strokes. She's going to be sore tomorrow. Our bodies are covered in sweat, and she's a devilish delight, writhing in my arms. I feel her start to quiver and I know she's close.

"Come for me again, baby. I want to feel you," I say as I massage her clit with strong fingers. Her eyes close briefly just as her orgasm builds, causing her to moan in revelry.

Her eyes open as I feel the first spasm and tightening of her pussy, strangling my cock. "Fuck, Elijah, yes, yes!" she wails, eyes locked with mine. For these brief seconds, I feel as if she can see my every thought, every wish, and I close my eyes to shut her out.

I shake my head. Bending, I cup her ass, pulling her up just where I want her as I feel my orgasm building. She's open, exposed in this position, and I pound into her. I feel my orgasm barreling down and I explode. "Fuck!" I hold myself deep inside of her as I come, and I feel my cock jerk repeatedly.

I finally release her, hoping she doesn't bruise. I bend, taking her lips in mine in a languid kiss, as we try to catch our breath. I rest my forehead against hers.

"Have I told you I'm fucking ecstatic I came out that night and we reconnected?"

She smiles, suddenly shy, and shakes her head.

"Well, I am, because look where we are now."

I kiss her once more before pulling out. She winces a little but looks pleased with herself. I remove the condom and place it in the trash next to the bed before rolling back to her. I lie on my back and pull her to me. I lose track of how long we lie there kissing.

This woman is so unexpected.

CHAPTER NINE

GEMMA

I stumble into my apartment around 6 am. I'm sore and exhausted. I can't wait to shower and climb into my bed. I feel thoroughly fucked. It's a thin line between pain and pleasure, and I've now straddled that bitch. I've heard people talk about this feeling and it is not what I expected, but it was worth it.

I strip on the way to my bathroom, leaving a trail of clothes in my wake. I giggle to myself as I step into the shower, and I cover my face with my hands because I still can't believe what happened.

I recall all the delicious moments from last night and this morning. Shit, I forgot to check the pictures on my phone. Those are now my most prized possessions. I can't believe he actually let me take them. Doesn't he know you aren't supposed to show your face in nudes? Even with his beautiful face buried in me, I'm sure I have several clear pictures of him. Dreams do come true, all my wildest ones.

He took me twice more before we finally collapsed from exhaustion, missing out on that amazing smelling lasagna. I slept for a couple of hours and when I was sure he was asleep, slipped out of the bed. I had to get out of there. I didn't want to be that girl who stayed the night and got labeled as a stage five clinger. Mission Promiscuous means no sleepovers, right? Summer Slut 101. So, I grabbed my clothes, got a Lyft, and here I am.

Elijah

I blindly reach for Gemma, ready to pull her into my body, and I'm met with nothing but cool, empty sheets. Thinking maybe she's just in the bathroom, I doze for a few more minutes. When I wake again, and she hasn't returned, I start to grow concerned. I turn to check the clock, and it's about 7 am. I get up and check the bathroom. She's not there either. I look around and I don't see her clothes, but I see that my clothes have been picked up and are neatly folded and placed on the chair. She also cleaned up the gold condom wrappers that littered the floor. I head downstairs to see if I can find her but no luck. Again, I see that she has cleaned, but this time in the kitchen. She cleaned up our salads, the uneaten lasagna, and loaded everything in the dishwasher. I continue to look around until I see that she sent me a text.

Thanks for dinner. I'll call you later.

Thanks for dinner? What the actual fuck? I guess she did eat my dick, but did she really sneak out while I was asleep? I fully planned on fucking her again this morning. I almost laugh, this would be hilarious if I weren't so pissed.

I jump in the shower. I need to have a chat with Ms. Gemma Davis.

Gemma

After the longest, steamiest shower and a hearty breakfast, I mean I had a strenuous night, I finally climb into bed. Looking at those pictures again had me too amped up to sleep. Instead, I tidied up my apartment a bit, but now the effects from my late night are hitting me. I'm just starting to feel myself drift off when I hear my door buzzer.

"Nooo, go away!" I yell. But it continues to buzz incessantly.

I jump up and run to the intercom. "What?!" I all but snarl.

"It's me." I hear a male voice say.

"Who's me?" I ask, confused.

"Elijah. Who the fuck else would be here at 8 am?"

My eyes bulge. What in the world? I press the button to let him in. I race to my room to grab something, anything to cover my half-naked body, clad in nothing but my polka dot panties. I only have time to grab a fitted black tank before I hear him knocking. I throw it on and go to open the door.

He's standing there and he looks pissed. *Oh boy.* He storms past me.

"So, I fucked you so senseless, you just left in the middle of the night? Not only am I disappointed because I had plans for us this morning, but it is not safe for you to be out by yourself that late...or early. You know what I mean."

I take a second to process his words before I burst out laughing, "Excuse me? You did not fuck me senseless! Get over yourself. We're doing the no strings, casual thing, so I took that to mean no sleepovers." I shrug my shoulders.

He takes a deep breath and runs his fingers through his hair before reaching out to stroke my cheek. "Well, I wanted you to stay the night. I wanted to wake up to this beautiful face this morning. I wanted to cook you breakfast and spend a little more time with you. I thought I conveyed that?"

I nuzzle into his hand. "No, I had no idea."

"I'm enjoying the time I get to spend with you. I know we're doing this "casual thing" but let's make our own rules and have some fun, yeah."

I just nod. *Mind. Blown. Heart. Aflutter.*

"So, if you're at my place, I fully expect you to stay the night. Ok?"

I smile shyly. "Ok."

He raises a brow. "And?"

"And what?"

"What about me? Am I invited to sleepover? My cuddle game is A1, just like my dick."

I burst out laughing. "I guess."

"You guess?" he growls.

I shriek as he picks me up, and the next thing I know, he has my body pressed against the wall, and my legs are around his waist. I wrap my arms around his neck and hold on as he takes my mouth in a rough kiss. My body responds instinctively. I writhe before biting his lip and pulling his hair. He groans before biting into my neck, his warm breath heating my skin.

"You guess? You would deny your body what it wants, what it clearly needs, because you're following some stupid rules?" His voice a growl as he grinds into me.

I can only whimper. The only thing separating our bodies are my panties and his basketball shorts. He has the upper hand here and I surrender completely.

He carries me to my living room and places me on my feet. "Are you still guessing?"

Goodness, he's really hung up on this, but if I'm going to be rewarded like this, I'll just keep guessing.

I shrug, but before I can make a smart-ass comment, he tears my shirt over my head, turns me around and pushes me over the back of the couch, with my face in the cushions and my ass in the air. Seconds later, I feel the cool air hit my body as he rips my panties down my legs.

He spreads my legs and bends and bites my ass.

Thank goodness I stay current with my laser hair removal treatments and that I sprung for the Brazilian.

"Look at this pretty pussy. She's already wet for me. You would deny her what she wants?" He runs a finger through my wetness, and I shudder.

"Oh baby, you're swollen," his voice is soft as a caress as he strokes me again. "Let me kiss it better."

He bends down, and I hear him inhale deeply before I feel a soft kiss, then the first slip of his tongue across my clit.

Whoa. My eyes rolled back in my head as I try to steady myself, tensing and anticipating the next lash of his tongue. Fuck, this almost feels indecent. My ass is right there at eye level, but I let those thoughts go as his tongue sweeps through my folds again. He sucks deeply as I bite the nearest cushion to muffle my cries.

I squeeze my eyes shut, wishing I could see. I wish I could see him right now, him, down on his knees worshipping my body. I moan just thinking about it, so I try to snap a mental picture for later.

He cups my ass with both hands and gives me a squeeze as he sucks and licks me into oblivion.

"Does that feel better, baby?" he whispers into me.

I barely get out a whimper before I feel him take his thumbs and spread me open, kissing me deeply, right there, before he inserts two fingers and begins to finger fuck me.

I cry out and clutch the pillow as I feel my orgasm invade my body and I submit, pulled under the waves of rapture.

He stands and kisses up my back before I hear the condom wrapper. *Yes!*

I don't have a second brace myself as I feel him sink into me. "Ah, baby!"

He pulls out and plunges in deeply again, and I feel every inch of him. He pulls out slowly. The drag against me has my body shuddering again already.

I grow greedier as I push back into him. He leans over me and kisses my back before grabbing my face and kissing me over my shoulder. His huge body envelops me, overwhelms me.

His hand goes around my neck with a squeeze as he continues his punishing rhythm as we go hard at it. The sounds of our ecstasy and skin slapping echo throughout the room.

"Do" *Thrust.*

"You" *Thrust.*

"Still" *Thrust.*

"Fucking" *Thrust.*

"Guess?" *Thrust.*

He asks as his hands go to my shoulders to grip me for leverage.

I can't speak words through this pleasure dome I'm floating in. I think I shake my head no.

"Is this what you want?" he asks as he reaches around and rubs his fingers over my clit.

"OH, god. Yes!" My orgasm has been building since he entered me, and I know this one is going to shatter me.

He presses on my clit. I detonate around him as my

body is wracked by what feels like a never-ending orgasm. My toes curl as I cry out, as waves of euphoria flow through my body.

Elijah continues fucking me hard and deep, and I can feel how close he is. I reach back and cup his balls in one hand, and I dig my nails into his thigh with the other. He hisses and I feel him lose control. His rhythm falters as I feel his cock pulse. He holds himself deep in me as he comes with a loud shout.

He kisses me along my back as he continues to move in and out of me.

"Bad girl. Look what you made me do," he whispers.

"Please feel free to do that to me any time you want."

He kisses my shoulder and trails a few more kisses down my back before he pulls out.

He walks out of the room, I guess to get rid of the condom, but when he returns, he finds me in the same position, because my damn legs don't work.

"What are you doing?"

"I can't move my legs; your dick was too good. Your mouth too."

He chuckles. "Sorry, not sorry, love."

He lifts me easily and carries me like a bride to my bedroom.

He sets me down and looks around. "I like your room. It's very you."

I look around too and nod. My bedroom is a mix of teals and corals, patterns, and polka dots, with white accents. The textured teal accent wall was a must-have. It just may be my favorite part of this room. Showing him the real me, him being here, is overwhelming. Never mind that I'm naked.

"Another fantasy fulfilled. I've lost track of the number of times I fantasized about you being in my bedroom growing up. It's surreal to have you here right now."

He kisses me softly before discarding his clothes and sitting on my bed, legs opened wide.

"You have me here, now what are you going to do with me?"

I drop to my knees.

We collapse onto the bed, exhausted and slick with sweat. Elijah pulls me to him, and I drape over his body as we try to catch our breath. He strokes my hair and I smile dreamily up at him.

"What? He smirks.

I sigh. "You were right. I apologize for sneaking out after you fell asleep. I don't know what I was thinking. You really must have fucked me senseless because a naked you in a bed shouldn't be wasted."

He chuckles. "Thank you. I could say the same about you," he says as he kisses my head.

I close my eyes and try to gather the courage to say what I'm about to say, "Elijah?"

"Yes, lovely."

I smile softly. I love when he calls me that. "I'm glad we ran into each other."

I feel him smile against my head. "Me, too."

His hand stroking up and down my naked back helps me get the rest out.

"I would love to continue to get to know you better, especially this body." I laugh, "In the last 24 hours, you've given me more orgasms than I've ever experienced with anyone else, combined. I know you're not looking for anything serious, neither am I, but I don't want to let go of my fantasies with you." I feel a full body blush come over me. I hope he understands what I'm trying to say.

He's quiet for so long I look up at him.

He kisses me softly. "What are you offering me?"

I scrunch up my face. "Friends with benefits?"

His beautiful blue eyes darken as he watches me. "With pussy perks?"

"Absolutely. Fantasy fuck buddies. Sleepovers included." I stretch up to kiss him, and his hand comes to my face and strokes my cheek.

"Deal."

I feel relief flow through me, and I squeeze him a little tighter. "My first fantasy fuck buddy. And don't worry, there are no strings attached, but let's agree to communicate openly when we want to end this or if we meet someone else."

"Sure."

I smile into his chest. With that unpleasantness out

of the way, I feel myself drift off into an exhausted sleep.

* * *

What feels like minutes later, I awake to Elijah kissing my shoulder. I finally open my eyes and see that he is fully dressed.

He brushes the hair from my face. "I have to go, lovely."

"No." I give him a pout.

"An actual pout on top of these pouty lips? You're not playing fair." He rubs his thumb roughly across my lips before bending to kiss me.

I pull him down to me. "Nope, never."

He nuzzles my neck.

I hold him tightly for a few more minutes, then release him with a sigh. "Fine, go."

"Don't act like that. Get some rest." He kisses me once more and stands and leaves. I hear my front door close behind him as I check my bedside clock.

I'm meeting the girls later this afternoon, but since it's only a little after eleven, I snuggle back into my bed. Someone wore me out last night and this morning.

I smirk, look at me, casually dating and shit.

* * *

Hours later, I'm with the girls. Sasha and I play creative directors/assistants as Mia poses for picture after picture for her blog. She's shooting three different looks today and getting candids walking around the city. Which means Sasha and I are lugging her crap around. I won't complain, though. We get tons of perks from being her friends and showing up in pictures on her blog. She tagged us in a picture on her Instagram in the hot new workout gear. The brand then sent me and Sasha free clothes, too. Our followings are not as huge as Mia's. She has about 70,000 followers, but we're well on our way to being mini influencers, so I'll take the free or discounted stuff.

Mia is currently trying to get pics of herself in the street. Sasha is watching for traffic, and I'm holding all the gear. I'm missing brunch and bottomless mimosas right about now.

We've finally snapped the last picture, and we walk back to Mia's apartment. After helping her put everything away, Mia heads straight for the kitchen. She owes us some frosty beverages. Mia makes us a pitcher of Frosé and a margarita for herself. We're all exhausted and lounge on her couch with our drinks.

"Mia, what's going on with you and Drew?" I ask her.

"Nothing really. Don't get me wrong, he's hot and super sweet, but I feel like he's the settling down type and I'm not interested in that right now. Plus, he hasn't really made a move." She shrugs.

"He's *respectful*? What a loser." Sasha laughs.

"No, I can't explain it. The chemistry is there, but I

feel like I'm holding back. Maybe he is too. I don't know. I haven't spoken to him since the beach."

"What about you, Sasha? Did you chat up Ty yet?" I wiggle my brows at her.

"No, I still can't read him. Plus, he makes me so nervous. He's gorgeous. And sexy. And successful. And gorgeous."

"Babe, he's all of those things, but so are you. If he doesn't see that, then it's his loss." I tell her.

"Yeah, and if he does see that, then he's as smart as I think he is. Plus, you guys would look so good together," Mia adds.

We cheers to that.

"So, I have a status report on Mission Promiscuous."

They watch me expectantly.

"Something may have happened at his place last night...three times, I think, and then again twice at my place this morning."

"He sounds like a winner!" Mia exclaims.

Sasha bounces in her seat. "Why are we just now hearing about this? We need all the details."

"I don't want to share too much, but just know he makes me feel as good as he looks."

"I'm impressed. You never know with pretty boys. They usually don't have to work too hard to get laid, so they don't work hard when they do." Mia shares.

"Yeah, or they get laid so much they have to be good, or they'll get a bad reputation. It's a pride thing." Sasha adds.

"I don't know. He is very tactile. Maybe he gets off on giving pleasure because he got me off multiple times. I'm really looking forward to sitting on his face the next chance I get."

Mia holds up her glass. "And what a pretty face. Perfect for sitting."

Elijah

I try to stifle my yawn. I'm tired, but it's well earned. I smile inwardly. My time with Gemma last night and this morning are burned into my memory. It's currently living rent free in my mind.

Ty returns to the table and slaps me on the back. "You look like shit, man."

We're meeting for drinks to discuss our work week. We have several meetings and projects to prepare for this week, but sometimes we like to keep it casual and away from the office.

Ty and I have amassed an impressive portfolio of industrial, retail, and residential investment properties in the last six years. I have an eye for the property or location and the details, while Ty handles the money and negotiations. We are a formidable team and have been since we were kids. Fortunately, we complemented each other perfectly and found success early and often throughout our careers. And with this latest deal, we'd be skyrocketed to the upper echelon of real estate development companies. All before the age of 30.

"I didn't get much sleep last night, but I'm good. I'm heading home after this to prepare for the week, then I'm just going to chill. We have too much shit going on for me to flame out."

This week, we had several meetings to finalize our bid for a luxury apartment complex, with space for retailers and restaurants, in a new trendy up and coming neighborhood. This was another huge move for us.

"We got this, bro. I'm not worried about Eli Adler flaming out. What had you up last night? Are you stressed?"

I typically told Ty everything, but I wasn't in the mood to talk about Gemma. I was still processing everything myself.

"Not any more than usual. I don't know what it is, man."

"Well, I propose we have a wicked weekend once we get the go ahead for this project, because once we get the ball rolling, we're going to be swamped. I'm thinking a quick little trip to Vegas or Miami to get our dicks wet before shit gets crazy."

"Deal."

CHAPTER TEN

GEMMA

I can hear the music blasting from Sasha's apartment from the hallway. She swings the door open just as I'm about to knock. My sweet angel baby Sasha is the biggest music lover and a huge hip hop head. It doesn't matter if it's new or old, she plays it proud and sings it loud.

She pulls me into her apartment, and she starts singing along to the song.

We dance around her apartment to *Ho* by Ludacris. She exclaims, "I played this especially for you. It's your new anthem."

I crack up and sing and dance with her. I'll take it. I'm a Promiscuous Summer Slut, after all.

Tonight, Sasha and I are going on a double date with these guys we met a few weeks ago. They are both personal trainers, so at the very least tonight, I can get a few pointers and tips for a flatter stomach and firmer ass. Sasha finally turns the music down so we can chat without yelling.

"I love your look tonight. Hey, gorge!" she exclaims.

I look down at myself, and I smooth my dress with my hands. I'm wearing a fitted violet dress that comes down to my knees and has spaghetti straps with a low draped back. My hair is piled on top of my head in a bun, and I'm wearing these multicolored chunky earrings that I picked up today.

"Same to you, doll." Her sexy little body appears to be floating in a beautiful aqua off-the-shoulder dress that shows off her toned legs in sky-high stilettos. I don't want to toot our horns, but toot toot. I think we look damn good tonight.

We head to her bedroom for finishing touches. She sprays herself with perfume and grabs her clutch as I check myself out in her full-length mirror.

I'm back on track and have stuck to my workout schedule, and I'm loving my results. I mean, I have the biggest motivation... Elijah. He looks amazing in a suit or t-shirt and shorts but naked, he's utter perfection.

"Are you ready to go? I'm going to order the Lyft," she asks.

"Yep, but let's take a shot or something before we go. I have bat-sized butterflies in my stomach."

She agrees and we head to her kitchen. Her drink of choice is vodka, so I prepare myself for the yuck of it all. I'm surprised I don't have a drinking problem between Mia's tequila and Sasha's vodka preferences

We each down two shots and I have a feeling Sasha is just as nervous as I am. She orders our Lyft and we both decide to grab a roadie for the ride. No sense in wasting our buzz.

"Sasha, I honestly don't remember anything about these guys," I tell her as I take a sip of my vodka soda. I've been in Elijah-land as of late and all men seem to pale in comparison. I picture his gorgeous face with his piercing blue eyes, square jaw, and his pleasure giving mouth and I shiver.

"To be honest, I don't remember much myself. It's been a few weeks since we set this up. They were both cute, and we were all flirty, so I guess we'll just have to see how it goes."

"Well, you have dibs on whichever one you like. I'll just be over here keeping it casual."

We giggle as we pull up to our destination.

We decided against dinner since that seemed too much like a date-date, so we went with drinks at a trendy new bar. It's supposed to have a speakeasy vibe, so we thought this would be a perfect spot for our double date. We walk in and are immediately impressed with the venue. The lighting is low, and the decor is everything you'd imagine it would be. All deep dark reds, gold, and black. There's a stage, with a piano, at the far end and I cross my fingers in the hope that there's some live music tonight. The walls are lined with large booths, down the center of the room are smaller tables, and there is an array of stools lined up at the bar. The amazing bar is stocked with every drink imaginable. There are also cool light fixtures that resemble bourbon bottles above the bar and across the ceiling. This will certainly do.

Sasha sees the guys sitting at one of the smaller tables in the center of the bar, close to the stage.

I whisper to her, "What are their names again?"

"The blond one is Aiden and the dark-haired one is Franco," she whispers back.

"Sit next to the one you're into. I'll take your castoff." Casually dating means dating different people to see what you like, right? You never know unless you give it a chance. Both guys are attractive, and this date will just be fun practice.

Both men stand as we approach the table. They both get a point there. We all hug and kiss in greeting. Sasha takes the offered seat from Franco, who looks as if he won the lottery. Aiden pulls out a chair for me and I sit. I grab the drink menu and happily peruse all the cool prohibition themed drink options.

Aiden leans over to check out the menu. "What are we drinking?"

I look up and meet his gaze. He really is quite handsome, in a wholesome, boy next door kind of way.

"I don't know. I'm typically a wine or champagne girl, so maybe something fizzy."

We chat about the options, and I steal a glance at Sasha and Franco. They look very cozy. Our waitress comes by, and I decide to try a French 75. It's one of the only options with champagne, so it can't be bad. Sasha orders a vodka gimlet. The guys decide that they want us to try all the specialty drinks on the menu, so Aiden orders the first two drinks listed on the menu and Franco orders the last two drinks, and we'll see if we'll meet in the middle.

These two just got more interesting. It is going to be a boozy night.

Elijah

Ty and I have just finished up a business dinner. Now we're enjoying a celebratory drink when I get a text from Xander.

Hey, twat. Your girl is here, and it looks like she's on a double date with Sasha. She looks smoking hot.

Two photo attachments ping and I open them. The first is a picture of Gemma and Sasha sitting at a table with two dudes. They are all laughing, and some blond asshole has his arm around the back of her chair, trying to show ownership or some shit. The next is a zoomed in picture of Gemma smiling at her date.

Xander is right about one thing. She looks fucking phenomenal all dressed up. Her slender neck is exposed with her hair up. She's edible.

She's not my girl but keep an eye on her for me. From the looks of it, those guys can't be trusted.

He replies.

Sure, no problem.

I show Ty the pictures and his eyes linger for a moment. I tell him, "It looks like the girls are on a double date with these two."

Ty takes a sip of his drink. "How do you feel about that?"

I shrug. "I don't. We hang out, no strings."

He continues to watch me.

"What?" I ask.

"You like this girl, don't downplay that. I've known you for a lot of years, and she's the first girl I've seen you publicly acknowledge. The usual women you fuck, I never meet. They are completely separate from your tidy little life."

I think about that for a minute.

"In just a few short weeks, you're going out on dates with her, dancing with her, kissing her, *in public.* You never do that shit, man. I think it's something about this one." He takes another sip of his drink while I consider this.

He's right. I love women. I love spending time with them. But I do all of that in private. That has always worked for me. I've spent years building a successful business. This delineation is probably a big part of that.

I take a sip from my drink. "Have you ever been so sexually attracted to someone that you can't think straight? I want to *own* her, *fuck* her, *claim* her, all the time."

Ty raises a brow. "No, you caveman, but it sounds fun."

An hour later, we've just settled our bill when my

148

phone goes off again. I see Xander's name light up the screen.

"Hey," I answer.

"Dude, your girl is well on her way to blackout and this guy is all over her. What do you want me to do?" Xander says.

"Fuck. Don't let her leave with him. Drop a pin. We're on our way." I say before ending the call.

I look at Ty. "Gemma is apparently wasted, and I would guess Sasha is too. I'm going to get Gemma and make sure she gets home safe."

Ty nods and grabs his things. "I'm coming with you."

Gemma

I've lost track of the number of drinks we've had. I'm having a blast with Sasha, but the guys, or at least Aiden, is a dud. He's nice enough, but he's no Elijah. I sigh. Now that I've had a taste, I know everyone else is going to be blah in comparison.

I take another sip of my prosecco and check my phone; sadly, there are no calls or texts from Elijah. I wonder what he's doing tonight. I put my phone away and try to get back into the conversation.

Aiden puts his hand atop mine and smiles. He's cute, but I'm too distracted and he's just not interesting enough. I move my hand and lift it to get the attention of our waitress. I need another drink.

. . .

Elijah

We walk into the bar, and I can hear Gemma before I see her. She's laughing loudly like she's having the best night of her life. I see Xander standing near the bar watching her and we head over to him.

He slaps me on the back. "Hey man, she's over there," he gestures with his chin.

I spot her at a small table with Sasha and two assholes. They are all laughing and talking excitedly. I continue to watch her, she seems to be ok, but then I see the guy next to her run a hand up her thigh. She eventually pushes it away and laughs.

This motherfucker. I'm sure he's just testing the waters to see how drunk she is before he makes his move and I'm officially done with this shit. I quickly stride over to the table.

Gemma sees me approaching, "ELIJAH," she screams. She throws her arms up in excitement, stands, and wraps me in a hug. I see the asshole next to her scowl.

With her arms wrapped around my neck, she looks up at me. "You're looking real snack-ish, Mr. Adler."

I smirk down at her. "Snack-ish?"

She nods and hiccups. She's so fucking cute.

"I have a table over here. Tell these guys goodbye. You're coming to sit with me."

She giggles and pouts her plump lips. "Ok, Bossman."

She turns back to her table and slurs something along the lines of, "Sasha, I'm gonna sit with Elijah for a few minutes. Are you cool here or want to come join?"

I reiterate. "Party's over. Gemma's coming with me. Good night."

Ty steps forward. "Sasha, I want to make sure you get home safely."

I lead Gemma to Xander's booth. Ty and Sasha join us soon after. We sit down and I order water for the girls. I sit back with my arm on the back of the booth and Gemma snuggles into me. She inhales deeply into my neck and bites my ear. Her hand runs up and down my thigh.

Drunk Gemma is a lot of fun.

I lean down and whisper in her ear, "If you keep doing that, I'm going to bend you over this table and fuck you in front of everyone."

She looks up in shock and giggles again. "Don't threaten me with a good time."

The waiter returns with our waters, and I offer one to Gemma immediately. "Drink this; then we're leaving."

She attempts to brush me off, but I continue to hold it out to her. "Now."

She sticks out her tongue but eventually drinks it.

I stand. "We're heading out. I want to get this one home before she passes out."

Xander starts to protest, but as he watches Gemma and Sasha lean on each other in hysterical laughter, he decides against it and nods.

"Come on, Gemma, let's go," I say as I start to lead her away.

"No, I'm not leaving without Sasha."

"Ty will get her home. Let's go."

"No, we came together, and we'll leave together. Girl code. Plus, I don't know Ty. He's hot, but no."

For fucks sake. "I know Ty and he's a standup guy. He'll take care of her. Trust me."

She reaches up and tries to caress my face but almost pokes me in the eye. "I do trust you, but I can't just leave her with two guys we barely know," she says before turning and walking back to the table.

I try not to roll my eyes as I follow her. She's whispering in Sasha's ear, and Sasha nods before Gemma turns back to me. "Ok, now we can go."

Exasperated, I take her hand and lead her toward the exit but not before I see her date scowling in our direction. I shoot him a wink. *Fuck off, asshole.*

Thankfully, the black SUV is waiting outside for us. I help Gemma in before going around to the other side. I buckle her in, and she takes my hand.

"So, you think Ty is hot?" She just laughs and minutes later, she's mumbling about White Castle and chicken rings before she passes out. Yep, called it.

Gemma

I awake to the smell of bacon and a horrible taste in my mouth. I'm afraid to open my eyes. Gosh, what did I do last night? My head is already pounding, and I just want to remain snuggled under the covers, after I drink my weight in ginger ale. But the bacon is calling my name.

I slowly open my eyes. I'm not in my bed. Duh, who would be cooking at my house? I look around and am instantly relieved. I'm at my love's, erm, I mean Elijah's place. I stretch and notice I'm completely naked under these heavenly sheets. Hmm, sadly, I'm not sore or sticky, so no fun was had last night.

I sit up and see a glass of water and aspirin on the nightstand. Elijah is the sweetest. I swallow the pills and chug the water, but it does nothing to quench my thirst. I'm a complete camel today.

I rise unsteadily and make my way to the bathroom. Yikes, I look and feel very *Death Becomes Her*. I really need to take better care of myself. A shower is necessary before I face him. I scan the massive counter and see he's left me a toothbrush. He knows what mama needs. As I brush my teeth, I notice that not only did he remove my clothes, but he also took my hair down from my bun and removed all my jewelry. I hum. I would have loved to feel his hands in my hair, on my body.

I jump in the shower, his amazing shower with the multiple shower heads. I grab his body wash and soap myself. I inhale deeply, smelling like Elijah all day may be a gift and a curse. I reach for his shampoo and quickly wash my hair. I need to get to Elijah and that bacon.

I reach over and grab a warm fluffy white towel. Of

course, he has a towel warmer. I wrap myself in it and step out of the shower, and of course, he has heated floors. I head into his walk-in closet. Surprisingly, it's immaculate; his sandalwood scent engulfs me. Rows upon rows of suits are on one side, along with beautifully polished shoes. The other side is more of his casual wear. I find some drawers in the island in the middle of the room, and I find white tanks and boxer briefs. I grab one of each and a pair of socks and throw everything on. I take one more look at myself in the mirror before heading downstairs. I still look like I was rode hard and put away wet, but I no longer smell like a brewery, so I'm going to lead with that.

I trudge down the stairs to face the music. Elijah is at the stove shirtless, wearing low-slung basketball shorts. I can't resist his beautiful broad back. I immediately go to him, wrapping my arms around his waist. He tenses as I plant tiny kisses all over his muscular back. This body should be illegal; it's doing all kinds of things to me and I'm powerless to stop it. Not that I want to.

He inhales deeply as my hands begin to roam his abs and chest. He slowly turns to face me, and I refuse to let him go. He's just going to have to make it work with me attached to his warm body. When we're finally face to face, we take a moment just to stare at each other.

He strokes my face. "Good morning, lovely."

I shake my head and lean into him, kissing his chest. "Thank you for taking care of me last night."

He doesn't say anything, and I can tell he's upset with me as he pulls away.

"Have a seat. It's time for breakfast."

I do as I'm told, and he brings me a slice of avocado toast.

"Start with this. Something hearty will help you with what I'm sure is a monster hangover."

I happily dig in as he goes back to the stove and starts dishing up food. I finish my toast as he brings me a glass of orange juice. I smile softly at the sweetness of this man. Even though he's pissed, he's taking care of me without complaint.

He returns with two plates laden with hash browns, scrambled eggs, and crispy bacon.

I take his hand and kiss the back of it. "Thank you for breakfast."

He grunts a "you're welcome," before sitting at the island next to me.

I immediately dig in as I'm starving, and everything looks and smells delicious. We eat in silence for a few minutes, and I can feel the anger radiating from Elijah.

He puts his fork down and turns to me. I try to ignore him, content to keep shoveling food into my mouth so we won't have to have this conversation.

"Gemma, what the hell was last night?"

How do I answer that? Is he talking about my date or the copious amounts of alcohol I consumed?

I turn to him. "It was a double date."

"Fuck the date. Why were you so drunk?"

I shrug. "We were just having a good time. Sasha

155

and I took a couple of shots before we got there and then the guys ordered just about every drink on the menu."

He shakes his head. "So, because they ordered them, you felt obligated to drink them? That's irresponsible and dangerous."

Alright, now he's starting to piss me off. "I didn't feel obligated, I wanted to drink them, and I was having a good time." I go back to eating my yummy breakfast in an attempt to get him to do the same, but it doesn't work.

"Yeah, it looked like you were having a great time when I arrived. That asshole couldn't keep his hands off you."

I cringe. Yes, that part wasn't fun. "I'm dating, Elijah. Not every date is going to be a love connection. Give me a break."

"That's not the point. You can't trust other guys like you can trust me. I don't want you putting yourself in these dangerous situations."

I frown. "You don't want me going on dates? You can't tell me what to do."

"I'm not trying to. Go on your fucking dates. I don't care. But I do care if something happens to you. I told Greyson I would look after you, and that's what I'm doing."

Oh, hell no. "Sorry, *dad*. I don't need a babysitter. You and Greyson can fuck off." I stand. "So, you've just been keeping an eye on me for Greyson?"

He looks contrite. "That's not what I meant."

I'm too furious to care right now. "Screw what you meant; I'm going by what you said. I don't need another big brother, Elijah, or a daddy. Where's my stuff? I need to get out of here."

He rises without a word and grabs my purse and phone from the coffee table in the living room.

His jaw ticks in anger, but he doesn't look at me. "Your dress and shoes are upstairs." He turns and goes back to the kitchen while I head upstairs.

I order a Lyft that, fortunately, will be here in five minutes. I hurriedly grab my dress from the chair it's folded on, along with my shoes, and get dressed. Where the hell are my panties? Ugh, two minutes until my Lyft arrives. I rush downstairs. I need to get out of here.

Elijah's waiting at the bottom of the stairs. "Gemma, don't leave like this. I'm not trying to control you. I'm just worried about what could have happened last night."

Here we go again. "I appreciate your concern, Elijah, but there really isn't anything left to say."

He nods and turns away, and I can't quite make out what he mutters.

I go to the door; my Lyft has arrived.

"Goodbye, Elijah."

CHAPTER ELEVEN

ELIJAH

*W*ell, that went to shit quickly. I shake my head as I return to the kitchen. I try to finish my breakfast, but it's useless, I've lost my appetite. I clean up the kitchen as I go over what I said that pissed her off. I'm not trying to control her. Obviously, I was annoyed to see her on a date, but that's not why I was upset with her. Right? I'm upset because she was drunk and could have been taken advantage of. Why doesn't she understand where I'm coming from? If anything had happened to her, I would never forgive myself. I pace the length of the kitchen, my stomach queasy at the thought of any harm coming to her.

I scrub my hand over my face. This is why I don't fuck around with younger women. This is why I don't date or bring women to my home. I'm not into the drama. I have too much going on in my life to deal with this bullshit. If she thinks being an immature brat is something I'm interested in, she is sadly mistaken.

Gemma

Ok, so *maybe* I overreacted. It's been a few days since my fight with Elijah, and I can certainly see his point of view. I had too much to drink while out with some random. I can see now how badly things could have turned out.

Elijah hasn't contacted me since I stormed out of his place. He hasn't been responding to my calls or texts, which I guess I deserve to some extent, but this radio silence is really starting to get to me. In just a few weeks, Elijah has become an important part of my happiness. We may not see each other as often as I would like, but we frequently text, even if it's just a picture or a meme. I'm trying to abide by the casual code, but he's on my mind from eight until...Fuck, now I'm quoting Drake.

Mia and Sasha have confirmed that I was an ass, and an apology is necessary. I just don't know what to do. Sasha says, from what she remembers, we were pretty obnoxious. Which I agree with. Hello, we were Drunk One and Drunk Two, but I still don't think I was reckless enough to be scolded. Either way, I want to move on from this.

Tonight, we're hanging at my house to watch Bravo, but I can't concentrate on the show. I'm driving the girls crazy. "How do I apologize? He's not responding to my calls!" I whine.

They consider my question.

"Show up at his office in nothing but a trench coat and spiked heels," Mia suggests.

"No."

"Send him a handwritten note," Sasha recommends.

I roll my eyes. "No."

"Text him a picture of your tits covered in his favorite ice cream toppings. I'll write sorry in syrup for you." Mia volunteers.

"Maybe." I snicker.

"How about an edible arrangement?" Sasha adds.

"No!" I flop back onto the couch.

"Think about when Elijah sent you those La Perla's. It was something private, just between you, and it was unexpected. Find something similar." Sasha says.

I continue to consider this as they go back to watching women scream at each other across the table during an otherwise lovely dinner. I think back to that moment I received those panties. It was shocking, sexy, and funny. I want to give that to Elijah, and I think I have the perfect surprise.

Per Drew, Elijah is traveling for work, but I don't think I can wait until he gets back to put my plan into action. I beg Sasha to contact Ty and get Elijah's travel itinerary. I rub my hands together as I finalize my plans.

. . .

Elijah

I haven't spoken to Gemma in over a week. I'm on an extended trip for work, looking into prospective locations and properties. She's contacted me a few times, but she hasn't apologized for her behavior. I voiced my concerns regarding her drinking, and I've moved on from that. My major concern now is her behavior at my home. She stormed around, refused to hear me out, and left abruptly. Childish behavior is something I will not tolerate.

I've just returned to my hotel when the concierge approaches me.

"Mr. Adler, you received a delivery today. Someone from our staff will bring it to your room at your convenience."

"Thank you." I check my watch. "I'll be available in an hour."

I head up to my room and jump in the shower. I've had a miserable day. Not seeing or speaking to Gemma is taking its toll on me. I'm angry with her, but my desire for her is stronger. I wrap a towel around my waist and drag one through my hair. I'm starving; dinner is next on my agenda. I order room service and start to get settled for the evening. I have to prepare for a few meetings tomorrow. Then I'm going to call it an early night.

There's a knock at the door. Yes, dinner.

I open the door and am greeted by the concierge.

He presents a chilled bottle of Dom and a card. I accept them before additional staff arrives with an array of flowers. I step back and allow them into the room. Who would be sending me flowers? The staff leaves as I take a look at the display.

The first arrangement is full of red flowers, red flowers that look like lips. The card attached states this flower is called Psychotria Elata, also known as Hooker Lips.

I laugh loudly. Holy fuck. What is going on?

The next arrangement looks like small purple men, in hats, with erections. The attached card says they are Orchis Italica, more commonly known as the Naked Man Orchids.

Yes, I can definitely see that.

And the third arrangement looks like a woman in a robe with large breasts. The card states they are Angel Orchids.

I finally open the envelope the concierge handed me hoping to find some clues to this mystery.

Elijah,

*I want to apologize for being a raving bitch (I know you
would never call me that, but I'm nothing if not honest).
There are times when I have trouble admitting when
I'm wrong, but today is not that day (it was that day,
though).*

*So, I am offering up my "hooker lips" and my "angel
bosom" to you and your waiting "erection." (See what I
did there?) Come home soon. I've missed your face, your
touch, and just about everything else about you.*

*Accept these perfectly lovely and wholesome flowers
and a bottle of our favorite champagne as a form of my
sincerest apology for being an asshole."*

Your Fantasy Fuck Buddy,
Gemma

I throw my head back and laugh. Well, shit.

No woman has ever sent me flowers before, and
provocative ones at that. Gemma, Gemma, Gemma.
What am I going to do with you? This woman is always
a pleasure. I debate giving her a call, but I think I'll let
her sweat it out a little more.

Gemma

I lie in bed, unable to sleep. I received the
confirmation that Elijah's flowers were delivered today,
yet I haven't heard from him. He must really be pissed

at me. I huff and roll over on my back and look up at my ceiling. This uncertainty is driving me crazy.

Mia, Sasha, and I met Drew and Ty out for drinks tonight. Nothing too crazy, we went to a sports bar to watch the game and so I could drown my sorrows in hot wings and nachos. I thought Elijah would have contacted me once he received his flowers, or at least he would text his friends to share the news, but nope. And I can't take it anymore.

I grab my phone. I sit up and strike a sexy pose; maybe Mia was right about a tit pic. Plus, I owe him for the pictures of him I have from our night at his place. I'm smarter though and keep my face out of it.

I attach the picture and text him. ***You up?***

His response is immediate. **I am now.**

I can't tell by that response if he's happy to hear from me, so I press on. ***I saw your friends tonight. It was weird hanging out with them without you.***

They told me. My boys are always keeping an eye on you for me.

Why?

I just want to make sure you're safe. You keep me on my toes, but I like taking care of you. Thank you for my flowers. I think I like when you take care of me, too.

Swoon. I'm over this. I need to see his handsome face, so I FaceTime him.

He answers and there's light coming from

somewhere, so I can see he's perfectly rumpled lying in bed. He's all messy hair with one arm behind his head with his broad chest on display. His olive skin and dark hair are such a beautiful contrast to the white sheets. His body, his virility screams at me, taunts me.

"Hi." I smile.

"Hey," his deep voice rumbles. I think I really did wake him up.

"I wanted to see your handsome face."

"Oh yeah? I want to see more than just your face. Let's have a redo of that pic you just sent me. I didn't get to give that enough of my attention."

Elijah

Gemma sits up in bed. She's wearing a thin pink tank that I can see her nipples through, even with the dim lighting. Her hair is a disheveled, dark cloud around her shoulders, and her face is scrubbed free of makeup. She looks incredible.

"You're beautiful," I murmur.

"Let me see you."

I hold my phone out and pan it down my body. I'm naked except for the white sheet covering my dick. I slide my other hand under the sheet and take it in my hand.

"I wish I was there to bury my face in you."

I see her breathing quicken at my words.

"Touch yourself," I tell her. "Show me what you'd want me to do if I were there."

She hesitates. At that moment, I know she's never done this before, but I can tell she wants to. A jolt of pleasure hits me in the chest. I lick my lips, and I see her nipples harden through her shirt.

"Don't worry baby. I'll tell you just how I like it. Let's start by getting you naked. Then lie back for me."

She does what she's told. *Good girl.*

"Knees up, legs open. Show me that pretty, little pussy."

Gemma

I'm sitting at my desk at work, too distracted to actually do any work because I can't stop thinking about last night. I blush as I recall Elijah's hand gliding up and down his dick while he watched me touch myself. Watching his muscles flex and tense and the roughness with which he stroked himself was my filthiest fantasy. My body is still covered in goosebumps at the memory of his deep moans as the cum spurted onto his abs and chest. I had such a strong orgasm I dropped the phone and Elijah missed watching me fall apart. He then made the executive decision to use our laptops or iPads next time, so we have both hands free. *Next time.* This man makes me crazy.

I shake my head and try to concentrate on getting at least some work done when my work husband, Cameron, approaches my desk. I met Cameron my first day here, it was his first day too, and we were both nervous as hell. I dropped my purse, spilling things everywhere. We both bent down to pick it up when we bumped heads so hard we fell to the floor. We were those two weirdos in the lobby, on the ground, crying from laughter. We've been friends ever since.

Cameron approaches with the biggest smile on his face. I can't help it, I mirror his expression. Cameron just may have the prettiest teeth and deepest dimples I've ever seen. He's a handsome guy. I'll never tell him, but he reminds me of a young Taye Diggs.

"You're looking suspiciously happy at work. I had to come over to see if it would rub off on me," he says.

"I spoke to Elijah last night, he accepted my apology, and now we're back on track."

"Did he like the flowers?" he asks as he sits on my desk.

"He did. I'm quite sure it was the first time he'd ever received flowers. Flowers are my new game-changer. All my men won't know what hit them."

We both laugh.

"All your men? You have one man. If everything you told me about him is true, your Summer Slut plans are over."

"Nope, not happening. It's not like that with us."

"Sure. When are you going to see him again?"

"He gets back in a couple of days," I say as I look down.

"And?"

"He's going to stay the weekend with me."

"I rest my case."

* * *

Mia's taking me shopping today after work. Sasha's coming too, but Mia specifically said I *needed* her help for my weekend with Elijah. I guess when you spend so much time with your friends looking ugly in mismatched pajamas with food stains, they think you can't clean up well enough for the gorgeous man from your wildest fantasies.

We walk into the lingerie store, and Mia heads straight to the back. Right to the dominatrix section.

"No, this is not me." I stop on the spot.

"That's the point." She rolls her eyes.

"I'm looking for a few bra and panty sets and some loungewear. I don't need all of this."

Sasha chimes in, "You may not need it now, but it may be good to have, just in case." Mia and I turn to her, but she moves away as she continues to browse.

"Yes, exactly, thank you, Sasha. Just get something as a backup. You may not even use it this weekend, but it's always fun to have. Especially if you have to apologize again."

Or have a virtual booty call. She may be right.

"Alright, alright." I concede and start shopping.

I buy a few silky nightgowns, with spaghetti straps and semi-fitted bodices, that stop about midthigh. I also get cute little shorts and cami sets and two sexier lace corsets and thongs.

After shopping, we get mani-pedis at our favorite salon. I accept my glass of prosecco, pick my polish colors, and jump in my seat. I need this pampering so I can relax. I'm so freaking wound up about my weekend with Elijah. It will just be him and me together, all weekend. This will be the longest amount of time we've spent together. I really want it to go well. Plus, I have a few fantasies in mind.

We're all quiet today, lost in our own thoughts as our nails are done.

I return home after we had our mani-pedis and dinner. Elijah gets home tomorrow afternoon, and then I get him all to myself. I already told the girls not to bother me. No calls. No unannounced visits. I do not want my time with him interrupted.

With all this nervous energy running through me, I start cleaning my apartment from top to bottom. I wash my bedding and make sure there are fresh towels. I'm counting down the minutes until he arrives. I place an order for my groceries to be delivered tomorrow afternoon. I picked up champagne and candles yesterday. Do men like candles? Maybe not, but maybe they are more appealing if they are lit while you take a steamy bath together. That's it. Everything is perfect for my weekend with Elijah. I've thought of everything. I fall back onto my bed. What could go wrong?

Elijah

This has been the longest work trip that I can remember. Thoughts of Gemma have been running through my mind for days, ever since her apology and our impromptu FaceTime. She confuses me on every level. She says she wants casual, and I'm all for it. But then she does something like send me flowers or invite me to spend the entire weekend with her, that takes us outside of that casual box, and yet, I'm still all in.

She's a mystery. Is she telling me she wants to date casually because she thinks that is what I want to hear? Or does she truly mean it? I've had a few women tell me they know the score, but after a few nights together, they wanted more and thought I would change my mind. Is that her play here? I try to shake these thoughts from my head. Either way, I want her. I enjoy spending time with her. I'm not going to stress myself out with what-ifs.

I catch a Lyft to the airport. I have an early flight, and I should arrive back in Chicago in the early afternoon. I have a few things to check on in the office, but then I'm all hers.

Hers. It doesn't feel as foreign falling from my lips as I thought it would.

Back in Chicago, my driver takes me directly to work. I walk into my office and plop down in my chair. I respond to a few emails, upload meeting notes to the server, and make myself available in case anyone needs anything. I always like to be present for our staff, so they have an opportunity to seek guidance or share information with me.

I check my watch again. I'm out of here in twenty minutes to go home to shower, pack an overnight bag, and then head over to Gemma's.

Ty walks into my office. "Welcome back, E."

I smile. "Hey, man. Solid trip. I have some great ideas I want to share with you." I check my watch. "Monday. I'm out of here." I start to clear my desk and shut down my computer.

"Damn, you just got here. What's the rush?"

I stand. "I'm going to see Gemma. I'm staying at her place this weekend, and I need to shower and change."

He watches me since I'm not making eye contact. "A whole weekend, huh? Interesting. Well, I won't keep you. Have fun. Take lots of condoms," he says before walking out.

No need for that reminder. The way I'm feeling, I may just show up with one already on.

CHAPTER TWELVE

GEMMA

I pace my apartment as I wait for Elijah to arrive. I left work early so I could meet him here and he just texted that he was on his way. I exhale. My butterflies have butterflies. I wring my hands and roll my shoulders in hopes of calming my nerves.

I go to the kitchen and chug a glass of prosecco to take the edge off. I continue to arrange the charcuterie board with an array of meats and cheeses. I got all my favorites, which he seemed to enjoy during our picnic.

My intercom buzzes. It's him. I clap and skip to the buzzer allowing him access to my building. I look at myself in the mirror. I fluff my hair, smooth my skirt, and take a deep breath to calm myself. *Here we go.*

He's barely knocked on the door when I fling it open, and I see his gorgeous face.

His blue eyes meet mine as I take him in. My heart

gives a little flutter at the sight of him. Tan skin, full lips, square jaw, dark hair, and that stubble. *Damn.*

We continue to eye fuck each other, no words passing our lips, but I see a hint of a smile on his, and he cocks his head to the side. He knows I need a few minutes to take in all of his gorgeousness.

He's wearing a pale blue linen shirt and navy shorts. I scan down his body and take in his broad shoulders and tapered waist. I'm even turned on by the dark hair on his arms and legs. But the showstoppers, for me, are his hands. Big hands. Long graceful fingers. I know what those hands can do, and I'm slightly obsessed with them. I need to feel them on my body soon.

I glance down to I see that his dick is standing up to greet me. I lick my lips.

My eyes finally make their way back up to his and I smile. "Hi, handsome. You know how to make an entrance."

"Hi, lovely. May I come in or do you still need a minute?" He gives me a dazzling smile and my breath hitches. This is casual dating done wrong. This weekend is going to kill me. Abort mission.

I push that thought aside. I'm going to continue to shoot my shot and worry about the rest later. I reach out to take his hand, pulling him to me. "Yes, come in."

He comes in, closes the door, and takes me in his arms. He crashes his mouth to mine and *inhales me.* There's no other way to describe his kiss. There's no teasing, maybe more of a claiming. He's exuding sex and power. I let him consume me, submitting to every stroke of his tongue.

He swallows my moans and explores my mouth with that tongue; there's nothing playful about this kiss. He holds my face in his big hands. I don't know how he does it, but he deepens the kiss. My hands go to his hair, and I rake my nails across his scalp as he bites my lip. Yes, this is what I've been missing. I'm breathless as his lips leave mine and trail to my ear. He sucks my lobe before sinking his teeth into my neck. I gasp. He licks and sucks to my collarbone. I throw my head back and stare at the ceiling with wide eyes. I feel a laugh bubble up inside of me. We're still standing in my entryway.

Elijah drops to his knees, and his hands go to my hips.

"What is this skirt?" he says huskily.

I look down. I'm wearing a two-piece outfit, a crop top and a long skirt with a thigh-high slit.

His hands run up my legs as he parts the slit. He leans in and buries his face between my legs, deeply inhaling my aroused scent. I grab onto his shoulders to stay upright.

Holy fuck. He's been here for less than five minutes.

He grows impatient and rips my thong down my legs, puts it in his pocket, and before I can say anything, his mouth finds me. My eyes close in pleasure.

"Baby, you're soaked," he mumbles into my skin.

I can't respond. My brain has left the premises. He's stolen my words as well as my panties. I lean back against the wall and try to steady my shaky legs.

He lifts one leg over his shoulder and sucks me deeply. He greedily licks, sucks, and bites me. The scratch of his stubble between my sensitive thighs is the sweetest hell.

"You taste..." he mumbles between licks and nips. "I can't stop. I never want to stop."

I'm not sure if he's talking to himself or me, but I'm too consumed with pleasure to respond. My body starts to quiver, and he must feel it.

"Yes, come for me, baby. I want to taste all of you. Drink you down." He bites my clit and pulls, and that's it. I fall apart, my body starts bucking, and I fuck his face. His strong hands support me as he continues to suck and lick me to pull every last bit of pleasure from my body.

He kisses me once more, fixes my skirt, and stands. He takes my face in his hands and kisses me again.

"Thank you again for my flowers. No one has ever sent me flowers before. It was a perfect surprise."

I'm still in my orgasm fog, so I just kiss him back and try to gather my thoughts. "Noted. For mind-blowing orgasms, send flowers."

He chuckles into my neck. "No, that was because I missed you and I haven't been able to stop thinking about tasting you since our FaceTime."

Yes, I recall him talking about burying his face in me then. He has a one-track mind.

He finally pulls away, my body feels the absence immediately, but he takes my hand, grabs his bag, and walks further into my apartment.

I giggle. He sure does know how to make an entrance.

I lead him to my bedroom and show him where he can put his belongings.

"Get comfortable. I'm going to grab us some drinks. I have some snacks prepared if you're hungry."

I turn before I leave the room. "I missed you, too."

Elijah

I missed you, too. *Fuck.*

Something stirs in me at her words, at her expression. This girl. This perfect woman. I shake my head as I look around her room. It's colorful and bright, just like her. Varying shades and textures of teal and coral decorate the feminine space, making me feel like a giant in a dollhouse. I just know I'm going to stain something or break her delicate things. I remove my shirt and shoes and climb into her inviting bed. I'll just rest my eyes for a few minutes. I'm sated now and still exhausted from travel. Now that I'm with her, maybe I can finally relax and get some rest.

I awake a while later with Gemma's warm body pressed against me. It's darker in the room, a few hours must have passed, and there are candles lit.

My hands go to her body, fuck, she's so warm and soft and completely naked.

"You're awake. I've missed you," she whispers as she kisses down my chest.

"Sorry, love. Apparently, I couldn't relax until I got you back in my arms."

"Well, I'm here, now what are you going to do with me?" she says, throwing my words from my last visit back at me.

I put my arms behind my head and looked down at her kissing my stomach. "I'm going to fill that smart mouth of yours with my cock and watch you choke on my cum."

She laughs. "You're such a romantic."

I reach down and stroke her hair. "It's actually a fantasy of mine. To watch you struggle to take my cock. To fuck your mouth."

Her eyes rise to meet mine. "A fantasy?"

I nod. "I want to feel my cock beat against your throat. I want to watch your eyes and see that moment of panic when you struggle to breathe and swallow around me."

"Ok, what do you want me to do?"

Fuck, I didn't think she'd agree so quickly. I hesitate for just a second. She's so inexperienced, but she needs to learn.

"On your knees, on the floor."

She immediately complies, kneeling on the floor, her eyes wide.

I swing my legs to the side of the bed and stand. Without breaking eye contact, I take off my shorts and then my boxer briefs. Her gaze finally shifts to my cock, hanging thick and heavy between my legs. I grab it and stroke it a few times. It's aching for a release.

She licks her lips.

"You look like you need my dick in your mouth."

She nods and licks her lips again.

I take my thumb and roughly rub it across her pouty lips. "I've been thinking about this, punishing you, since I saw you on your little date."

She bites her lip but maintains eye contact.

"Open for me."

She does and I plunge into her mouth, making her gag.

"You're ok, baby, relax and take me."

She places her hands on my hips, closes her eyes, and starts a nice slow rhythm.

Giving her a few moments to adjust to the intrusion, I caress her cheeks and run my fingers over her stretched lips as she takes me deeper and sucks. Her desire to please me makes my heartbeat that much faster.

"Baby, I'm going to fuck your mouth now. Relax and breathe, or don't. You know I like the struggle."

She nods again, and I begin thrusting into her mouth. She gags a little, her eyes widening, before she steels herself and takes me to the hilt. Her eyes begin to water, and that first tear falls.

Fuck, yes.

I grab a fistful of her hair, and I hold her head in place as I continue to thrust. Stroking her face again, I hold myself deep in her throat before letting loose with long smooth strokes. I feel a sheen of sweat cover my body as my strokes intensify. I moan and take deep breaths. The slick heat of her mouth is unreal.

Looking into her eyes, I tell her, "You're beautiful. You're doing so good."

She gets messier as drool continues to spill from her lips and down her chin. It sparks an image of my cum spilling out, overloading her mouth and I lose it, ready to make it a reality. I grab the back of her head and pull her to me, and I let her have it. She digs her nails into my hips as I plunge into her mouth again and again and I feel the beginning of my orgasm deep in my stomach. It barrels down so fast that I can't give her a warning and I explode in her mouth. "Fuuuuck. Yes, baby. Yes, fuck!"

She chokes, but she doesn't stop, and I feel her throat bobbing as she repeatedly swallows to get it all down.

"Good girl. Swallow it all."

She continues to lick and suck me dry, and my knees give just a little.

I look into her watery eyes and the tears escaping. I pull out of her mouth and drop to my knees in front of her. I take her face in my hands and wipe away her tears with my thumbs.

"You did so good, baby."

I bend and kiss her, swiping my tongue through her mouth. I moan when I taste her and me on her tongue.

I hold her face in my hands. "Did I hurt you?" I ask, searching her eyes.

"No," she shakes her head, "I loved watching you fall apart and lose control."

I kiss her again as my hands trail down her body, and I slide my fingers through her pussy.

"Fuck, you're dripping wet."

Gemma

Closing my eyes, I grab his wrist. I'm so turned on right now. I will come with the slightest caress. Watching Elijah's slick body tense and thrust into my mouth is forever burned into my brain. He was an animal, an animal that wanted to pound the fuck out of me and come hard. It was the sexiest thing I'd ever seen. He completely lost control. I feel a sense of pride that I could bring him to his knees, crack his shell.

Stroking me again, he says, "Did you like that? You like to be punished?" I jerk as he inserts two fingers and starts to scissor them.

"Yes," I moan.

When he inserts a third finger, I gasp at the burn of it. He pumps me deeply as my body starts to quiver. I lean forward to bite his neck and nibble his chin.

He whispers in my ear, "You feel so good. My dick is jealous of my hand. I can't wait to get inside you again."

Oh god. I moan long and loud as my body detonates and I lurch forward as my body shatters into a million pieces.

Elijah finally removes his fingers and strokes my

folds, making me jump; I am so sensitive. I wrap my arms around his neck as he kisses me deeply.

"Come on, baby. Let's get you up. This floor can't be comfortable."

He stands and pulls me to my feet and into an embrace. He kisses the top of my head. "Do you want to get back in bed or take a shower?"

A wet and slippery Elijah Adler? This is a no-brainer.

"Let's shower," I say as I smile into his chest.

Showering with Elijah is everything I anticipated and so much more. I turn on the water and adjust it to a comfortable temp. I love an extremely hot shower, but I'm not sure Elijah would enjoy hot ass water on his manly bits. I go to the closet and get out clean towels for him and turn back to the shower.

Elijah is already inside, and my mouth falls open. I knew it. Elijah's hard body by itself is perfection. Elijah's hard body, slick with rivulets of water running over his pecs and down his abs, is my eternal wet dream. I watch in what appears to be slow motion as Elijah stands in a cloud of steam as the water flows over his shoulders and chest, down his abs, and even lower. With his eyes closed, he tilts his head back and wets his dark hair. I watch as he pushes his hair back and then those sky-blue eyes open and find mine.

He catches me staring and he smiles sexily. He tilts

his head to the side and reaches for me. "Come join me, love."

Yes, please.

I set his towels nearby and climb in. Instantly I feel heat and longing radiate from his body. My shower is a decent size, but Elijah's large, powerful frame almost overwhelms the space, me included. He takes my hand and pulls me to him. My arms go around his waist and my chin to his chest as I look up at him, smiling. He kisses my forehead before he steps back to get me under the water. He pushes my wet hair back from my face and kisses me softly.

"You're perfect," he murmurs against my lips. I shiver at his words. I don't know what he's doing to me, but I want more. More of him. More of this.

He releases me to grab my body wash. He smiles as he looks at it and squirts some into his hands. "My girl needs to be taken care of. She just took quite a beating."

I scrunch up my nose at him as he lathers his hands.

"Turn around. I want to wash your back."

I oblige, moving my hair to the side. I feel his soapy hands caress and massage my shoulders and trail up and down my arms.

"Arms up."

I hesitate for a second before I reluctantly lift them. *Again, I'm so thankful for laser hair removal.*

He bends down and whispers in my ear as he

washes under my arms. "Don't be shy with my beautiful body. I will lick your pits if I want to."

I feel myself blush. He's a nasty little freak and I love it.

His hands slide from under my arms and around to my breasts. He takes one in each hand and squeezes them before he starts massaging them with his soapy hands.

I let out a soft moan as my head falls back to his chest. My hands go to his hair, pulling him to me so I can kiss his lips. He kisses me deeply over my shoulder as he continues his assault on my breasts, pinching and pulling my nipples. I feel his erection grow against my back. Eventually, his hands trail to my stomach and hips, avoiding the place where I want him to touch me most.

"Turn around," he whispers in my ear. I shiver as goosebumps prick my flesh.

I comply as he adds more body wash to his hands. He goes down on one knee, leans forward, and kisses me softly, right there, before he begins to wash my legs and my feet. I sigh at the contact of his strong hands on my skin and the sight of him kneeling in front of me. *Worshipping me?*

My hand goes to his head as I run my fingers through his hair, scratching his scalp, and he hums softly at the contact. He finally stands, pulling me into his body as he massages my back. I happily wrap my arms around him and nuzzle into his chest. I sigh at the feel of his dick digging into my stomach.

He steps back again and puts us directly under the spray of the water, rinsing away all his hard work. He grabs the soap to lather his hands before they seek the heat between my legs. I wasn't expecting him to go there; it seems too intimate. He uses his hand to wash between my legs before reaching around to cup my ass. I gasp as I feel his hand move, I thought him washing my vagina was intimate, but this just feels taboo. His fingers stroke back and forth along my entrance, and I tense and close my eyes, still clinging to him. "I can't wait to take you here," he says softly.

My eyes fly open, and I try to step back, but he doesn't allow it. "What?"

He meets my gaze. "I said, I can't wait to take you *here*," he repeats as he touches my opening again.

"My *ass*? Like, anal?" I exclaim, my eyes wide as I stare up at him.

"Yes, you're going to love it," he says, firm and confident.

I gulp. When he says it like that, I believe him.

"I'm saving that for my husband. Sorry." I flutter my eyelashes.

He pulls me back under the water. "Your husband?"

I nod.

"Well, where do I sign up?"

Not knowing what to say to that, because I know he's not serious, I ignore him. "My turn to wash you," I say as I go to pick up the body wash.

"No, I still have to wash your hair."

I look up at him again. "You want to wash my hair?"

He bites his lip and nods. "I've wanted to since that first night when I saw you all wet from the rain."

"Ok," I whisper.

I stare up at him as he grabs the shampoo. This is, without a doubt, the best shower of my life.

CHAPTER THIRTEEN

GEMMA

I add some conditioner to my wet hair before throwing it up in a high ponytail to air dry. Elijah gave me the best shampoo and scalp massage as I rested against his hard body. I may never let him leave. Has anyone ever been forever ruined by a scalp massage? That wasn't a fantasy of mine, but it has now been added to the list.

He's out in the living room waiting for me to finish up. We're going to Netflix and chill tonight. I'm wearing the silky cami and shorts jammies I just bought. I look at myself in the mirror. This is me, polka dots and all. Hopefully, he likes this stripped-down version of me. He typically sees me dolled up for a night out but this girl right here, with her wet hair, no makeup, ready to lounge around, is the real me.

I venture out into the living room to join him on the couch. He has the charcuterie board, glasses, and the bottle of Prosecco already on the coffee table. I sit on the other end of the couch, facing him. He watches me with dark eyes but doesn't say anything. He pours me a drink and hands it to me, our fingers touching, and I feel those sparks flicker between us.

"Why do all of your fantasies involve head?" I ask him, looking over my glass.

He throws his head back and laughs a deep belly laugh, and I feel the richness in my bones.

"It's one of my favorite things to do with you, especially with that mouth of yours," he chuckles again. "Just remember, if I'm ever upset, blowing me will release the pressure, so to speak. And then I'm putty in your hands."

"Thanks for the advice." I take a sip of my drink. "What are some of your other favorite things?"

He looks over at me and his eyes sweep over my face, "I can't tell you all my secrets, but I'll tell you one more." He leans over and strokes my cheek. "You. You just maybe my favorite thing."

Swoon.

I feel the biggest, goofiest smile spread across my face that I can't stop. There's no way to play this cool. Not only am I shocked, but I'm pleased. I'm relieved. This beautiful man that I've longed for, dreamed about, for years, just may be as into me as I'm into him. I stop myself from straddling him. I know exactly where that will lead. Instead, I want to just spend this time with him. Soak him in.

I stretch and kiss him softly on the lips. "Who knew you were such a sweet talker?" I murmur against his lips. "But we have something in common, you've always been my favorite, since the first moment I saw you."

He shakes his head and pulls me in closer for a deeper kiss. "And here we are now."

Here we are.

Elijah

We're supposed to be Netflix and chilling, but I can't take my eyes off this beautiful girl. We sit on the couch, her facing me, she has her feet in my lap as I give her a foot massage, and she tells me about work. She just read a new book that she's really excited about. She thinks it has the potential to be a huge bestseller. She's explaining the premise about vigilante psychics that solve unthinkable, brilliant crimes. She's so animated and passionate that it almost pulls me in. I want to read it, even though it's typically not my thing. It's just another thing about her I love, I mean, I like about her. She just has a way about her. I've been drawn to her, to her energy, from the moment we reconnected.

I press a knuckle into the arch of her foot, and she moans and closes her eyes. She was so resistant to this foot massage at first. She's still so shy about her body with me. *My body.* She still hasn't learned to trust me completely, to trust that I will take care of all her needs and ensure her pleasure. *But she will.*

She watches me for a moment, her beautiful brown

eyes scanning my face. "Tell me about your ex?" I ask her. She appears surprised at the change in topic.

She sighs. "There's not much to tell. Dustin and I were friends first. We dated for a while, and then we broke up." She shrugs, not making eye contact.

"Why did you break up with *Dusty*?" I question her.

She laughs. "*Dustin* and I broke up for a number of reasons." She counts them on her fingers. "It was a long-distance relationship after college. We were just content. There was no passion. I guess we loved each other, but we weren't *in love*. We were probably better off as friends."

"Was the break-up the catalyst for you to avoid relationships?"

"Probably, or the aftermath. My friends said I would regret not experiencing more once I was married with kids." She shrugs. "So, we came up with Mission Promiscuous aka Operation Summer Slut."

I clench my jaw at the mention of that. She has not figured it out yet, but she's done with that shit. She can slut it up for me all she wants, though.

"I know you haven't been in a relationship in a while, right?" she looks at me and I nod. I guess I could consider some of my college hookups as relationships.

"If you were looking, or when you're ready, what will you be looking for?" her voice drops to a whisper. "With your busy life, I imagine you'd want someone who sits at home waiting for you."

I smirk. "Wow. Really? I guess we never did finish

this conversation. Well, I want someone to be my equal, not only mentally but sexually. I love sex. I love fucking. I want a woman who wants it just as badly as I do so I can keep her well-fed with hard dick. I would love a woman who is ambitious, someone with their own passions and drive, a woman that could teach me something. So, to answer your question, that's what I want right now. Not someone who just sits home and waits around for me."

Gemma

I replay the words that left me dumbfounded a few minutes ago as I head into the kitchen. *I want someone to be my equal not only mentally but sexually. I love sex. I love fucking. I want a woman who wants it just as badly as I do so I can keep her well-fed with hard dick.*

After the whole spiel, I could do nothing but blink at him. Fuck me. I was wet just thinking about that hard dick. Hello, I'm always hungry. I volunteer as tribute. I finally just nodded like an idiot and said, "Good to know."

I grab another bottle of prosecco and search for more snacks, but nothing is appealing. Maybe we should order a pizza?

"Babe, do you want to order a pizza?" I yell toward the living room.

He doesn't respond and I freeze. Did I just call him *babe*? I feel my face start to flush, and I break out in a sweat. Why did I just do that? Maybe he didn't hear me. I cross my fingers.

A second later, he walks into the kitchen with a knowing smile on his face.

"Babe?" he asks.

I laugh. "Bae?"

"Maybe not, sweetheart."

I shake my head. "Boo?"

He smirks. "Use it in a sentence, darling."

"Hey boo, you want to order a pizza?" I smile at him; I can tell he hates it.

"Try again, baby girl."

"Honey?"

He laughs. "You can call me whatever you want to, dumplin'.'"

I wrap my arms around his waist and put my chin on his chest to look up at him. "I'll keep working on it, but I think babe is a winner." I giggle.

He holds me tightly and kisses my nose. "Let's order that pizza, doll face."

I know he was just being silly, but I melted a little at each endearment. He's so swoony.

After our pizza, we start going through our Spotify playlists, and I have an idea.

"Let's play a game. Share a song with me that holds a special memory." I pull up Sean Kingston's *Beautiful Girls*. "I remember going to a school dance and dancing to this song with my friends. Back when we were just getting interested in boys, but we were too scared to talk to them. This song came on, no one asked us to

dance, but we had a blast dancing with each other."
With a smile, I press play, waiting for the song to blare
through the Bluetooth speakers.

Elijah smiles over at me. "Gemma, would you like
to dance?" and he holds his hand out to me.

I smile shyly and accept it. "With you, always."

We start dancing, Elijah is singing along too, and
we both start cracking up, falling into each other, as we
listen to the words. Kids, we would just sing along to
anything. We had no idea what we were singing about.

For Elijah's turn, he selects Pitbull and Ne-Yo's
Time of Our Lives. He pulls me close as he recalls the
memory. "I remember Ty playing this song one night
after we'd busted our asses for about 12 straight hours.
We had just launched our company the year prior, and
we were working like crazy. Ty decided we needed a
break, a night out to blow off some steam, and this song
came on as we were getting ready. It was like the
universe agreed with him. We had a great time that
night."

I watch his beautiful face as he smiles,
remembering that night. Wishing I were there to
witness their hard work firsthand. I feel a sense of pride
flow through me. He made his dreams come true.

And that's how we spend our evening. Each of us
picking a meaningful song or a random one—and
sharing a memory while we dance crazily around my
living room.

. . .

Elijah

I awake the next morning cuddled up behind my girl. I didn't realize I was a cuddler until our first night together. I never spend time with women in bed, unless we're fucking, and I've never stayed the night with someone. But my body just seems to gravitate towards hers, whether we're awake or asleep, and I must admit, I'm more than ok with it. I kiss her shoulder and pull her closer while burying my face in her neck. She's already so familiar to me. I kiss her a few more times before she sighs and pushes back into me.

Waking up to her luscious body is something I could quickly get used to. I slide my hand up and down her body, gliding over her curves. I kiss her right below her ear, in the spot that makes her shiver. I feel her body waking up, and my arousal starts to flow.

I had planned on taking her out for breakfast, but it wouldn't hurt to have a little taste before we go. I kiss her shoulder once more before I roll her onto her back and kiss down her stomach.

And she called me a snack.

Gemma

After the best sleep ever and an even better wake-up call, we decided to get out of my apartment for breakfast. I feel so rested, and I'm surprised because being a light sleeper usually means I don't sleep well with others. There must be something about him, or maybe I'm just exhausted from all the sex.

As we walked to a little cafe near my apartment, Elijah took my hand in his. I tried to play it cool and hide the smile that wanted to beam off my face as we walked hand in hand, and I must have succeeded because he didn't poke fun at me. Obviously, we've held hands before. I've spent enough time with him to know his preference for physical touch, but this is sweet, maybe even innocent, almost natural. And that both thrilled and terrified me.

Elijah holds the door open for me once we arrive at the restaurant. I approach the hostess stand and greet the staff. She starts to smile at me until she gets a look at my companion. She does a double-take, her eyes bugging, and then she breaks out in a nervous giggle as she licks her lips. I roll my eyes and sneak a look at him too. He looks fucking edible today, so I can't blame her. Tousled just rolled out of bed hair, sexy stubble, light gray V-neck tee that does nothing to hide his broad shoulders and ripped everything. Yes, I'll let her have this one.

He takes off his sunglasses as he looks around. I see her flush as she gets a peek at his dazzling blue eyes. Fortunately, he doesn't notice as he's looking around and reading the specials written on the chalkboard.

Her gawking time is up. I clear my throat. "Table for two, preferably on the patio, please." She finally brings her eyes to me and smiles guiltily. "Of course."

She checks her seating chart, grabs a couple of menus, and says, "Right this way."

Elijah gestures for me to walk ahead of him. He puts his hand on the small of my back as we follow her through the restaurant and out to the patio seating. I can feel the shift in energy as people get a good look at him. I see a group of women, and a few men, turn to stare, and there's a ripple of whispers following us out of the restaurant. I glance up at Elijah, and again he doesn't seem to notice the effect he's having on everyone. Instead, he leans down and kisses me on my temple.

She takes us to a small table for two. Elijah pulls out my chair and pushes me in once I sit before taking his seat. She hands over the menus and hurriedly turns away, flustered. Hmm. I look at him for a moment to see his reaction, but still nothing.

We've barely had a chance to look at the menu before our waitress arrives. She greets us, tells us her name is Kim, before she shakily fills our water glasses. I roll my eyes, not her too.

Elijah orders a coffee and I order a kale tonic. He makes a face, and I stick out my tongue at him.

Kim leaves us as we go back to our menus. He peers at me over his and asks, "What do you usually get here?"

"I usually get the meat lovers skillet with scrambled eggs and toast." You can't go wrong with meat and potatoes, am I right?

"But you ordered the kale tonic."

I laugh. "It's all about balance."

"No, I'm happy. I thought you were going to order a fruit bowl or cottage cheese. I've heard women don't really eat on dates."

I burst out laughing again. "Is this a date?"

He doesn't respond but has a small smile on his face.

"Just about every time we've hung out, food has been involved, so if you haven't noticed, I'm a huge fan of it," I tell him as I sip my water.

He chuckles. "Glad to hear it," he says, and goes back to his menu.

Kim returns with my drink and a carafe of coffee. She appears nervous. Her face is bright red, and she spills a little coffee as she pours it into his mug. She's immediately apologetic, but Elijah assures her it's fine. She rushes off to grab a towel and returns quickly and with another apology.

"No problem. It was an accident," Elijah assures her.

We place our orders. I get my skillet and Elijah orders the steak and eggs, with waffles as an appetizer. A man after my own heart.

I smile at the gorgeous man sitting across from me. I have to ask.

"Do you notice the effect you have on people when you walk into a room?" Do men like to hear about how beautiful they are? Because I would love to tell him all the reasons why I'm a huge fan. Or do they like to be called hot or sexy? Maybe they prefer hearing about their big perfect dicks, because he has one of those, too.

He shrugs. "I notice, but I know they are just reacting to my face, or suit, or my nice watch. They don't know *me*, so their reactions or attention don't spark or hold my interest."

Hmm, spoken like a person who has been hot their whole life. I look at him. He's leaning back in his chair, legs open wide, his large body dwarfing everything around him. He's the perfect picture of sex on legs.

"Well, I look at you with lust in my eyes. How is that different?" I ask, my voice husky.

He leans forward then, his blue eyes darkening, probably recognizing the want in my eyes and voice.

He licks his lips. "That's different because our attraction is mutual. You took some time to get to know me and didn't just throw yourself at me. I guess I'm not into that anymore."

"Oh yeah. What are you into now?" I ask, leaning forward.

He pauses and looks at me for a second, blue eyes shining as he assesses me. "I'm supremely attracted to a confident woman. A woman I look forward to talking to just as much as I look forward to seeing, touching, tasting. A woman that pulls me to her with her infectious laugh and energy. A woman I can stay up all night fucking but also laughing and dancing with. A woman whose lush body calls to mine, submits to mine. I'm very into a woman with warm brown eyes, long dark curls, pouty lips that curve up into an enchanting smile. A smile that makes me feel like I'm bathed in sunshine on a winter day."

I swallow. *Holy fucking shit.*

Before I can respond, the waitress returns with our food, interrupting our moment.

We lean away from each other as she sets our plates down, but we don't break eye contact. After she leaves in a huff, disappointed that Elijah doesn't look at her, we lean toward each other again.

I clear my throat. "Well, she sounds lovely."

He smiles and picks up his fork. "She is indeed."

We eat in silence for a few minutes, watching each other, unsure what to say next, when alerts ping on our phones, almost simultaneously. I hold up my phone to show Elijah as her picture, and the name Sasha flash across the screen. He holds up his phone to me. I see the name Ty on his. Interesting. We both hit decline.

"I wonder what that's about."

He shakes his head. "I have no idea. I told him I was busy this weekend."

"Same. The girls know we're together and I want you all to myself." I smile sweetly.

"Don't worry, love. You got me."

I shiver. *Do I? Do I have you, Elijah?*

While Elijah pays for breakfast, I head into the restroom to wash my hands. I stand and stare at myself in the mirror. What is wrong with me? I have the hottest man on the planet giving me the sweetest compliments and I freeze? I wanted to return the sentiment, but I don't want to scare him off by saying too much. I take a deep breath and stare at myself in the mirror. He's who I've always wanted. Can I actually have him? He's perfect and perfect for me, but this is still a casual thing. Isn't it?

The more time we spend together, I just don't know.

CHAPTER FOURTEEN

ELIJAH

"Where to, lovely?" I ask Gemma as we exit the cafe. I take her hand in mine, and she happily squeezes mine in return. I haven't done this since middle school. I don't know what this gorgeous girl is doing to me.

Before she can respond, my phone rings. I've had a flood of text come in, that I haven't checked yet, but now I'm getting curious. This time it's Drew calling. Seconds later, Gemma's phone goes off.

She looks at me. "Should we just answer it, so they leave us alone?"

I let out an exasperated breath. "We might as well."

We both answer our calls, and we continue strolling down the busy sidewalk.

"Hey, Drew. What's up?"

"Hey, man. I'm glad you answered. We've been texting you all morning."

"I know. We were trying to enjoy our breakfast." I say meaningfully.

"Sorry to interrupt. How is everything going?"

I look over to Gemma. "Very well. What do you want? And no, I haven't checked my texts."

He snorts. "Ok, I'm sorry. But we want to get together tonight and hang out. We haven't seen you and Ty in forever, so I spoke to Mia, and we want to get the crew together tonight for drinks."

I look over to Gemma again. She's watching me. I can only assume her call is the same as mine.

"Dude, I told you guys I was busy this weekend. I haven't seen Gemma in a while either."

Drew pauses. "This is getting serious. You and her?"

My instant reaction is to deny, deny, deny, but as I look at Gemma's beautiful face, watching me, I can't.

I sigh. "I'm not talking about this now. I'll get back to you." I tell him as I end the call, stopping and moving away from the bustling sidewalk.

Gemma takes that as a cue to end her call as well and follows me to the secluded area.

"I told them I wanted zero interruptions this weekend," she says.

"Same, but I think they are ignoring our requests. So, what do you think?" I ask her.

"Sasha and Mia both gave very convincing arguments. I don't think I can say no. Unless you're completely against it, I'm in."

I pull her to me and kiss her softly. "I'm in. Luckily,

I have you to myself for the rest of the day. What should we do until then?"

She looks up at me as she thinks. "I need to find something to wear tonight. Let's head over to Southport."

"Shopping? You're making me go shopping? There are so many other things I want to do with you, and they don't involve clothes."

Gemma

I drag him to one of my favorite boutiques. I'm having a brain fart and can't think of anything to wear tonight, so I'll grab something just in case nothing in my closet calls to me. Yes, my clothes talk to me.

We walk into the store and immediately, all eyes are on my beautiful man. I roll my eyes; how annoying. I'm the only one of us that can shop here, but he's getting all the attention.

I head over to a clothing rack of jewel-toned dresses and start flipping through it. I love this shop; they carry a limited inventory, so I rarely have to worry about someone wearing the same thing as me.

I continue to browse when two large hands reach from behind me and pull out a dress for a better look. I look over my shoulder to find Elijah standing behind me.

"What are you doing?"

He looks at me quizzically. "We're shopping."

Surprised, I ask him, "You're going to help?"

He nods. "If I'm here, I'm shopping. Plus, whatever you buy, I'll get to peel it off you later," he says before biting my neck.

I shiver and look up to see the salesgirls watching us, eyes shining green with envy.

"Ok, I'll give it a try." I take the dress from his hands and continue shopping. Elijah trails me around the shop, pointing out things that he likes. Guys usually complain while shopping, preferring to find a seat and play on their phones. Elijah is fully engaged and has great taste.

I go check out the accessories as see him continues to peruse the clothing racks. I've stacked up about five dresses, two of which I'm considering for tonight, a few casual sundresses, and a couple pairs of earrings and midi rings.

"Babe, I'm going to go try these on," I call out as I hold up the dresses for him to see.

He follows me to the small dressing room area and takes a seat on a chaise.

"Are we going to have a *Pretty Woman* moment right now?" he asks.

I turn around, shocked. "You've seen *Pretty Woman*?"

"Who hasn't? I love Julia Roberts."

I nod. *Same.*

"Wait, are you calling me a whore?"

"No, but you are a slut. At least a summer one."

I giggle and stick my tongue out at him. "Watch it,

Mr. Adler. I'll be right back. Park it and stay out of trouble."

* * *

I start with the sundresses. I found a short white dress with large black heart-shaped polka dots covering it, and I'm obsessed with it. Polka dots are my weakness. I'm for sure buying all the casual dresses. Now, onto the sexy dresses. Elijah picked out a gorgeous little black dress, you can never have too many, and it fits me like a glove. It is low cut in the front with a sheer high back and sheer cut-outs along the thighs. After a quick look in the mirror to fluff my hair, I head out for a little help from my shopping companion.

He's staring at his phone when I walk out, and I keep my eyes on him for his reaction when he sees me. I call out, "Elijah, what do you think about this one?"

His eyes snap to me. He bites his lip as he gives me a slow perusal. Awareness unfurls in my stomach. He leans back against the chaise, widening his legs, and looks me over again from head to toe. I can see the approval in his eyes, the arousal, and I clench my thighs together. I wonder if this is how he feels when I take my time and eye fuck him. I continue to watch his face as I see all the dirty thoughts in his eyes. He absolutely approves of this dress.

I ask him again, my voice a whisper, "What do you think about this one?"

He meets my gaze. "I'm captivated. You're

breathtaking in that dress. I knew you would be."

I look down at that, suddenly shy, my hands smoothing over the dress. Elijah stands and stops in front of me, lifting my chin. "This one is a definite yes. I can't wait to see you in the next one," he says before kissing me softly. Then he turns me back to the dressing room with a firm pat on the butt. He may just be my favorite shopping companion.

I head out a few minutes later. I'm getting every single thing I grabbed. I'm quite sure I have a shopping addiction. I don't need any of these things, but I'm going to treat myself. Treating myself to books, clothes, and food is my weakness. I look up and see Elijah already at the register. I join him and place my items on the counter. The sales associate rings me up, and Elijah hands over his card. I frown and look up at him.

"What are you doing?"

He returns my stare. "I'm buying these for you. They are as much for you as they are for me." He bends and kisses my nose. "Just say, 'thank you, Elijah,' and let's go."

I continue to stare at him, mesmerized by his blue eyes, before the sales associate clears her throat. "Is this the card you're using?" she asks us.

Elijah quirks a brow at me and waits for my answer. I turn to her and nod.

She completes my purchase, Elijah takes the bags, and we head outside.

"Thank you, Elijah." I finally say as I stand on my tiptoes to kiss his stubbled cheek.

"Good girl."

Elijah

Gemma and I spend the rest of the day walking around her neighborhood and browsing the shops and restaurants. I bought her a few more things and even found some items for myself. Thankfully, there wasn't a baseball game, so we only had to contend with typical Saturday foot traffic and not the typical rowdy drunk crowds.

I dropped her back at her apartment after an early dinner. Since I didn't have anything appropriate to wear, we'd decided that I would get dressed at my place and we'd meet up later at the bar. I don't think either of us was ready or comfortable with this step of arriving at an event together. It would spark too many questions from our friends.

Mia and Sasha showed up at her apartment soon after we'd arrived back. They'd decided to get ready together, so my goodbye was cut short, and I'll admit that it was frustrating. And now, sitting alone in my home, I watch the clock. I'm so ready to get back to my girl.

I was already so attached to having her with me, having free access to her. Her laugh. Her touch. Her attention. I feel a rush of unease in my stomach. She claims she wants to see each other casually, like so many others. Does she mean it, or is she just saying it because she thinks it is what I want to hear? Is it what I want to hear? I rake my fingers through my hair. I've never wanted more before. Are you supposed to feel like this? Shouldn't it be simple, easy? I don't want to make a mistake and ruin this. I don't want to move too fast or too slow. I like the progression of things right now.

I take a sip of my drink. We'll see how tonight goes, then I'll decide.

Gemma

We take the elevator up to the rooftop bar, Nevaeh. The last time I was here was when Elijah and I were reunited. I shiver as I remember that first shock of electricity when we touched. We see the guys immediately, sitting across three white couches with a low table in the center. The Four Fucksmen all look delicious, and I already see several women circling them like sharks. Aw, fuck. This should be fun.

They all stand when we approach the table. We make our way around the group for hugs and kisses, and I end up in front of Elijah, who looks edible in a slim cut black on black look, his shirt unbuttoned at the collar. He smells good, too, like clean laundry, sandalwood, and his own distinct scent.

Standing in front of him, I'm nervous. Do I go in for a kiss? A hug? I freely touched him all day, but this feels different. Being on a date is different than running into a guy you're fucking, right? And I don't want to stake a claim on him in front of everyone...well, that's a lie, but I don't want to upset him. I'll let him make the first move.

Elijah smiles down at me and pulls me into a hug, his body pressed against mine in all the right places. He nuzzles my neck, kissing me below the ear, and asks gruffly, "What the fuck are you wearing?"

I laugh to myself, jackpot. I decided against wearing any of the dresses he bought for me today, wanting to surprise him. I actually had the perfect dress in my closet, something I had purchased forever ago and never worn.

He runs his hands down my back, touching my exposed skin. I'm wearing a two-piece white lace dress; the top has a sexy scoop neck. It fits me like a glove, molding to my curves. The high-waisted skirt stops just above the knee, so I don't feel too exposed since it has the illusion netting, so it looks see-through and shows off every curve.

"A dress," I say innocently as I feel my body softening against his. My soft pressing against his hard.

I feel his hand drift down to my ass, giving it a hard squeeze. I return the favor, maintaining eye contact.

He smirks and leans down again, whispering in my ear, "Enjoy it now and take lots of pictures. I'll be ripping it from your body as soon as we get home and you'll be on your knees soon after."

Home, that has a nice ring to it. Being on my knees does too.

I swallow as he bites my ear and kisses my shoulder before pulling me down to the couch next to him.

Everyone looks away when we look up, except for Mia. She's staring at us with a huge grin on her face.

Elijah pours me a glass of Dom. I wonder if he got this because he knows it's my favorite, as I take a look around at our friends. Mia is sitting on a couch between Drew and Xander. She looks like a sexy nymph tonight. Her long blond hair is wavy and full, and she's wearing a beautiful flowy green dress. The guys are fawning over her, and it looks like a competition to see who can hold her attention the longest or who can make her laugh loudest. She said Drew was too nice for her taste; I don't get that at all. But I think Xander maybe just rough enough around the edges for her.

I laugh to myself as I see her try to discreetly scratch her head, then her legs, and back to her head. Earlier tonight, Mia told us about her recent hookup with a guy she'd been talking to for a few weeks. She said after they hooked up, his dog climbed in the bed with them, and now she's convinced she has fleas. She does have a few red marks on her legs. Sasha and I checked her hair, like how the school nurse checked our hair for lice when we were younger but didn't find anything. But now she's paranoid and can't stop scratching. I laugh to myself as I see her scratch again.

Over on the other couch are Sasha and Ty. Sasha looks fab in an off-the-shoulder fitted black dress that skims her body perfectly, her hair pinned back on one side. If I were a body language expert, I would say they are totally into each other. Their bodies are turned toward each other, they are both leaning in to speak, and they are completely oblivious to the rest of us. I really like Ty. He seems so genuine, and he's drop-dead gorgeous. Tall, dark, and handsome. Go, Sasha.

Elijah pulls my attention back to him, growling into my ear, "Love, you're a fucking stunner. I'm going to have to keep you close tonight."

"Just tonight?" I ask softly.

He doesn't respond immediately. I'm not sure he heard me. He puts a strand of hair behind my ear. "You're perfect. I don't think I can let you go."

I look up to meet his gaze and as if in slow motion, he bends down to kiss my lips softly, reverently, in front of everyone.

Elijah

The girls are out on the dance floor. I watch as Gemma's body moves to the beat of the music, her long dark hair swaying with her hips. I keep her in my line of sight. The last time we were here she had assholes all around her. I know she may not want my protection; she is more than capable of handling herself in any situation, but she shouldn't have to and she's not.

Gemma looks up and catches me staring again. She smiles and bounces her tits at me. This one is fiery, like the devil. She's opening up, blossoming before my eyes. She's letting go of the innocence and exhibiting her more carnal nature, and I love it.

Ty leans over. "You guys look good together."

"That's not too hard with her."

"She is a beauty," he says softly. I look at him sharply then follow his gaze, but he is not looking at Gemma. His gaze firmly on Sasha, dancing. My eyebrows raise.

He finally turns to me. "What's going on? This looks like more than fuck buddies; it always has, in my opinion."

I don't respond immediately, because I don't know what to say. Gemma is an enchantress. Initially, I thought it was just our fun fantasy games or the amazing sex. But now I know it's her.

I run a frustrated hand through my hair. "Dude, I don't know what I'm doing. It's easy between us now, but will that be the case when I'm working all the time? Traveling? I can't afford the distractions, nor do I want her to feel like one."

Ty shakes his head at me sadly. "Take work out of the equation because, in some form, it will always be a part of the equation. Do you want this girl?"

I look up and see her at the bar with her friends. I take in her animated expressions as she talks with her friends. Her big smile a bright beacon. I note other eyes on her, drawn like I am to the shining star at the bar. Again, she doesn't seem to notice.

I turn back to Ty. "Yes, that's not the problem."

"I know you're not ready for kids and the lot, but could you be happy for her if she has those things with somebody else? If you can, keep it casual. But if the thought burns you up like a double shot of cheap whiskey..." he trails off.

My eyes flick back to her. I imagine her belly swollen, full of life. I see her holding a perfect little girl, an amazing mix of the both of us, and I feel a twinge in my stomach. I imagine worshipping that ripe body, kissing her rounded belly, and massaging her sore feet. I feel the arousal start to thrum through my body and my dick twitches. Fuck, I can't get the image of her pregnant and happy out of my mind now. I can't even consider her having those things with someone else. It makes my blood boil.

"No, definitely not. She's mine." I tell him, not taking my eyes off her.

"What are you going to do about it?" he asks.

I lean back on the couch, considering this for a moment. I feel something soft brush against my arm thrown over the back of the couch. I ignore it, deep in thought. I feel it again, then a second later, I feel that soft thing resting on top of my hand.

I look over to see an ass in a tight blue dress sitting on my hand. I pull away immediately, and she jumps, pretending to be embarrassed. She comes around the couch immediately, to apologize. Yeah right. I'm used to these tricks for attention, these tricks for a reaction. I try to quickly reassure her that everything is fine, to cut this interaction short. Out of the corner of my eye, I see Gemma watching us.

This could be interesting. I smile up at the woman.

CHAPTER FIFTEEN

ELIJAH

I'm not going to try to make her jealous, but if she happens to get jealous, that's not my fault, right? I turn my attention back to the woman who is still attempting to apologize for brushing against me. She even takes my hand in hers.

Gemma's eyes remain locked on us from her spot at the bar. Her usually expressive face is unreadable, and I know I've fucked up. She does not like this one bit, and I know I need to terminate this little game immediately.

Smoothly pulling my hand away, I assure her everything is fine, no harm, no foul. I'm being presumptuous, but I tell her I really didn't notice her because I was too busy staring at a beautiful woman. Then I point her in the direction of Gemma.

Gemma and I are locked in an intense stare, and I tell the woman, "I only have eyes for her."

I don't know if she read my lips or she picked up on

the sentiment, but I see her face soften. The woman apologizes again and excuses herself.

Before I know it, I'm headed toward Gemma and her to me, and we meet somewhere in the middle.

I cup her cheek; she closes her eyes and leans into my hand. I feel like the biggest asshole. Why would I want to test her, possibly hurt her? She doesn't have to prove anything to me.

"I told that woman, I only have eyes for you." I kiss her softly before continuing. "So, what do you say we pause your Summer Slut movement for now? Maybe you could be a Fall Floozy or an Autumn Thot'em." I laugh, knowing I'm lying. She's mine. I lean down and whisper into her ear. "I want you all to myself, Gemma Davis, all the strings attached."

She giggles and I know I've got her.

Gemma

I had been happily telling the girls about my time with Elijah after Mia asked how the fuck fest was going. I felt like I was on such a high. Elijah had been attentive all night. Even while I danced and spent time with my friends, I felt his eyes on me. Whenever I looked up, I met his greedy gaze. It didn't feel oppressive. It made me feel wanted, cherished, protected, sexy.

When I saw the woman in the blue dress make her move on him, I felt my heart stop for the briefest second before I realized I wasn't worried. I've never felt more secure in a relationship, or non-relationship, in our case. He's eased any possible fears because even though I couldn't make out what he said to her, I could feel it. And that stopped me from joining them and telling her to go kick rocks with no socks.

And now he's shocked the hell out of me. *He wants to be exclusive. Yes, please. You're all I've ever wanted.*

I laugh as I nod yes, overwhelmed at the surge of emotion that rushes through me. The relief I feel that just maybe he feels the same way. I crush my lips to his. He's just as greedy for me, and we're all thrusting tongues and clashing teeth. Our bodies are flush, and he pulls me closer still, hands on my ass, as he grinds me onto his hard cock.

I whimper as his mouth goes to my neck, licking and sucking. I want to climb this man. I grab his hair roughly and pull him back to my mouth, biting his lip.

We stand there lost in a moment when I hear Drew say, "You guys are making a scene."

Elijah pulls back to look into my eyes and says, "A scene? Fuck that. We'll make a fucking movie." I can only nod my head in agreement.

Drew laughs before pulling us over to the dance floor, where they are all dancing. Sasha is living her best life. The DJ is playing a good mix of top 40 and throwback hip hop and R&B songs, and she's loving it. I see her and Ty gravitating toward each other as they get caught up in the music.

As soon as we make it to the dance floor the song changes to Frank Ocean's *Thinkin Bout You*. I *love* this song; it gives me all the sexy vibes. Elijah is in luck because I'm about to grind so hard all over his dick.

My arms go around his neck, and I press my lips to his throat, giving him a lick, practically purring at the taste of him. He grabs my ass and pulls me closer as I slow wind against him. He looks down at me, bends, swiping his tongue through my mouth, before he nibbles my lip.

I feel a rush of arousal between my legs. I need to get this man home and put us both out of our misery.

The song mixes into Beyonce's *Naughty Girl* and deciding to be naughty, I turn in his arms, my back to his front. My skirt is too tight to get crazy, thankfully, because, in this moment, I really want to be spread-eagle on the floor.

Instead, I undulate into his hard body before he fists my hair, making me bend at the waist. His hands go to my shoulders as he holds me in place, pounding into my ass, repeatedly.

Alright, I can take the hint. It's time to go.

We crash through my front door with a bang, my skirt up, legs already around his waist. He kisses me deeply and thoroughly as he carries me to my bedroom, hands on my ass, grinding me into his erection.

He sets me down near the bed, and before I can think, he grabs my top, his fingers tearing right through the lace, and rips it from my body, shredding it completely. His hands quickly go to my skirt, still bunched up around my hips, and he does it again.

Shocked, I stand in front of him in my white thong. His eyes slowly travel down my naked body. My nipples harden as he appreciates my body. My thong is soaked, and I can feel the moisture gathering between my thighs.

"Undress me," he commands. His voice a rumble in his chest.

I obey immediately and with shaky hands, I reach for the first button. I struggle with it. Losing my patience, I pull his shirt apart, sending buttons flying, before I tear it from his body.

I drop to my knees, fully submitting to him. I meet his gaze as I gently remove his shoes and then his socks. His hands go to my hair as I wet my lips and start on his belt.

Still on my knees, I undo his pants and pull them down his muscular legs, his hands still on my hair as he steps out of them.

He stands there in his black boxer briefs and my eyes scan his hard body. Even in the darkness, I can see every hard line of his body. I caress that sexy V that disappears into his briefs. His abs flex as he breathes in and out and I lower my head to his cock. I kiss and nuzzle his cock through his boxers, as it strains to get to me. Finally, I reach up and pull them down, exposing his cock to my hungry gaze. I exhale noisily, my breath fanning against his body. I've been eye to eye with this monster a few times now, but the sheer size of him always takes my breath away. I take him in my hand, and I relish the power I feel as he hisses at my touch, loving the smoothness and his surrender as I caress him.

I pepper light kisses across his hips and thighs. I kiss his tip once, licking his slit. I give him teasing, playful licks like he's my favorite flavor of ice cream, still not taking him into my mouth.

He fists my hair tighter, moving my head to look up at him.

"I have a fantasy I want you to fulfill," he growls.

"Ok," I whisper. I don't care what it is. I know I'll do it.

He bends, lifts me, and throws me onto the bed. I squeal and laugh as I bounce a few times and I see him go to my nightstand and take out a few condoms.

He joins me in bed, lying on his back, and pulls me to him. I turn my face to his expectantly.

He offers me a savage kiss before he says, "Tonight, you're going to ride my cock, but first, you're going to sit on my face."

Shock races through me. Sit on his face? What if I kill him?

I shake that off. This is happening. I want to fulfill all his fantasies, just as he has fulfilled mine.

He doesn't wait for my answer. He kisses me again before lifting me so I can straddle his head, my thong still in place.

I feel clumsy and awkward as I grab onto my headboard and climb over his face. The only sounds I hear are our heavy breathing and my thunderous heartbeat. Knowing he wants this sends a warm thrum through my body, and I feel another rush of arousal between my legs. I want this too. I've wanted this for a while.

Elijah's big hands cradle my ass as he brings me down to his mouth. He licks me through my thong, then a teasing bite and my eyes close immediately. *Oh My Gah.*

I feel his fingers go to my ass to pull on my thong, pulling it tighter, and it roughly rubs all of my spots. I moan as pleasure shoots through my body, and I start to move. Elijah groans into me as I tremble.

He moves my thong aside, fully exposing me to his mouth, and he slides his tongue and lips through my creamy folds. I try to start a slow rhythm, but his large hands hold me in place.

"Look at me," he growls. "Watch me eat your pussy and love every fucking minute of it."

Holy fuck, I'm going to drown him.

My eyes fly open, and I look down between my legs. His blue eyes are dark as he meets my shocked gaze as he licks up everything I'm giving him.

He pulls me down harder and parts me with his tongue. I want to throw my head back and close my eyes. But watching him genuinely enjoying this is something I can't look away from.

This moment will be forever committed to memory, my dark fantasy come true.

His grip tightens as he slides me back and forth

against his mouth as he bites, licks, and sucks intensely, his stubble scratching my delicate skin and my thighs. The sound of my wet arousal confirms how much I am enjoying this treat. My hands grip the headboard and my body begins to quake. I feel his finger glide through my spread cheeks, adding light pressure.

Oh fuck, is he? I shudder. Why does something so naughty feel so good?

My body marvels at the delectable sensations running through me as I feel my orgasm barreling down. I truly begin to fuck his face, my body's natural instincts taking over, chasing my orgasm, because I need to come. I reach down with one hand and fist his dark hair, holding him in place as I grind and slip and slide all over his face. He pulls me down harder into him, sucking and biting, and I explode with a scream, my movements wild and rough. And he accepts it all, eyes closed in pleasure.

As my quivers start to recede, he plants one more deep kiss right there before he lifts me and slides me down his hard body. Proving my immense pleasure and appreciation, I leave a wet trail along the way. I collapse on his wet chest, eyes closed as I try to gather my thoughts, reign in my emotions.

"You're amazing," he whispers.

I look up into his beautiful face, covered in my cum. I lick his lips, his stubbled face, and suck his chin, before he grabs my face and captures my mouth. He groans, and I can't get enough of my taste on his tongue, so I suck it.

He finally pulls away, ripping my thong off. "I need you on my dick, now." He grabs a condom, tearing the wrapper with his teeth, sheathing himself.

I have a moment of panic. If I sit on that thing, it's going to rip me in two.

He must sense my trepidation because he strokes my hair for a moment before reaching down to pinch my clit. I'm still wet and slippery when he thrusts two fingers inside me. I cry out, still sensitive from that bone-shattering orgasm.

"I won't hurt you, baby. Now, get on my dick," he says as he strokes me twice more before withdrawing his fingers.

I rise on shaky legs to straddle him. I grab him roughly, closing my eyes on a moan as I rub the wide head of his cock through my folds and against my clit. I slowly start to lower myself onto him, inch by inch, and we both moan. Our eyes are locked on where our bodies are joined.

Elijah keeps his hands on my ass, his face strained, as he lets me get accustomed to his size, taking him at my own pace. He stretches me completely, and I swivel my hips to loosen myself up to take those last few inches. He massages my clit, sending pleasure through my body, and I relax as he slides in those last few inches.

Oh god. I sit there for a moment with my eyes closed, pleasure and pain overload.

"Ride me, baby. Take what you need from my dick. I want to feel you come all over it."

I experimentally lift myself up and down, my eyes still closed, as my body is wracked with pleasure at how full I feel. I sigh as I rock forward then swivel my hips again.

He sits up suddenly, and I moan at the change in position. He kisses my mouth, my face, my neck, hands in my hair.

"You're perfect. You feel amazing. Don't stop, baby." He bends and takes my nipple in his mouth, biting and sucking hard. I cry out and arch into him, seeking more, as my body clenches around his cock.

"There she is, my baby," he whispers around my nipple. His big hand goes around the back of my neck, gripping me. His other hand pinches and twists my other nipple. "Yes, baby, just like that." He guides me up and down on his dick. So cocky.

I follow the easy rhythm, clenching and rolling my hips. He's so deep like this, hitting every possible pleasure point. I know I'm not going to last long.

He kisses me deeply before he falls back on the bed and my hands go to his chest for leverage, my head thrown back. I grind onto him and clench again. He massages my clit, and my body shakes uncontrollably, the smell of our sex an added aphrodisiac.

Elijah's mouth forms an O, watching where our bodies are connected. He grips my hips fiercely, slamming me down on his cock and thrusting up into me. I cry out as the air is knocked from me.

He pulls me down until my breasts are pressed against his chest while kissing me greedily, before biting my neck. Our sweaty bodies slide against each other as I drive down, and he thrusts up. My pussy slides up and down his length, milking his cock, begging for his cum. I can't get close enough.

I feel another orgasm barreling down and my body writhes and clenches around him. "Oh god!"

"Come with me."

I scream before I bite his shoulder as we explode together. His deep grunts in my ear send goosebumps over my body.

I collapse on his chest, exhausted. We're both panting like we've just run a marathon. I lick his sweaty neck, loving the taste of him and the saltiness on my lips, as he strokes my hair and down my back. He pulls me even closer, and we kiss languidly like we have all the time in the world.

He finally pulls out and disposes of the condom before immediately pulling me back to his warm body. I snuggle into him as he kisses my head before pulling my face to his for a deep kiss.

Tonight, has been so intimate, it feels like a new beginning, and I don't want it to end.

CHAPTER SIXTEEN

ELIJAH

I wake to find Gemma cradled into my side, her face in my neck. I rub my hand over my face. After Gemma blew my mind fulfilling my fantasy, we showered before doing it all over again. Then we collapsed from exhaustion.

I peer down at her naked body, blankets long gone after last night, and I stroke her silky skin. This feels right, waking up with her in my arms. I'm not thinking about work or deadlines. I'm happily here in the moment with her. I'm happy. She makes me happy.

Ty's words come back to me from last night. I feel a pit in my stomach at the thought of her moving on with someone else. The thought of her sharing her body with anyone else and starting a family with them turns my stomach. I've never considered those things before. Or maybe I had, but I thought I'd pull a Clooney and settle down later in life when I was free to travel, free to enjoy life more. Maybe it's time to reconsider everything and enjoy life right now.

No longer able to stop myself, my hands roam her body, and I see goosebumps rise on her flesh. I kiss her before I get up, covering her with the blanket, and head into the kitchen. I need sustenance.

I make us omelets and prepare mimosas before rejoining her in bed. I kiss her mouth, morning breath and all. "Time for breakfast, lovely."

She stretches sexily and opens her eyes. "Breakfast? The true way to my heart."

We spend the rest of the morning in bed, dozing on and off, watching a little TV. And it is heaven. I rarely have time to do the things I need to do, let alone the time to do nothing. I've been missing out.

The afternoon rolls around before we get out of bed and shower together. I'm shampooing her hair, one of my new favorite things to do, when the idea comes to me.

"I have to leave for a short business trip in a few days. I'm not ready to let you go. Come stay at my place until then."

She freezes for a second before relaxing back into me. "Ok," she says, and I can hear the smile in her voice.

After we shower, she starts packing for the few days she's going to spend at my place. To be honest, I would love for her to stay and to be there when I get back. I scrub my hand over my face. Dude, slow down. You don't want to scare her off.

· · ·

Gemma

My alarm goes off on my phone, a reminder it's time for my FaceTime with my parents. We chat every Sunday to check in with each other. I sit with my back against my headboard and call my mom. She answers immediately, excited to tell me all about my brother's upcoming wedding. She is having the time of her life helping with the planning, all while driving my future sister-in-law crazy.

"Hi, baby," she beams at me. She looks away from the phone, "Honey, it's Gemmie." My dad appears behind my mother. "Hey, baby girl."

"Hi, mom. Hey, dad. What are you guys doing?"

They tell me about some veggies they've grown in their garden that they are excited about, and I laugh. I forgot all about their new obsession with gardening. Or my mom's new love of gardening. My dad just tags along with whatever she's doing because he is obsessed with her.

I tell them about work and a few of the new books that have come across my desk. I feel like I've really hit my stride at work. While we chat, I make sure to keep my phone on my face so they can't see Elijah, who has his head in my lap as I mindlessly run my fingers through his hair.

"How's all the wedding stuff going?" I ask.

My mom bounces in her seat. "Everything is

perfect. I'm so happy Brooke is letting me help her. It's going to be beautiful."

Before I can respond, she continues.

"Speaking of the wedding, are you bringing a date? How are things with Dustin? Have you made up?" she fires at me.

Oh, fuck. I feel Elijah stiffen. Originally, I had not planned on taking a date, let alone Elijah. But I think we're officially dating, so I should, right? It would be rude not to ask him now. Plus, he and Greyson are friends. It would be a great surprise for Grey.

"Actually, I'm seeing someone new, but I'm probably not going to invite him." Elijah takes the opportunity to bite my thigh, and I flick the back of his head.

My mom pouts. "Why not? We would love to meet him. What's his name? Is he cute? Where did you meet? What does he do?"

Elijah turns and looks up at me expectantly as I cover his face with my hand. I am not having this conversation with him here.

"Mom, I have to go. I need to get ready for my week. I'll call you tomorrow."

"Sure, sweetie. Do you have a busy week? Any dates or plans with your mystery guy?" she asks, stalling. I should have known she wouldn't let me rush her off the phone.

"Besides my doctor's appointment tomorrow, my week is pretty dull. Just work, add I'll probably go to kickboxing this week." I barely pause before I ramble on. "Gotta go. Talk to you later, mom. Bye, dad. Love you!" I yell because I know he's somewhere nearby.

They let me go and I end the chat.

Elijah sits up and leans against the headboard. "I forgot how sweet your mom is. Do you see them often?" he asks.

"Not as often as I would like, so we make sure to talk a few times a week, if we can, with our Sundays being mandatory."

"Did your parents like Dusty?"

I shrug. "They liked him well enough, although they only met him when they came to visit me at school. He's the last boyfriend that I had and the last guy I mentioned to them, so he comes up sometimes."

Elijah nods but doesn't look at me, and I can't read his expression.

I lean into him, putting my head on his shoulder and looping my arm through his. "So, would you do me the honor of being my date to Greyson's wedding?"

I look up at him as his face lights up in a boyish grin that makes the butterflies in my stomach flutter a little faster.

He pulls me to him, kissing me deeply. "I would love to."

We arrived at Elijah's a couple of hours ago. We ordered an early dinner. Now we're soaking together in his enormous bathtub with a bottle of champagne, candles, and soft music playing.

We face each other, my legs between his, and he massages my feet.

"Do you want to have kids? If so, how many?" I ask him.

"Yes, I've always wanted four kids."

"Four? That's a small army."

"Yeah, I like the idea of a big family, so they have each other growing up. Plus, I like even numbers." He smiles at me. "I always assumed I'd be an older dad, so lots of kids to take care of me when I'm old." He laughs.

"Why do you want to be an older dad?"

"I don't think it's something I wanted, but with how busy I am with work and no relationship," he shrugs, "Means no kids. Waiting until I was older, with more time to devote to a family seemed the right thing to do."

He cocks his head to the side as he asks, "What about you? What does your future look like?"

"I'm all about that happily ever after, and hopefully that includes two kids. I would love to be a stay-at-home mom initially or continue my career less formally so I could devote my time taking care of my family."

"What does 'happily ever after' mean to you?" his voice huskier now.

I hum as I try to formulate my response. "I know people talk about being best friends with their spouse, don't get me wrong, I want that bond too. But I also want us to be so head over heels in love and lust with each other. I want passion and romance because our connection will keep our foundation strong so that my kids grow up in a home so full of love that they feel it. I want what my parents have. They are still crazy in love and dote on each other all these years later. Maybe it's a fantasy, but I want the fairy tales. I want that forever kind of love. I want to be his world, as he would be mine."

I smile at him before adding, "I've always wanted to be a wife and a mother, and I assumed I would be a young one so I could be around for my kids as long as possible."

"We're the exact opposite."

I sigh. "Looks like it."

He grabs my other foot and pulls me towards him for a kiss. "Two kids, huh? That's light work. I could manage that in my sleep."

I kiss him back. "Four kids? Sounds easy enough."

I turn and rest my back against his broad chest, his arms around me. Something has changed between us since last night. There's an intimacy, a vulnerability that wasn't there before.

"Tell me about your week. You told your parents you have a doctor's appointment tomorrow. Is everything ok?"

"Yes, I have to see my gyno for my annual exam. That's the only reason why I've been keeping my hands to myself today. No sex until after my appointment."

He looks at me, incredulous. "Is that a thing?"

"My doctor recommends it."

"Is your doctor male or female?"

I roll my eyes, this guy. "*She's* going to be examining me, and I don't want to be in there with a bruised cervix." I joke.

"What time is your appointment?"

"First thing in the morning. Quick exam, blood test, then I'm heading straight to work."

He nods and kisses my neck. "Well, she's not going to be examining your throat, is she?"

I burst out laughing and try to splash him.

Tonight feels very couple-y and normal, and I didn't realize how much I craved that, craved him. After our bath, we lie in bed together and search Netflix for something to watch. The search takes forever, and we both give up.

We're tempting fate here, both naked since Elijah told me the rules of no clothes in our bed. *Our bed.* All I want to do is crawl all over his body, but with restraint, I sit up on my elbow and look over at his gorgeous face. He mirrors my actions and faces me.

"So, I said yes to all the strings. What does that mean?" I ask him, avoiding his gaze.

"What do you want it to mean?" he responds, maneuvering to meet my gaze.

"I want it to mean we're exclusive, monogamous. No more Mission Promiscuous for me and no more single moms or divorcees for you."

He shakes his head vehemently. "I haven't been with anyone since we reconnected and probably weeks before that. I don't really remember anyone before you."

"Yeah?" I murmur.

"Yeah." He leans forward and swipes his tongue through my mouth before whispering against my lips, "Mine."

I shiver, and just like that, I'm claimed. But I've been his since we were kids. He just doesn't know it.

CHAPTER SEVENTEEN

ELIJAH

I bend to kiss a still sleeping Gemma. I rub my nose along her cheek as she stirs. I pull away, not wanting to wake her up so early. Ty and I have an early breakfast meeting, then the guys are meeting us to play basketball before lunch. Since I'll be traveling later this week, I convinced them to play an earlier game.

I walk into my favorite diner. Ty is already in a booth, reviewing some reports.

"Morning," I say as I slide into my seat.

"Morning," he looks at me with assessing eyes. "Stop smiling like that. You look creepy."

I chuckle. "I don't look creepy, asshole."

He retorts. "You're not looking at your face right now. Why do you look so weird?"

"I don't feel weird. I'm happy. This is called a smile."

"Ok, why are you smiling creepily?"

"Gemma stayed the night last night. Actually, she's staying with me for a few days. I left her warm and naked in my bed to come here, at the butt crack of dawn, but I'm smiling because I know she'll be there when I get home."

Our waitress, Dottie, returns with a smile and a coffee for me and a refill for Ty. She knows our orders since we're regulars and puts it in now that I'm here.

Once she leaves, Ty turns back to me. "That must mean your weekend with her went well?"

"It went better than well. We decided to be exclusive. She's mine. She always has been, but now it's official."

Ty's brows shoot up to his hairline and he whistles. "Look at you. You finally took my advice and stepped up. Good for you, man. I like Gem. I really like her for you."

"What's not to like? She's perfect."

He shakes his head. "Alright, you ruined it. Are we done with your love life? I have some shit I want to discuss with you."

I take a sip of my coffee, nodding. "I'm listening."

"We have a lot of irons in the fire right now, not sure if you noticed. But I think it's time we hired some additional help. We need to hire someone, or multiple someone's to oversee projects in and outside of Chicago, so we can focus on the big picture and additional projects."

I nod; the travel is becoming my least favorite thing. "I like it. Let's review the numbers once we're back in the office." We probably should have made this decision a while ago with our growth and success, but we're both control freaks and wanted our fingers in everything. Now, I'm a little more interested in having my fingers, and other things, in Gemma.

Our food arrives, halting our conversation for a few minutes while we dig in.

"You didn't respond to my text about basketball today. Are you coming?" I missed the last few basketball days while traveling and I really need to fit some time in with my boys.

He grins. "Those assholes have been talking so much shit about you the last few weeks. I wouldn't miss seeing what they say to your face."

My eyes narrow. "Is that right?"

We destroyed their asses on the court. Ty and I have played together since we were kids, and we usually play on opposite teams to make it fair for the others but not today.

"I heard you guys were talking shit, so I decided to really give you something to talk shit about."

Ty laughs as Xander throws his towel at me. "I was off my game today, don't take too much pride in this victory."

Drew scowls. "I thought you'd be a little rusty, but clearly, I was mistaken."

"Swimming in new pussy will do that to you, keeps you loose and buoyant," Xander retorts.

My gaze swings to him as I take a step toward him. "Watch your mouth, motherfucker," my voice dripping venom.

His eyes widen as he raises his hands in surrender. "Are you serious about her? Shit, my bad, dude. I like Gem. I was kidding."

I turn and wipe my face with my towel. "Yeah, we're exclusive."

Drew and Xander look like cartoon characters as their eyes practically bulge out of their sockets. Ty chugs his water, uninterested. He's listened to me talk about her all morning.

Drew slaps me on my back. "Congrats, dude. She's a good girl, a definite keeper."

"Well, this makes sense now that I think about it. You were following her around the club all night like a little puppy," Xander says.

We all laugh. "No, I wasn't, fucker."

Xander nods. "You totally were. And the way you were dancing with her and kissing, you totally were pissing all over her, so to speak. Salute to you, my friend, nicely done."

We all laugh at the mental picture we conjure. This fucking guy.

"Alright, assholes. I know it's hard, but enough about me. What's going on with you? Ty, are you still seeing that chick?"

He turns back to his bag, packing things away. "Nah, not for a few weeks."

"Anyone new?"

"Nope, not really," he says, still averting his gaze.

Xander jumps in, "Well, I met the hottest fucking chick Saturday. She took me back to her place and introduced me to some new shit."

That piques our interest. I love Xander, but he's a whore of the highest caliber. If she taught him something new, he's probably in love.

He sits on the bleachers and takes a swig of his water. "We get back to her place, and she immediately wanted me to undress. She was especially persistent about taking off my shoes and socks. She then goes to change into something more comfortable."

We're all listening in rapt attention.

"She comes out of the bathroom completely naked, *covered* in oil, with a bunch of fucking stockings or nylons, whatever they're called, draped all over her."

We all nod. "I'm sitting in her bed when she crawls to me and goes right for my fucking feet. She's kissing and nuzzling my feet and moaning like I'm balls deep in her, right."

We all roar with laughter, only this guy.

Drew finally pulls himself together to ask, "What the fuck did you do?"

Xander looks at him with a raised eyebrow. "I did what any self-respecting man would do. I put the stockings on, rubbed my feet all over her body, clit included. Then I stuffed them in her mouth and fucked her stupid."

We lose it again; I'm gasping for air as I laugh at this idiot.

He closes his eyes, shaking his head. "Fuck, guys, she may be the one."

Gemma

I smile to myself as I recall my morning. I'm on the L heading to work after my gyno appointment. Fortunately, it's not too busy, so I get a window seat. I catch my reflection in my window, and I have a goofy smile on my face.

Elijah left me a key to his house, and I know it was for a practical reason. I am staying with him for a few days, but this feels huge. Especially for Mr. Fantasy Fuck Buddy.

My smile starts to hurt my face as I remember my shock when I woke up. On my nightstand, he'd left me the key on a keychain of a jewel encrusted capital E and a note.

"So you'll always have a piece of me with you..."

"Babe," I whispered. I mean, I can't even right now.

He'd spent the weekend with me, so when did he have time to get a key made and buy the keychain? Had he been planning this? What does this mean? Ugh, my mind was going a mile a minute.

I almost miss my stop, but I jump off just in time and trek to work. I check my phone as I walk, reading the messages from Mia and Sasha. I sent them a picture of me with the key and a shocked expression on my face. After we got over the "what the fuck is that" of it all, they were happy for me and the same questions I asked myself started rolling in. We'd already made plans for lunch because this weekend needs to be dissected.

I work at my desk until just before my lunch hour. Fortunately for us, Mia has a more flexible work schedule than Sasha and me, so she usually gets to the restaurant early to order our food so we can maximize our time.

Sasha and I finally make our way to our favorite low-key lunch spot down the block. Mia sits sipping an iced tea. Our fries and salads are already at the table.

We sit down, and she eyes us excitedly. "Tell us everything."

And I do. Between bites of my lunch, I tell them about my incredible weekend with Elijah, *my new boyfriend*. From the craziness that followed our night out, me inviting him to the wedding, and the amazing time at his place.

Mia leans in. "Ok, so how did the key come into play?"

I shrug. "I woke up and it was just there. We didn't talk about it. He invited me to stay at his place until he leaves for his business trip. When I woke up, there was the key and note." I swoon a little just thinking about it again.

Sasha leans over and takes my hand. "You sound and look so happy. I love this look on you."

I squeeze her hand. "I am happy and a little scared. He's who I've always wanted. I'm all in with him."

They nod and say together, "We know."

* * *

The rest of the day passes without incident. I stay to myself, working at my desk, and counting down the hours until I can go home. Well, Elijah's home. The place I now have a key to.

Sasha and I walk out of work a little after five when I see Elijah's driver, Thomas at the curbside.

"Ms. Davis, Mr. Adler's meeting ran late, and he requested I pick you up and transport you to his home."

Sasha and I manage to hold in our squeals, and she shoos me to the car. I offer her a ride, which she declines, and I climb in. Thomas closes the door, and I spot the single red rose tied with a red silk ribbon. *Swoon.*

I pick it up gingerly and inhale it. I sit back in my seat, head on the headrest. Having a boyfriend is better than I remember.

We arrive at Elijah's. Thomas opens my door and tells me, "I'm returning to gather Mr. Adler. He should be here shortly."

I give him my thanks and let myself into the house with *my key*. I set my things aside and wander around.

I have an hour or so until he gets home, and I don't know what to do with myself. I start to head upstairs and explore a little more.

His place is massive. Three stories and a finished basement. Five bedrooms. Game room. Theater room. Home gym. Huge office.

Again, I wonder why he needs so much space. He said he wanted to marry later in life, but I don't believe it by the look and size of this place. He built this for a family, even if he doesn't know it yet.

I head to his master bath to take a soak in his huge tub before he gets home. I start the water and search his cabinets for bubble bath. Fortunately, I find a basket full of body wash, shampoo, lotion, and bath salts and bombs, in all the brands and scents I have at my apartment. "No, he didn't," I whisper.

I grab my favorite bath bomb and throw it in the bathtub, and I sprinkle in some bath salts because I can. I shake my head and I begin to strip. He really is thoughtful and clearly observant. He's so secretly sweet. I hold in a squeal as I think about his handsome face and beautiful heart.

Elijah

I arrive home and quickly discard my belongings. I take the stairs two at a time. I need to see my girl. I follow the sound of music to my master bathroom, and I inhale deeply as I catch sight of her. Her hair is piled on top of her head, her eyes are closed as she leans back, resting her head against a towel at the side of the tub. She's completely relaxed in the fragrant water as she sings along to the music.

I smile as I listen to her soft, tone-deaf wailing. She's a horrible singer, but she's so damn cute. As I continue to watch her, I have this sudden yearning for her, this sense of protectiveness and the desire to fulfill her every wish washes over me. I want her here. I need her here with me, every day. It's an odd feeling, and I stumble from the room before she catches me.

I scrub my hand down my face and remove my suit jacket and tie. I need a drink. I head down to the kitchen, grabbing her favorite champagne and two flutes before returning upstairs. She's in the shower now, rinsing herself. Her back to me, still singing her heart out. I place the bottle and glasses on my nightstand, remove my clothes and step in the shower with her. She must hear me at the last second because she turns quickly before immediately relaxing when she sees me.

"Babe," she whispers with a soft smile.

I step into the spray of the water and pull her to me.

"Love," I say as I kiss her shoulder. My hands roam her body. "I could get used to coming home and finding you already wet for me."

She laughs softly, kissing my chest. She looks up at me with her big beautiful brown eyes, "I'd love to make all of your dreams come true."

We stare at each other for an extended time. I don't

know what it is I see in her eyes, but I want more of it.
Before I can say anything, she reaches around me for
my body wash. She squirts some onto a loofah and
begins to wash me with long slow strokes. I've been
hard since I saw her in the tub, but I ignore it as she
rinses me. I pull her to me, loving the feel of her breasts
sliding silkily against my chest.

I kiss her nose. "Did everything go well at the
doctor? Am I free to fuck you again?" I whisper in
her ear.

She shivers as I watch the goosebumps spread
across her shoulder. I bite it softly until she moans.

She nods. "Everything is fine," she whispers. She
places both of her little hands on my chest, one palm
directly over my beating heart. She meets my eyes.
"Back to making all of your dreams come true. I'm
always wet for you, hot for you, greedy for you. And
that includes my mouth." She stretches to lick my neck
before kissing down my body and dropping to her
knees.

We only emerged from the shower once we were
both sated, and the water had turned our skin pruney.
Yes, I could get used to this.

It's early still, but we decide to lounge in bed and
order takeout. I leave soon for my business trip, and I
just want some uninterrupted time with my girl.

We order some Thai food, before I head down to
the kitchen to grab some water for my love. *Fuck, is
that what this is? Love.*

After dinner, I remind her of the rules, no clothes

in bed. She obliges with a playful roll of her eyes, and I watch as she slowly removes her thin tank and panties. She crawls across the bed on all fours. I watch the sexy sway of her tits and hips as she moves towards me.

I'm sitting up with my back against the headboard, clothes already discarded. She crawls right to me, taking my lips in a hard kiss, her mouth spicy from our dinner. Still, on all fours, she reaches over to my nightstand to grab a condom. I take the opportunity to run my hands over the shape of her body, my cock already so hard it's painful. I cup her pussy as she leans back to open the little gold wrapper. She's soaked, and I can't stop myself from swiping through her wet folds. She gasps before pushing my hands away, sliding the condom down my shaft, and straddling me. Before I can react, she sits on my dick, impaling herself, and I hear her soft whimper.

My hands fly to her hips, attempting to hold her in place to give her a second to adjust, but from the look in her eyes, I can tell it's the last thing she wants.

I reposition her legs to put her feet next to me on the bed, so she's in more of a squat position. I lean back against the headboard, arms behind my head.

"Take it, baby. Work for it," I growl.

I awake a few hours later, tangled in her arms and legs. I pull her closer to me, kissing her head. I feel a level of contentment I don't think I've ever felt before. She's only been in my home for a couple of days, but I know I don't want her to go. I cover her little hand with mine on my chest, directly above my heart, and I feel my heart rate increase. Yes, she's made her way there too.

A moment of panic washes over me, but...

No, I want her here with me...*always*.

CHAPTER EIGHTEEN

GEMMA

*I*f I were the type of person to excessively swoon and say the last few days have been magical, I would. Who am I kidding? I'm absolutely that person. The last few days with Elijah have been magical, maybe even perfect. I feel like screaming it from a grassy hilltop. Boyfriend Elijah is kicking Fantasy Fuck Buddy Elijah's butt. As if a switch has been flipped, Elijah is even more attentive, protective, and caring. Loving? He's still the sexiest man alive to me. He gets hotter with each blissful day.

I roll over and squeeze the pillow that smells like Elijah. I'll never tell anyone this, but I stole one of his worn shirts to capture his scent and yes, I stuffed a pillow into it so I could sleep with it. Don't judge me.

He left for his business trip yesterday. I put on a brave face but as soon as he left, I cried in the shower - an ugly slide down the shower wall cry. We'd been wrapped in this little cocoon, only leaving each other for work, but even after just a few days, my new routine was ingrained. I pull his pillow to my face and smell his shirt again. Ugh, he can't get back soon enough.

I finally pull myself together to head to the shower to get ready for work. Stepping out of my apartment, Thomas is waiting at the curb to drive me to work. Did I mention Elijah is spoiling me? Thomas has been at my disposal since Elijah left. I also received a beautiful bouquet of purple picasso calla lilies at work yesterday and a few more dozen bouquets of orchids and peonies when I arrived home.

I greet Thomas with a smile, and we head down the street to pick up Sasha. She's been enjoying helping me bask in Elijah's generosity. She climbs in with a smile but is quiet on our way to work. I don't mind it. I'm not a morning person. My mind is on the delicious memories of a hard and naked Elijah from our FaceTime call last night. I started my period right before he left and he's the world's biggest tease. The man is devious, and I'm not mad about it, at all.

Friday finally rolls around. I'm grateful for my shortened workday. I'm exhausted from this week, and I've had the worst cramps. I'm finally starting to feel better, but I want to get some rest today because I finally get to see Elijah again tomorrow, thank goodness.

Thomas makes a few stops for me before he takes me home. I give him the rest of the night off because

I'm probably not leaving my bed, let alone my apartment, for the rest of the night.

I walk into my apartment and I freeze. *What the hell?*

I hear soft music and voices, several voices. I hesitantly peek my head around the corner, and I hear, "surprise!"

I give a little scream and scan the room. My living room has been converted into a spa with low lighting and lit candles. I see white massage tables set up in my living room and three women leaning against the wall. Sasha and Mia are also here and dressed in white robes and slippers. Sasha holds out a glass of champagne to me.

"What is going on?" I ask them, happily accepting the champagne and taking a generous drink.

Mia steps forward. "Elijah set this up for you. He thought you needed a little pampering and we agreed."

Sasha leans in. "I hope you don't mind. We used our 'in case of emergency' keys to get in."

"No, of course not. Wonderful surprises like this are absolute emergencies and keys should be used."

I introduce myself to the estheticians. They review the services they are there to provide; massages, facials, and mani-pedis.

I scan the room, and I see more flowers and a card with my name on it. I grab it and head into my room for some privacy and to get changed into my robe.

Lovely,

Since I couldn't be there to take care of you, I sent in a few substitutes. Relax and enjoy tonight and know I'm in agony thinking about anyone else touching your body. I'm counting down the hours, minutes, and seconds until you're in my arms again.
Always,
Elijah

I hug his note to my chest. *This man is everything.*

I grab my phone to call him, and he answers after the first ring.

I jump in before he can speak. "Babe," I whisper.

I hear the smile in his voice. "Love."

I shake my head. "Why are you so sweet? Thank you. This was such a thoughtful surprise."

"No need to thank me. I still have the perma-grin that you gave me, people think it's creepy, but I wanted to give you something to put a smile on your face." I swoon just a little bit more and he continues, "Now go enjoy it. I'll see you tomorrow." He hangs up before I can respond. So bossy.

I strip down, get into my robe and bound out into the living room. This is just what the doctor ordered.

We're on our backs, having just finished our massages, about to get our facials when Mia says, "Elijah is a keeper."

Sasha giggles. "Yes, lock him down, girl."

I turn to them. "Believe me, I know and I'm trying."

They look around as Mia adds, "I'm pretty sure you've succeeded but if it gets any better than this, I'm going to fight you for him or officially become a sugar baby."

We all crack up.

I've officially been buffed and rubbed into submission. My body feels like a melted marshmallow when I finally climb into bed, my thoughts on my man. I clench my thighs together in anticipation. It's only been a few days, but I've missed him so much. It's not just the sex, either. I miss the intimacy we're building.

No matter how tired he is or what he has going on, Elijah makes it a point to talk to me about my day every night. We speak and text several times a day, yet he listens to every mundane thing that I share, and he lets me ramble before going to bed. That consistent us time has been a major key in the growth of our relationship, and I look forward to it every night.

I smile to myself; Elijah returns tomorrow, and I think it's time I take care of him.

I let myself into Elijah's home sometime in the late morning. His flight gets in this afternoon, and I want to be here waiting for him. He talked about coming straight to my place, but I know how much he loves having me here. Instead, I told him I had plans and to call me when he made it home. He sounded disappointed, but I'm sure he'll find a way for me to make it up to him.

I take my time setting up candles in the bedroom and the dining room. I set the table with care, but hopefully, we won't even make it to dinner. I tried cooking one of his favorite meals, roast chicken and potatoes.

Elijah surprises me a few hours later. I'm checking the warming food, bent over in something short, black, and lacy, when I hear his sharp intake of breath, and his deep voice say, "Baby."

I turn. The hunger and warmth in his eyes almost melt me, and I swear my little heart skips a beat. I run to him, jumping into his open arms, and we devour each other's mouths. I hate when he leaves, but I love our reunions.

"I love that you're here. I missed you."

Those words are my undoing, and I take his face in my hands. "I missed you too. I'm so happy you're home."

He sucks my lips, and I wind up on my back on the kitchen island. I gasp as my skin encounters the cool surface and he takes full advantage, kissing me deeply. I moan and arch into him. He stands, his hands roaming my lace-covered hips and breasts.

"I don't think I can make it upstairs. I need to get in this pussy asap. It's been too long." He bends, fucking my mouth with his tongue, and he peels my flimsy lingerie from my body. The feel of his clothed body pressed into my bare flesh makes me whimper, and he groans at the sound. He kisses down my body, biting my nipple along the way, making me arch toward him in need. His tongue sweeps through my wetness before he gives me a deep suck. I practically sob as I buck my hips, seeking more.

He rises, pulling me up with him and one hand goes to pull my arms behind my back, the other strokes my pussy, roughly pushing two fingers inside. I throw my head back, moaning long and loud. He groans as I clench around his fingers, greedy for him, for more. I've missed this. I've missed him. He holds my wrists against my lower back as I spot the gold wrapper on the counter, too caught up to wonder where it came from. He removes his fingers, and I sigh, knowing he will fill me soon. He quickly undoes his pants, tearing the wrapper with his teeth before sheathing himself, and plunging into me in one stroke.

We both stop and stare at each other at that, lost in a moment of realization, at the rightness of this, of us. He kisses me softly, reverently, once before he starts to move. Short, hard thrusts bring our bodies together over and over again. My hands are still restrained behind my back, and I want nothing more than to run my hands through his hair, pull him even closer. I gasp and moan, between each thrust, each bite of his teeth to my neck, breasts. In this position, I can do nothing but take it, at his mercy as he pounds me. The sound of our bodies coming together and my cries echo throughout the room.

He licks my neck, growling, "Fuuuuck, baby, you feel so good. You...this pussy...welcoming me home... I'm home."

"Yes...home...welcome home," I gasp, feeling the tension building in my body.

Pulling him even closer with my legs, I feel my orgasm begin to unfurl through my body. Closing my eyes tightly, I throw my head back as my body goes taut as I come. Waves of pleasure pour through my body and gibberish leaves my mouth as I try to tell Elijah how he makes me feel.

He finally lets go of my wrists as both his hands come to my hips, fingers digging into my soft flesh, as the pace of his thrusts increases. I raise my hands to touch his face, pull his hair, and I feel him swell and pulse inside of me. He grunts my name once before his lips find mine as he lies me back on the island, his big body covering mine, as he continues to slowly slide in and out of me.

We both work to slow our breathing, foreheads pressed together. I sigh as he kisses along my jaw and neck, laughing when he bites my shoulder.

"Home," he whispers before burying his face in my neck.

I rub his back, laughing at how wham bam that was and that he's still fully dressed. And I loved every minute of it.

Home.

* * *

The next couple of weeks pass in a blissful blur. We spend time at either of our homes, never spending a night apart. Elijah continues to cherish me, from lavishing my body to surprising me with gifts of fresh flowers, jewelry, and handwritten notes. Elijah has long erased any insecurities that this is just some one-sided childhood crush. He feels it, whatever it is, too.

We wake up bright and early Thursday morning. We're getting on the road soon to head to my hometown for my brother's wedding. I'm nervous to reintroduce him to my parents, but I'm excited to see his reunion with my brother.

I try to steal kisses and caresses as we pass each other, packing our last few things, but Elijah never lets it stop there. After my second walk by with a hand sliding down his exposed abs and a slap to his butt, I'm spun around, causing me to drop whatever nonsense in my hands. Elijah lifts me, wrapping my legs around his waist, and we crash into the wall.

Elijah heads out back to his garage for his car, I didn't even know he had one, and I wait in the foyer with our bags. He pulls up a few minutes later with a honk, and I step outside. Elijah is sitting pretty in a black-on-black matte Mercedes G-Wagon. He looks sexy as fuck behind the wheel. He rolls the window down with a huge smile on his face. "Hey, beautiful, you need a ride?" he says while wiggling his eyebrows.

I giggle, this man. "Oh, I would love to ride you."

"And ride me you shall." He smirks before getting out of the truck and opening the passenger door for me.

I offer him a sweet kiss, climb in, and he buckles my seatbelt. He loads the trunk with our bags and locks up the house before he climbs in.

He caresses my thigh. "Ready, lovely?"

I nod. "Yep, and I put the address into your GPS."

We have about a three-hour drive to my parents' place. Elijah offered to buy us plane tickets, but I wanted this time alone with him. Our first official road trip.

Elijah keeps his hand on my thigh, holding my hand as he drives. I turn my body toward his. I don't know how but he's exuding sex right now, and I don't want to keep my hands to myself. I begin to stroke his hand and arm. He looks over to me, winking, before raising my hand to his mouth, kissing, and biting each of my knuckles. I clench my thighs together, stifling a moan. This is going to be a long three hours.

I was wrong. The drive flew by. Elijah and I sang and danced the entire drive. Usually, I fall asleep on long car rides, but uninterrupted time with a carefree Elijah is too hard to pass up. About 20 minutes from my parents', I turn down the music.

"So, tonight is Grey and Brooke's last chance bachelor and bachelorette parties. I'm fairly sure they are having separate dinners before joining the parties for a night out downtown. Friday is the rehearsal dinner, and Saturday is the big day. I want to apologize now for how busy I'm going to be. I'm helping out with last minute things today and tomorrow, and obviously, I'll have my bridesmaid duties all weekend."

I say all of that in a rush, looking over to him, wincing. He just kisses my knuckles again. "I'll take you any way I can get you."

Elijah

We drive up the long driveway. I can feel the nervous energy radiating from Gemma. I squeeze her hand again to reassure her. Hopefully, she's just excited to see her family, and she's not regretting bringing me along.

I take in the huge front yard and beautiful trees, and I imagine a little Gemma running around playing in the yard, chasing butterflies. I bet she was the cutest with that curly hair blowing in the wind. I want our daughter to look just like her.

I blink rapidly, waiting for the panic to rise in my throat, but it never does because this is what I want. I've never *really* considered having children or what they would look like. But in this moment, I can see Gemma with a rounded belly and our dark-haired baby on her hip.

I kiss her hand again in an attempt to calm us both. We continue up this never-ending driveway, and I see her mother's large studio further down the path. Gemma's mother, Delta, is an artist now, a damn successful one. When we first met years ago, she was a lawyer. Gemma's dad, Christopher, is a doctor, but I can't recall his specialty. I think my brain is in overload mode. I've never done the whole meet the parent's thing. I kind of forgot that was all a part of spending this weekend with Gemma.

We round the last tree, and her childhood home comes into view. I take in the large windows and brick facade, again picturing Gemma growing up here. I smile softly; the swing on the front porch and the bright flowers planted give it a homey, inviting vibe. Her family is already waiting on the front porch, waving. She must have texted them we were close while I was daydreaming about babies. They direct us to pull up in front of the house instead of driving around back to the garage.

I comply, and I can see her mother bouncing and clapping, they are excited to see my Gemma, and I know the feeling. My windows are tinted, so they can't see us yet and I can't wait to see the look on Greyson's face when we get out.

I slide the gear into park. Before I can get out and open her door, Gemma has thrown the door open and is enveloped in a hug by her mother and father. I take in the sight, noting Gemma and Greyson are the perfect mix of their parents. Gemma's father, Christopher Davis, is tall, his dirty blond hair mostly gray now, while Delta Davis has rich, deep brown skin and kind brown eyes. Her age shows in her hair, her long 'locs gray at the temples. Her parents are older as they waited to have children until their forties, after they'd had a chance to establish their careers, but the gray hair is the only sign of their age. They are both fit and appear active, and they are currently squeezing the life out of my girl.

I round the truck, and I hear Greyson exclaim, "Eli?"

"Hey man, congratulations." We do the whole dude-bro thing, hugging and slapping each other on the back.

"It's been years. What are you doing here?" The shock is evident on his face.

Gemma joins us then. "I brought him. He's my date."

He looks between us, his eyes narrowing slightly. "Sure, we'll get into that later. Come here." He wraps his little sister in a hug, and I turn to their parents.

"Mr. and Mrs. Davis. Elijah Adler. So nice to see you both again. You probably don't recall, but we met years ago." I extend my hand to them both.

Gemma joins us then, and I put my arm around her shoulders, pulling her into my body.

"Mom, Dad, this is my boyfriend, Elijah." I kiss the top of her head and meet her father's eyes.

Her mother squeals and pulls Gemma to her for a hug. I hear her whisper loudly, "Oh, he's handsome, Gem."

She laughs as they turn and walk into the house with Mr. Davis following them.

Greyson claps me on the back, hard. "We have a lot to discuss."

I nod, grabbing Gemma's bags from the truck and follow him into the house.

. . .

Gemma

Having Elijah in my childhood bedroom is like checking another thing off the old bucket list. He followed me to bring my bags up. I smile softly as I watch him walk around, looking at my poster and the pictures on my corkboard.

Not much has changed since I moved out years ago to attend college. My room is bright and cheery, everything white and yellow. I sit on my canopy bed and continue to watch him as he learns about my teenage years. There are tons of pictures of the girls and me. Pictures with our group of friends being silly. Pictures of me in my cheerleading and volleyball uniforms. Pictures from dances and prom. He stares at those the longest.

He finally turns to me with a smile. "I knew it. You really are the cutest."

I stand and hug him. "And you're the sweetest, but we need to go downstairs before my dad joins us. The rule still stands. No boys allowed."

I lead him downstairs, and we head out to the back patio for an early lunch. Greyson's fiancée, Brooke, has arrived. I run to give her a hug. I love her and am excited to have her officially join the family. She is a good fit for Grey, who can be a little uptight. They really balance each other out.

As I'm hugging her, I hear my dad say to Elijah, "There you are. I'm sure our Gem has told you, but there are no boys allowed in her room. We've set up a guest room for you to stay in this weekend."

Brooke and I look at each other and laugh at my dad. The same thing happened to her the first time she came to visit over the holidays.

"Of course, sir. I really appreciate it, but I actually booked a room at the hotel where the wedding is taking place. I wanted to give you all this time together as a family, without me to worry about."

I turn to him at that. He hadn't mentioned that to me. It is very considerate, but I don't like it at all. I was looking forward to sneaking into his room later tonight. My dad has moved on to interrogating him about any and everything. I stick my tongue out at him, teasing him behind my dad's back and he just smiles, not a care in the world.

CHAPTER NINETEEN

ELIJAH

I meet Greyson at the restaurant for his bachelor party dinner, and he immediately pulls me aside. I knew this was coming. I knew that as soon as his shock wore off, he'd have questions.

"Spill. What's going on with you and my sister? How long have you been seeing her?"

I don't hesitate. "Remember when I texted you a while back telling you I ran into her? We've been seeing each other since then. Initially, I didn't know where this was going, but we're serious now. *I'm* serious now."

He continues to watch me with an unreadable expression on his face. Fuck, I hadn't even had this discussion with her yet, but I push on.

"I care for your sister and my intentions are to be with her for as long as she'll have me. She's incredibly special to me. I would never hurt her." I stop there because I have no idea where I'm going with this.

Hopefully, he understands what I'm trying to say, what I've never said about anyone before.

He stares at me for a minute before squeezing my shoulder. "Alright, man. She's my little sister, so just know if you hurt her, I will hurt you." I laugh. He doesn't. "Let's go get you a drink. It's my bachelor party, after all."

I look around the table. Twelve of Grey's closest friends are here, and he appears to be in high spirits, no nerves. He seems content. He's been texting Brooke all night, and all the guys are giving him shit, which he happily accepts. Dinner has turned into a roast, and my stomach hurts from all the laughter. I've missed my friend. I'm looking forward to reconnecting with him.

After dinner, we head to a hookah lounge where we'll be meeting the bachelorette party, and I'll finally get Gemma back in my arms. I take in the room as we walk in. It's dark and smoky with sexy music and couches and cushions galore. They've reserved several areas for our large party, and I see Gemma already seated, sucking on her hookah. I make my way to her and take the cushion beside her on the floor. I lean in and kiss her neck before whispering in her ear, "I've got something even better for you to suck on right here."

My baby giggles and turns to me with hooded eyes. She brings her mouth close to mine and gives me a shotgun, blowing her smoke into my open mouth, before she licks my lips. Oh, we're going to have some fun tonight.

· · ·

Gemma

I awake the next morning with a groan. For some reason, I partied like it was my bachelorette party last night. Big mistake. Huge. I barely remember how I got home, but I think I recall Elijah throwing me over his shoulder, Grey doing the same to Brooke, and walking us out of the bar.

My phone begins to vibrate on the nightstand. I'm finally able to crack an eye open, and I see I'm in my childhood bedroom. My bleary eyes find the nightstand. There's a water, sunglasses, and Advil. Looking down, I'm completely naked. Shaking my head, I laugh. *Elijah.*

I reach over and turn off my alarm. We have tons to do today for the wedding. I have no time for this hangover. Groaning again, I sit up and head into my bathroom. I jump in the shower, turn it up to hell, and try to wash away the ickiness from last night. From what I remember, I had a grand time. I'd forgotten how much I missed my brother and I loved seeing him and Elijah reconnect.

I quickly wash my hair before jumping out of the shower. Today we have the walk-through of the venue, the grand ballroom of a posh hotel downtown, and mani-pedis. I'll also be chauffeuring grandparents and great aunts and uncles from the airport. They all refused car services because they are apparently dangerous. Then there's the rehearsal and afterward, dinner.

I pin my hair up on top of my head, throw some

concealer on under my eyes, add a little lip gloss, before dressing in a flowy sundress and white tennies. I grab my sunglasses and head downstairs.

Brooke and our moms are sitting on the back patio having brunch. Somehow Brooke looks fresh as a daisy, as if last night never happened. I grab a bagel and slather it with all things yummy before I sit to go over the game plan. Brooke hands me an itinerary that has tasks listed on both the front and back. *Fuck my life.*

Elijah

I'm dressed and ready for the wedding. I didn't get a chance to see Gemma yesterday. With all she was doing to help her family prepare for the wedding, I didn't want to distract her. Then I skipped out on the rehearsal dinner so she would have time with her family and not have to worry about me. She wouldn't relent at first, but I promised to make it up to her.

I walk into the ceremony space, and I take a seat among the two hundred fifty guests. I check my watch and read through the wedding program before I hear the music start. I turn to spot Gemma on the arm of a groomsman. She's smiling softly, a vision in a pale pink dress. I've never seen her hair straightened before and it's pulled back into a sleek low ponytail.

She scans the crowd, smiling and waving at friends and family. She makes it to the front, continuing to scan the crowd until our eyes finally lock. Her face nearly splits in two with her huge smile, and she gives me a little wave. I'm sure my face mirrors hers. I'm so fucking happy to see her. I cock my head to the side, looking her up and down slowly, and I mouth, "You're beautiful." She scrunches her nose, confused, so I mouth it again, a little slower. A sweet smile spreads across her face before she puckers her lips, sending me a kiss.

My eyes remain on Gemma for the entirety of the wedding ceremony. I'm sure the wedding was lovely, but I missed it staring at my girl. I at least stand and clap with everyone else after they kiss. I watch Gemma leave with the rest of the bridal party. The rest of us are herded to the cocktail hour. I've barely had my first sip of my scotch before a woman approaches me. Not this shit again. I really must work on my "Not interested, I'm happily taken" face.

I manage to make it through the cocktail hour without incident, and it's time to head into the ballroom for dinner. Thankfully, I'll get to see Gemma again soon. Her friends and family are nice, but I'm just here to spend time with her. Glancing around, I must admit that Grey and Brooke did an amazing job transforming what I'm sure was a nice ballroom into a glamorous one. The tables are covered in an abundance of white flowers and grand candelabras. It looks like they were going for a romantic look, and I idly wonder what Gemma and my wedding would look like. She'd be a vision, obviously, but would she want a large wedding like this or something more intimate. I ponder this as I grab another drink for me and a champagne for her before I take my seat at our table. Gemma did inform me that we'd get to sit together since Grey and Brooke were doing a sweetheart table, whatever the fuck that is.

I sense her before she touches me. Her scent of sunshine and citrus sweetness wafts to me a few moments before I feel hands slide down my chest and she bends to hug me. Without turning, I say, "Ma'am, I already told you, I'm happily enchanted with the lovely Gemma Davis. Please remove your hands."

She giggles and kisses my cheek. "I knew leaving you alone would be trouble, but I'm here to save you, handsome." I pull her around to sit on my lap. I know we're at her brother's wedding and her parents are here, but I don't give a fuck. I kiss her neck before leaning back, "Let me get a good look at you, love. You're a little siren tonight. What the fuck is this dress? I don't think you are supposed to look this sexy at someone else's wedding." My hand roams up and down her covered leg. I'm trying to avoid her bare skin exposed with the slit, because if I don't, her father and brother will kill me for the scene I'd cause.

She bends to kiss my lips before resting her forehead against mine for a few moments. "Stay with me tonight," I say, and she nods. My room at this hotel is only a few floors away. I can't wait to drag her back to it later. Gemma kisses me one more time before she stands to go speak with her parents and finish her bridesmaid duties. She accepts her champagne thankfully and offers me another kiss before she leaves.

I people watch as I wait for Gemma's return, and the people that are most interesting are Grey and Brooke. It's as if they are the only two people in the room. They are seated at a small table, front and center but away from everyone else, and they can't take their eyes off each other, speaking with just their eyes. Their food has been set on their table, forgotten and untouched in front of them. I look away, giving them some privacy, as Grey pulls her closer and strokes her face.

Gemma finally returns to our table, and I'm introduced to the rest of the bridal party and family members seated at the tables around us. A few women give Gemma conspicuously raised eyebrows and thumbs up as they each give me a thorough perusal.

After dinner, I pull Gemma out onto the dance floor for a moment alone. As soon as I pull her close, Rihanna's *Diamonds* starts to play. Gemma squeals and looks up at me and says, "Aww, this is the first song we danced to the night we met on the rooftop."

I smile down at her. "I know. I asked the DJ to play it for us." We're only swaying at this point, too caught up in our moment to actually dance. I lean down and kiss her nose before singing along softly in her ear, the words conveying my feelings for this beautiful gem of a woman. *Maybe we'll dance to this at our wedding.*

Gemma

We see the bride and groom off, cheering them

through the hotel lobby and out into a vintage car. They are heading out for some alone time and pictures with the downtown cityscape as a backdrop before returning to the hotel.

Elijah leads me to the elevator, barely giving me time to wave goodbye to everyone. If I treated the bachelorette party like my own, he's treating tonight like it's our wedding night and we need to hurry to consummate it. I smile up at him. It has been a couple of days since we not only slept in the same bed but also *slept* together, so I understand his urgency.

The lights are low when we walk into the room. We're high above the city, and the floor to ceiling windows give us a beautiful, twinkling view of downtown. He's booked a large suite, because of course, he did. I walk further into the suite, taking in the view, the spacious seating area, kitchen, and dining room to my left. The walls are a bright white, the furniture in a soft neutral gray, but the yellow and black accents, art, and retro armchairs give the space character. Elijah closes and locks the door behind us before saying, "Let me get a better look at you in this dress, love."

I preen under his appreciative gaze. This dress is sexy for a bridesmaid's dress, but Brooke picked it out. It's a sleeveless pale pink dress that's beautifully draped for the perfect amount of cleavage, with delicate spaghetti straps, cinched waist, and leg exposing slit. I turn around, giving him a full three hundred and sixty degree view of my body. His heated gaze on me throughout the wedding was so distracting, but here, right now, I crave it.

"Fuck." He steps toward me before wrapping his hand around my ponytail twice before lifting my face to his, my neck exposed for him to take what he wants.

"I have a couple of fantasies that need to be fulfilled, love."

My eyes close from the heat of his gaze and I nod. He should know by now that I will do anything; he doesn't have to ask.

He pulls me to the bedroom, the only light in the room coming from the windows before he turns on the bedside lamp, one of two long pendant lights hanging from the ceiling. He comes back to me and runs his fingers through my ponytail before he starts removing all the pins and elastics, helping to hold the style together. My hair is styled in a sleek low ponytail with a deep side part, and I immediately feel relief at the removal of the pressure, and I sigh as I lean into him. He runs his fingers through my hair and starts to massage my scalp. He kisses me deeply after a moment before he brings down the zipper at the back of the dress and he steps back and sits on the end of the bed.

"You're stunning in this dress, but I want to see you out of it." His body screams want and need to mine as he sits with his legs wide, his eyes never leaving me.

I comply, because who wouldn't, and push the straps off my shoulders. "Hey, handsome, have I ever told you I love you in a suit?" He's wearing a dark charcoal suit, white shirt, and pale pink tie. Utterly delicious.

He smiles softly. "Yeah? Well, I love you. I love you in this dress or in your comfy pajamas. It doesn't matter to me, either way, I think you're perfect. I love your laugh and how you wrap me up in that blinding smile. I love doing everything and nothing with you."

I freeze and look at him with wide eyes as my brain short circuits. *Did he just say...* I tear up, my lip trembling, as his words wash over me; my heart so full it may burst.

A self-satisfied smile crosses his face at my reaction, and he quirks a brow as he undoes his tie. "One of my fantasies tonight was to tell you I love you. To tell you, I'm so fucking in love with you. I think I have been since the first time I heard you laugh." He pauses and licks his lips before continuing, "but I want to get to the next fantasy. I need you to take your dress off first, lovely," he says softly. His deep voice sends tremors through my body, jolting me from my shocked haze.

I look down, trying to suppress the biggest face splitting grin and try to focus on the task of undressing. My hands shake as I push the dress down, exposing my strapless bra. I shimmy the dress over my hips, and it falls to the floor. I step out of it, only wearing my strappy silver stilettos, bra, and panties.

I hear Elijah's deep inhale as he takes in my state of undress. "Are those...?" *The panties you got me.*

I stand proudly in front of him in the thong he

bought me after our first date and the matching bra I picked up. "You said, surprise you. How'd I do?"

He's on his feet in the blink of an eye. His hands go to my hair as he yanks my face to his as he ravages my mouth. I bask in the ferocity of his kiss. My tongue swipes at his greedily before I bite his lip. I rip his suit jacket from his shoulders, not breaking our kiss as his hands roam my body before lifting me by the ass and wrapping my legs around his waist. He walks me to the window and presses my body against it. I squeal as my fevered body meets the cool glass. He grinds against me, and I take the opportunity to try to remove his shirt. I attempt to undo the buttons with shaky fingers as he licks my neck.

"For my second fantasy, I want to have another first with you, another first period. I want to make love to you tonight, with nothing between us. You're mine. I want you bare, raw. I want my cock drenched with your cum."

He looks at me expectantly as I try to catch my breath, still wrapped up in shock and my supreme arousal fog. He takes my hesitation as a sign to continue.

"I know you just saw your doctor about your birth control and got tested. I would never do anything to hurt you, so I went and got tested, too. I have my results. I'm clean," he says as he grinds into me again and all I can think is that I'm ruining his suit pants with how wet I am.

I pull his mouth to mine and kiss him with all the passion and love I have for him before I nod.

He walks me to the bed and places me in the center before he starts removing the rest of his clothes. I watch him with hungry eyes and my gaze sweeps over his sublime body. I've kissed, licked, and sucked every bit of this body, but each time I see him in all his glory, it's like the first time.

I've finally found my voice, and I exhale deeply as I maintain Elijah's gaze. "I love you, Elijah. I always have. I want this. I want you. I don't want anything between us again."

He gives me a growl as he lifts my leg to his shoulder and unbuckles my shoe, throwing it over his shoulder before kissing my ankle. He grabs my other leg to remove my shoe, this time biting the top of my foot.

"This will be a first for me too, babe," I whisper.

He inhales sharply, before kissing, biting, and sucking his way up my legs to my thighs. I whimper with need as I feel his nose nuzzle me through my soaked thong. I blush when I hear him inhale deeply before he brings his lips to my pussy for a kiss.

His eyes rise to mine as he begins to peel the black lace down my legs. He smiles darkly as he says, "You know I'm keeping these, right?"

"Rude, you can't take back a gift!"

He shuts me up, giving me a deep lick before he begins to *feast*. I moan and buck as he sucks and bites my clit mercilessly before he changes his tempo and gives me long deep licks. He brings me to the edge of orgasm before he changes the tempo again. I shamelessly grab his hair to hold him in place as I grind into his face. He slips one, two, three fingers into me and pumps me hard and fast. He bites my clit once more. I lose it and shatter around him with a long cry.

He gives me one more kiss before he continues kissing his way up my body. His tongue flicks into my belly button, and I gasp as his hands come up to squeeze my breasts. He pulls my bra down, exposing me to him. He takes a pebbled nipple in his mouth, licking and sucking hard. I moan as I begin to writhe under him again. His hand goes to my other breast, and he gives my nipple a pinch, sending heat shooting through my body, and I cry out on an exhale. His body's sinful weight on top of mine is heady. I try to grind into him to relieve the tension already building again in my body.

Lost in him, I'm pliant as he removes my bra and tosses it over his shoulder. We're face to face now, and I rub my nose along his and we both pant. The smell of our arousal and the weight of our lust nearly suffocates us.

"Say it again," he growls.

I know what he means immediately, and I whisper, "I love y-." As he slides into me in one thrust.

Holy. Fucking. Shit.

CHAPTER TWENTY

ELIJAH

"*Fuck, baby,*" I groan.

My heart beats rapidly for her words and her body. There's nothing between me and my love, and there never will be again. I'm right where I was always meant to be.

I thrust into the hilt, and I take a second to breathe to calm myself before pulling out completely, Gemma's pussy clenching, grasping, trying to keep me sucked in. I push back in slowly, inch by fucking torturous inch.

I expected the heat, but this, I'm fucking consumed by it. Immediately addicted. The hot, silky slide of my body into hers, her body claiming me, squeezing, and milking me for my cum.

Gemma whimpers as I continued to stretch her, fully sheathing myself in her. I hold myself deep inside her again before grinding into her, swiveling my hips.

Her legs cradle my waist as I bend to kiss her,

slowly, deeply, as I try to convey the depth of my feelings. Now that I've told her I love her, I want to ensure she feels it every day, and I'll show her with my body, time, and actions.

Gemma

Elijah halts his movements as we kiss fervently. For several beautiful minutes, hours, our bodies connected, our bodies one, we kiss, and kiss, and kiss, and with each swipe of my tongue, I hope he can taste all the feelings and thoughts I can't express with words. He pulls away, and I caress his face, our eyes locked, as time stands still. I see awe and adoration on his face, and I stretch to lick his jaw and bite his chin.

We finally start to move. We move together so slowly, our foreheads touching, breathing the same breath. We're not actively seeking pleasure; it's just a bonus. Right now, it's about savoring our union, the significance of this incomparable moment, and the feeling of our hearts as they beat together as we make love.

Elijah peppers my nose, my cheeks, and the corner of my mouth with kisses. I feel every throb of his hard cock inside me, and I moan as he grinds into me before pulling out and pushes in again and finds an unfaltering rhythm. He finds my clit with a soft graze of his finger, and I'm surprised by an orgasm that quakes my body. "Oh, god." I clench around him, I hear his deep groan, but he continues to long, slow stroke me through it until I come down, only to be caught up all over again.

He rolls us until I'm on top, straddling his waist with my knees, chest to chest. "Sit up. Let me see you," his deep voice rasps.

I comply as he thrusts up and then his hands are everywhere. He runs a hand over my face, through my hair, circles my neck, before they trail down my body. One hand goes to my ass, giving me a firm squeeze, before he does the same to my hip. My pussy clenches and milks him, letting him know how much I love him inside of me, all around me. I moan as his hands travel my body again like he can't believe I'm here. That we're here together like this. He rolls and squeezes my nipples before reaching up to touch my face. His thumb caresses my lower lip and cheek before he reaches down to stroke my pussy, causing me to moan again and shudder. He brings his fingers to my mouth, and I know what he wants. He slowly slides them between my lips, and I lick and suck them just the way he likes it.

"Legs up," he growls, and I bring my feet up near his shoulders. His hands go to my hips as he repeatedly lifts me and brings me down on his cock. It's so deep this way. I shudder again at just the thought of his cum inside of me. I want to feel that more than anything in this moment.

He circles my clit before he grinds me against his

body. His fingers travel back to my ass, and he touches me there. He teases me, spreading my wetness before he breaks my seal. He slowly slides the tip of his finger in, and I come apart. I don't recognize my voice as his name escapes my lips, repeatedly, in a crescendo before it ends on a scream.

This seems to break his control and he growls, "Yes, baby," before he shoves my legs down and rolls us until I'm on my back.

He lifts my legs to his shoulders, to hold me in the perfect position for deep, pounding thrusts. I throw my head back in pleasure. This man, *my man,* is so fucking hard for me.

He spreads my legs before he brings his chest to mine. "Look at me, baby. Watch me as I fill you with my cum."

He kisses me once more, and I watch the ecstasy spread over his beautiful features as I meet him thrust for thrust, desperate for him to fill me. He finds my clit with a pinch and a pull, and I come again, triggering him, and we soar together as we both cry out from the intensity. I feel his cock jerk, and his warm cum spreads through me, making it wetter and messier, as our sweat slick bodies slide against each other, and I love it.

Elijah licks my sweaty neck and chest before planting a wet kiss on my lips. "Damn, woman. You taste good."

I giggle as I stroke his back, scratching along the

way. I feel him tremble as goosebumps raise across his flesh.

He kisses me again, this time deeper, his tongue sweeping through my lips before he pulls back to meet my eyes, "I love you, Gemma Davis."

"I've always loved you, Elijah Adler." He smiles softly before kissing my forehead and the tip of my nose. He finally pulls out and brings me to him, kissing the top of my head, his hands skimming my body. After a while, he goes to stand. "Come here, love. Let's get clean, so we can get dirty again." He picks me up, and I wrap my arms around his neck while he carries me into the massive bathroom.

Everything is clean and white. Marble practically covers every available surface. There's a huge bathtub in the center of the room, but he heads for the impressive shower that looks like it could fit six people easily. He sets me on my feet as he turns on the water to warm and grabs towels.

His eyes scan my body. "Fuck, baby. Let me look at you," his voice dark with desire. He bends to look at the mess we made. He watches in fascination as his cum drips from my pussy and runs down my inner thighs. He takes his thumbs and rubs it into my skin before he leans in, right against my pussy. "This is the hottest thing I've ever seen," he says as he kisses me repeatedly, right there. He caresses me briefly before licking his lips and standing. He rubs his wet fingers across my lips before he kisses me deeply. His voice gruff, he pulls away and says, "I love how we taste."

The old me would have blushed. Hell, the old me wouldn't even be here in a moment like this. The new me, confident and loved by this man, brings his fingers back to my mouth, licking them and sucking deeply. I hum, "Me too, babe."

His brilliant eyes darken as he watches me before he takes my hand and pulls me into the shower, "I like getting you clean almost as much as I love making you dirty."

I step straight under the spray of the water, wetting my hair. I look around for his shampoo when I spot mine, along with my favorite body wash, soap, and conditioner. I look up to his face. "You have all of my stuff?"

He scoffs like I'm being ridiculous. "Of course, what else would you use?"

I shrug. "I don't know, yours or the hotels." I wrap my arms around his waist, and my chin goes to his chest. "How did you know I'd agree to stay with you tonight?"

"I didn't, but I was hopeful. I wanted you to have everything you would need."

I pepper his gorgeous chest with kisses. "You're the cutest, yes you are," I say like I'm talking to a kitten.

I feel the rumble of his laughter in his chest, "Cute? I just had you screaming my name while I impaled you with my huge dick. You're still full of my cum. You can't call me cute."

I giggle into his chest. "Ok, whatever you say, cutie."

I grab the shampoo and step back to wet my hair a little more. Elijah takes it from my hands, dropping it to the floor of the shower before he pulls me to him, his thumb caressing my cheek.

"There she is. There's my love."

My straightened hair is long gone, and my curls are back. I sigh deeply. My man makes me feel so confident, beautiful, and loved.

"Let me wash you."

I do and I bask in every minute of the love pouring from him.

I awake the next morning with the sun heating my face. My body is exhausted after last night, but my spirit is vibrating with happiness. Elijah's arms are wrapped around me, his front to my back. I turn slowly, so as not to wake him. He's usually up before me, working out or rushing off to meetings. So, I'm going to take advantage of this uninterrupted time with him. I'm face to face with him now as I scan his sleeping form. He looks so relaxed, his full lips twitching a little. I reach up and stroke his cheek softly, immediately jealous of his long dark lashes and full brows. He doesn't even need them! I try to stifle my laugh, but my body must shake because Elijah's eyes start to flutter as he wakes. He stretches as a deep rumble of a groan escapes him and hits me right in the puss. My body is instantly ready for his.

His arms tighten around me before his eyes even open. I can't help but snuggle a little closer.

His eyes finally open and my smile nearly beams off my face.

"Love," he says, his voice raspy.

"You," I whisper back.

And before I know it, I'm beneath him. He massages my pussy, finding me wet and ready. He takes my nipple in his mouth, licking and sucking, before he slowly sinks into me. We both pause as the sensation overwhelms us.

"You're so wet for me. Is that left over from last night or fresh this morning?" I smile. He wasn't wrong when he said he was going to fill me to the brim with cum last night. I love that there's nothing in between us now, but the cleanup and upkeep are a hassle.

"Both," I tell him.

He makes love to me then, slowly, sweetly, with soft kisses and murmured words about how I make him feel. About how much he loves me. It's perfect.

I hold Elijah's hand as he drives us back to Chicago. He was going to let me drive his sexy truck, but I had too much on my mind to concentrate. I pretend to read for a while, but I've given up. I'm just openly staring at him now. He smiles softly before pulling my hand to his mouth to kiss my knuckles.

I smile as I think back to our morning. We

showered again before I realized I had nothing to wear, besides my bridesmaid dress. I say this to Elijah, and he just scoffs at me before taking me to the closet. Inside hanging up are three different outfit options for me. I look to him and back to the closet. There's an open suitcase on the floor. I see a few pairs of shoes, bras, panties, a little make-up, and hair styling tools. This man, *my man,* takes such good care of me. Straight to my knees, I went to thank him for being so thoughtful.

Later, we had brunch with my parents, Brooke's parents, and the newlyweds. I'm so happy for my brother and Brooke; they look so in love and are excited to leave for their honeymoon tomorrow. I also especially loved seeing Grey and Elijah reunite. I watched as they hugged goodbye, and Grey promised that he and Brooke would visit us soon. Afterward, we went to my parents' house to pack up my belongings. My mom had given me the warmest hug and whispered in my ear that I'd found a keeper in Elijah and seeing me so happy brought her joy.

I lean back in my seat and smile at him as I think about the whirlwind we've been in since we reconnected at the start of summer. I laugh to myself as I think about Mission Promiscuous, aka Operation Summer Slut. Boy, did that ever work out for me.

I gaze at his handsome face until I drift off to sleep with dreams of dark-haired, blue-eyed children running around.

* * *

Idyllic is how I'd describe the weeks following our love confessions. Mr. Adler just keeps getting better and sweeter, darker, and dirtier. We've pretty much moved in with each other, refusing to spend a night apart. We agreed to alternate between our houses to be fair but secretly, I love staying at Elijah's. He has more space, that huge kitchen to cook all my favorite foods, and that big bed where we can get as wild and loud as we want. Plus, he's worked so hard to make his place feel like my home. He's given me half of his massive closet and continues to buy me clothes, shoes, or whatever else he wants to see me in to fill it. I have such an extensive lingerie collection now. He knows me so well. Everything he buys me are things I would buy for myself.

I smile into my mug as I thought about our video session last night. He's amazingly lascivious, whether in person or across the internet. Elijah and Ty had a business trip to finalize their new hires and to begin training for the other new positions they'd recently hired. Elijah's required travel will decrease significantly, once they get their new staff up and going, and I can't wait.

My door buzzer rings. I'm expecting the girls later for a binge sesh, thinking maybe they're early. I grant them access by pushing the door buzzer. I soon hear footsteps in the hall. Running over, I fling the door open. Time stands still for an instant, before my chin practically hits the floor in my shock.

"Hi, Gem," he says, with a sweet smile on his face.

I blink as my brain misfires. I finally pull myself together.

"Hey, Dustin."

CHAPTER TWENTY-ONE

GEMMA

*D*ustin.

Dustin is standing at my door.

Dustin is standing at my door, smiling at me like he's happy to see me.

Dustin, the same guy who hates Chicago, even though I live here.

Dustin, my friend, the guy I dated for two years, but who hasn't spoken to me since we ended things, is standing at my door.

Now that Elijah is in my life, I know what I was feeling with Dustin was comfort, not love. The word complacency rolls around in my head as well. Even though we were in a long-distance relationship and only saw each other on weekends, sex became routine, maybe once during our visits with the lights off. There was no foreplay or teasing, no passion. I would get a few kisses, and he was ready to go... for about 5 minutes. We finally ended things when we realized we weren't enough for each other. It hurt at the time, but I know now that it was for the best. Dustin was a good friend. That's the only aspect of our relationship that I miss.

These thoughts flash through my head as I stare at home, mouth agape. *What the actual fuck is he doing here?*

"What are you doing here, Dustin?" I say aloud.

He smiles softly. "I'm in the city for the weekend. I just wanted to come by to see you and say hi."

I continue to watch him; I am confusion; confusion is me.

He sighs. "I've been thinking about you a lot lately. I want to apologize for the way I treated you. I was a jerk back then. You were one of my best friends. You didn't deserve my crap. I'm sorry."

I finally relax. This is the Dustin I remember, the sweet Dustin I miss.

"Thank you, D. Of course, I accept your apology. But you really didn't have to come all this way. A call would have sufficed."

He shakes his head, "Nah. You're worth more than that. I know you don't want me to come in, since we're still standing in your hallway. Would you go on a walk with me? Maybe get some ice cream?"

I exhale a deep breath and consider him. Honestly, I miss Dustin. We may not have worked as a couple, but we started out as good friends.

"Sure, let me grab my purse."

I do and we set out to walk the few blocks to an ice

cream shop. I'm in the mood for a double hot fudge sundae, and no one is going to stop me. I laugh to myself. Operation Look Good Naked is still a thing, but I think I deserve this little treat.

Dustin is quiet throughout our trek to the ice cream shop, but he always could be a little slow to warm up. I'm used to it and enjoy my sundae and fill him in on Mia and Sasha and the shows we're currently watching as we walk back to my apartment.

Once we return to my block, I hear him exhale before he looks at me. He puts his arm around my shoulder and pulls me close to him. "I've missed you, little Gem."

I lean into him a little, feeling nostalgic. "Yeah, our relationship didn't work out, but I'm glad we can work on being friends again," I smile up at him.

His brows furrow for a second, right as we stop in front of my apartment building. He finishes his ice cream cone, and he turns me to him, his hands on my shoulders.

"Gem, I don't think you understand what I'm trying to say."

I nod, prompting him to go on because he's right, I don't.

He meets my gaze, "I'm here in Chicago because I've been interviewing for jobs. I'm moving here soon."

I freeze for a second while his words sink in. He hates Chicago. He called it dirty. He said the people were rude. He complained that everything was too expensive. So many reasons why he rarely traveled here to see me. I almost always had to travel to see him when we were together.

I stifle those thoughts, though. "That's awesome, congratulations. I'm sure you'll get whichever job you're most interested in. What changed your mind about Chicago?" I ask, as I take another bite of my sundae.

"You. You're in Chicago. I miss you, little Gem. I want to move here and try again with you. I know I fucked up, but I can do better. I *will* do better."

He rubs his hands up and down my arms and my brain malfunctions again.

What the fuck?

He must take my silence as a positive sign because he starts talking again, but I can't quite follow what he's saying.

He misses me? Does he want to give our relationship another try?

We haven't spoken in months, and I don't know where this is coming from. I'm convinced men have some kind of dog-whistle alert system that notifies them when their ex is doing well and moving on, but this is extreme. He's moving to be near me.

I snap out of my fog as I hear him say, "I love you, Gem," right before he takes my face in his hands and kisses me.

I'm so stunned, and I don't want to drop my sundae; I stand frozen for a few moments, with his lips pressed to mine.

Before I can react, Dustin is yanked away from me

and my sundae splatters at my feet. I immediately jump back, and I look up to meet Elijah's furious face.

Shit.

He glares at me. "Fuck! Is this what you do when I'm away?" he spits out.

What? My heart begins to race as I see the look on Elijah's face. Oh no. He can't think I *wanted* to kiss him, right?

I shake my head, but Dustin jumps in, "What the fuck, man? Don't talk to her like that."

Elijah and I both whip our heads to him.

"Shut the fuck up," Elijah says, as I say, "Stay out of this, Dustin."

Elijah whips his head back to me, his face incredulous. "*Dustin?* You're out here kissing fucking *Dusty?*"

Dustin approaches us. "It's Dustin, asshole. Who the fuck are you?"

Oh no, does he have a death wish? I look to Elijah, his chest heaving as he tries to draw air into his lungs, glares daggers at him. If looks could kill, RIP Dustin.

Elijah meets him before he can get to me and steps between us.

"I'm her boyfriend, motherfucker. She upgraded. Get the fuck out of here."

Dustin scoffs at that. "Fuck that and fuck you. I want to hear this from her." Dustin goes to step around Elijah to talk to me, but I'm still standing there in shock at Elijah's anger. I've never seen him like this.

Elijah blocks his path to me and pushes him back. "No, don't talk to her. You talk to me, *Dusty*."

The venom dripping from his voice has a shiver running down my spine. I know he won't hurt me, but Dustin seems oblivious to the danger he's in.

"Fine, asshole. Gem is my ex. We were on a break, but I'm moving here so we can work on our relationship. You've just been a fucking placeholder."

Elijah turns around to me, shock and hurt displayed clearly across his face. I never want to see him look like that and I just cover my face with my hands so I can calm down and carefully explain. My heart is in my throat. I try to swallow a few times and take a deep breath.

I look up and reach out to take his hand. "Elijah, please..."

And Dustin takes that opportunity to lunge at us, trying to get in a sucker punch. Elijah evades the punch, but Dustin's momentum carries into me, knocking me to the ground.

And Elijah completely loses his shit.

Elijah

I can't recall what happened. I must have left my body or blacked out. Seeing Gemma, my love, my baby, thrown to the ground. Hearing her shriek in fear and the sound of her body hitting the ground sent me over the fucking edge.

I snap out of my haze when I feel blood splatter

across my face and Gemma's screams telling me to stop. I look down. There are arms of strangers trying to pull me off Dusty, who has a busted nose, split lip, and two swollen eyes. I can already see discoloration spreading across his face.

Heaving, I drop my hands immediately and shake out of the grasps of the guys trying to break up the fight. It's eerily quiet as everyone backs away from me. I can't bring myself to look at Gemma. I don't want to see the fear and disappointment in her eyes. I also can't watch her go to Dusty and comfort him. That will hurt almost as much as seeing her kiss him.

I turn and grab my suitcase and walk down the street. Never turning back.

Gemma

I drag myself out of bed after another night of restless sleep. I haven't spoken to Elijah in days, and it's slowly breaking me. After the shock and horror of the altercation between Elijah and Dustin finally diminished, I got angry.

Yes, we'd been in a love bubble the last couple of weeks. Yes, we'd fallen in love in just a short while, but I was disappointed in him and how quickly he jumped to the conclusion that I was cheating on him. I was happy to give him the silent treatment while I calmed down.

But after days of silence and looking at this from his point of view, I know I would be livid if I saw him kissing someone else. Especially his ex. So now, I'm giving him time to cool off. I remember his face as he walked off. He looked devastated, and I know I'll do anything to make sure he never feels that way again.

So, today's the day. I can't take the silence anymore, so I finally text him. I know he's up; he's been up for hours working out and is probably already at work.

Good morning.

I stare at my phone for a minute, silently begging him to respond. After another minute, I put my phone aside with a huff. I slowly get ready for work, eagerly checking my phone every 5 minutes. Nothing.

And so goes the next couple of days.

I text him good morning every day. I text him throughout the day to share cute or funny things that happen to me, or I read about. I call him before bed and leave messages telling him good night and that I love him.

He never responds.

I've gone mad.

Each day I awake more defeated than the last. I realized weeks ago that Elijah had become a big part of my life. My happiness. Having it ripped away so suddenly and without any kind of discussion is tearing me apart.

My girls have been incredible through this. They've spent these last few days letting me vent, cry, and brainstorm ways to get his attention.

We're at my place now. I'm elbow-deep in a tub of

cookies and cream ice cream. I'm not one of those people who stops eating when they are sad. Comfort food is a real thing. I'm already salivating at the mac and cheese I have baking in the oven.

I groan and fall back onto the couch, dripping ice cream onto my shirt. "You guys should have seen his face. He was so hurt and angry. I can't believe *fucking Dusty* just showed up here."

Mia and Sasha both nod before Mia hands me another drink. Tequila and ice cream don't necessarily go together, but I'm spiraling here. Besides, they are used to my rants and only provide support and more food or drinks when I pause for a breath.

"*Dusty* refused to visit me here, made me spend my money to visit him the majority of the time, dumps me, then he thinks he can just show up here and ruin my life? He *kissed* me, and my dumbass let him." I throw my arm over my face, covering my eyes.

"You didn't let him kiss you. Don't start blaming yourself for this. This was just poor timing. A misunderstanding. You guys will work this out," Sasha supplies.

I look up at her. "Yeah, you think so?"

They both say firmly, "YES," before Sasha hands me a shot of vodka. I take it and belch. Ugh, that was disgusting. I think I'm done drinking my sorrows away.

I fall back onto the couch again. "Why hasn't he responded to any of my calls or texts? He's reading them, so he knows I'm upset."

"Maybe he still needs time to cool off. You said he

lost his shit. Maybe he's trying to find it right now." I look to Sasha; she has a point. Elijah was a bit unhinged.

"Maybe he's working or traveling, and he wants to wait to talk to you in person," Mia throws in, distracted with her phone. She's been on that thing since she got here, but I know she's just busy with her own life.

"All of those things are probably true, but I just don't like us not speaking at all. He could say all of that in a text. Like, hey, I need a few days, or I'm traveling, and we'll speak once I return. I'd take anything. A carrier pigeon. Smoke signal. I'm desperate over here." They both laugh as we throw around all the ridiculous ways he could've contacted me.

Later, when I'm alone in bed, I replay that day over in my head, thinking about what I could have done differently. Wishing I had turned Dustin away when he showed up unexpectedly at my door. Elijah showed up at my place a day early. He'd obviously cut his trip short and came straight to my apartment to surprise me. But I surprised him by cheating on him, or so he thinks. I roll over on my side and cry myself to sleep, again.

* * *

Thursday after work finds me with Sasha and Mia at our favorite neighborhood patio bar. Summer's almost come to an end, so we're going to enjoy some cocktails under the sun while we can.

"Still haven't heard from Elijah?" Mia asks.

"No, and I'm starting to give up hope."

Sasha and Mia look at each other and share a look like they know something that I don't.

"Alright, spill, what's going on?"

"Well, what if we told you we knew where Elijah was going to be this weekend? Is that the kind of information you would be interested in?" Mia teases.

"Duh, of course, I want to know where he is. I can finally talk to him, face to face, where he can't ignore me."

Sasha reaches over and takes my hand. "He's in Vegas with his friends. They left yesterday."

I look between them, incredulous. "Hell no! I'm sitting over here heartbroken AF, and he's on a fucking vacation with his friends?! He's in Sin City with the *Fucksmen* of the Ho-pocalypse?!"

Mia hands me her phone, and she clicks Drew's Instastory. Drew is talking to the camera, showing off the view from wherever they are. In the next story, he's filming everyone around him in some nightclub. I see Elijah sitting with a group, sipping a drink as girls mingle around him, Ty, and Xander. I quickly close the app, unable to watch in case he shows interest in any of the girls and hand her the phone before pinching the bridge of my nose.

They watch me warily as I take out my phone and start looking up flights to Vegas.

"Where are they staying?"

"Planet Hollywood. Why?" Sasha questions, looking to Mia.

"Because we're going to Vegas." I gesture to our waiter for the check. "We need to go and get packed."

Both of their mouths drop as I hand my card to the waiter. "There's a 7 am non-stop flight to Vegas tomorrow, and we'll be on it. My treat."

They both immediately protest before I counter. "Either I pay for your flights or the room. This is my way of saying thank you for putting up with me and dropping everything to go with me." I smile at them, hopeful.

"Of course, we're going. It's not even a question."

I sign our receipt with a flourish, and we start walking home. "Who did you get to spill his location?"

"Drew. Apparently, Eli and Ty planned to take a trip with the guys when they closed some big deal. The deal closed, so they are off to celebrate all weekend," Mia tells us.

I feel like such an asshole. Elijah has been working so hard to land this deal. I smile as I remember how proud he was of telling me about their plans, and I wasn't even there to congratulate him. I'm hearing about it from my friend and not him. I drag my hand down my face as we reach Mia's apartment.

"We're video chatting in fifteen minutes so you guys can help me pack," I tell them before we offer Mia a quick hug and Sasha and I continue down the street towards our buildings. We stop outside of my building and Sasha squeezes my hand.

"Are you sure you want to do this?"

"Absolutely. Either we talk and move past this, or we don't, but at least I'll know, and I can stop worrying myself about it."

I watch her as she walks the two blocks to her building, then I head inside and go straight to my bedroom to grab my laptop. First, I need to deal with work and getting the time off, then I go ahead and book our hotel room for the weekend. Next, I get the video chat set up so we can talk while we pack.

I'm already in my closet with my suitcase open when they both join the video chat.

Mia jumps in immediately. "We're going to need bikinis, daytime looks, and sexy party dresses. They're doing pool parties every day and dinner and clubbing every night."

Ah, Vegas pool parties. They are basically just outdoor clubs. Instead of wearing tight dresses, you wear skimpy bikinis while you dance and grind. Plus, there's a large body of water in case you get too hot from dancing under the Vegas sun. Pool parties have become my favorite thing about Vegas.

I watch them both move around their closets, grabbing dresses and shoes. I know they are like me and wish we had more time to shop for this trip. I usually like to buy brand-new everything for a vacation, but I tell myself that this is more of a rescue mission than a vacation.

Mia prompts me to pack a couple of bikinis and dresses she got me recently that I refused to wear because they were too revealing to wear around people I actually know here in Chicago.

I start to protest, but she cuts me off immediately.

"Slut up or shut up."

We all laugh. I guess I'm dressing for battle.

Vegas, here we come.

CHAPTER TWENTY-TWO

ELIJAH

I can barely hear the guys over the music. The pounding bass is doing nothing to silence my thoughts. The sound of Gemma's shriek as she fell constantly reverberates in my head. I take another sip of my drink. I haven't spoken to Gemma in over a week. She calls and texts, but I just don't know what to say. I'm angry. Angry at her. Pissed as fuck at Dusty. Angry with myself for losing my cool. I don't want to take my anger out on her, so I've been avoiding her. Until I can get the image of her kissing *fucking Dusty,* out of my head, I'm keeping my distance.

I try to snap out of the negative vibe and take in the scene around me. Vegas, one of my favorite party destinations. If this can't cheer me up, I don't know what will. We have a huge cabana at this pool party. The sun is beaming down, the bottles are popped, and there are half-naked women everywhere. We caught the eyes of several on our walk up here, and of course, these assholes have gone fishing and reeled them in, offering them drinks and laps to sit on.

I watch Xander pour glasses of champagne for two blonds, while Drew is dancing with a beautiful redhead. We're here to celebrate the massive deal Ty and I closed. As I look around for him, he's standing off by himself, gazing over the railing down to the main pool. I grab him a drink and head over to him.

"Cheers, brother. We did it. We should be celebrating." I hand him his drink.

He accepts it before saying, "Is this how you'd really want to celebrate? We discussed this trip before you went and fell in love. I'd bet money that you want to be anywhere but here right now. So why are you?"

I don't say anything and take another drink.

He continues, "If you were really 'celebrating,' you'd want to do it with her. Have you spoken to her?"

I shake my head no.

"Why the hell not? You can't honestly believe she was cheating on you? Even if she were, be an adult and talk to her about it. I've never seen you run from anything."

"It's not that simple." I look down at my still marred knuckles.

"It is that simple. You love her. You were happy with her. You were sickeningly happy before this happened."

He turns to me and continues. "If this whole incident hadn't happened, would you be with her right now?"

"Yes." My response is immediate.

"Then there you go. Fix it. I'm tired of seeing your ugly mug and your new perma scowl."

I laugh softly, considering what he's saying.

"It may not be easy, but she's never given you a reason not to trust her. Hear her out."

I consider this for a minute. He's right; she hasn't, except for her Mission Promiscuous, Summer Slut, plan. But fuck. She's young. Maybe this relationship is too much, too fast, for both of us right now. Maybe we could go back to just having fun.

I shake my head. No, I don't think I could do that either. What I feel for her far exceeds hooking up. I can't go back to that. I rub my hand over my face, trying to unsee her hitting the ground. I don't know how she'll stand the sight of me. I left her, maybe hurt and scared, sitting on the ground. That is my biggest regret. Not losing my shit on Dusty but not being there for her, angry or not. Maybe I don't deserve her if I could do that. Maybe this is all for the best.

Fuck, I'm so confused and angry. Angry that she kissed someone else, not just someone, but an ex, and I'm angry at myself for how I reacted across the board. Guilt is weighing heavily on my shoulders.

I turn to face Ty, but he's looking intently at someone. From the look on his face, he likes what he sees, so I follow his gaze.

Directly across from us, down a level next to the pool, are Mia, Sasha, and my Gemma

Fuck me.

She's a walking fucking thirst trap, showing off all of my favorite things in the skimpiest of bikinis. My body instantly reacts to the sight of her. It's been too long since I last touched her, since our last kiss and I can already feel my resolve weakening.

I rub my hand over my face again. I can already tell she is up to no good.

Gemma

Our flight to Vegas was uneventful. Sasha and Mia slept the entire way, but I remained awake, thinking about my reunion with Elijah and all the things I wanted to say. I fantasized about him taking me in his arms when he sees me, but I know that is wishful thinking. Instead, I have to make him see that this all was just a huge misunderstanding. I want us to move on from this, but only after I let him know he hurt me as well. The flight gave me the perfect opportunity to work through my emotions, as they've been all over the place since all of this happened.

But now we're here. We checked into our hotel and got a room on the same floor as the guys. Drew has been the best and has delivered all the details of their weekend. I have their itinerary memorized in case we need to 'bump' into them wherever they go.

Through Mia's contacts, we were able to secure a daybed reservation at the same party the guys will be at. We rushed to get ready since Drew told us they were already at the pool.

Following Mia's suggestion to slut up or shut up, I'm wearing a bright white bikini with thin black straps. What makes it interesting are the bottoms. The bottoms are strategically cut to only cover the hot spots, and the rest is just made up of three tiny strings of materials, exposing a lot of skin. I kept it playful with a half-up, half-down 'do with my pony on the top of my head. I feel a little like a genie, ready to grant wishes with the nod of my head. I'm rocking big, dark sunnies, so I can disguise my stares, just like I did when we were younger.

We're escorted to our daybed, in a prime location next to the pool, across from Elijah's cabana. I felt a lot of eyes on us as we walked over here. I think we all took Mia's advice to heart and slutted it up. We're here to fuck shit up.

We sit down, and I immediately but nonchalantly look up to the upper level. I can't see Elijah from here, but I have no problem catching sight of Xander and Drew already grinding with a few girls. It's barely noon, but it's Vegas.

We pull out the menus to get our own party started. We quickly agree on frozen grapes, a bottle of champagne, and a pitcher of their featured fruity cocktail. In the cab ride over, we game-planned on how to get Elijah to talk to me. If he thought he could ignore me, me of all people, he has another thing coming.

Mia appears and says, "We've made contact. He has you in his sights."

I feel a thrill race through me. I'm so ready to talk

and move past this. Without Mia telling me, I would feel Elijah's gaze on me. The hair on the back of my neck stands at attention, but I don't look up to meet his eyes. I want to draw him to me. I want to take us back to the first night we met. That night we were just having fun, and he watched me dance before he couldn't stop himself from joining me.

I shoo the guys away that are standing around us. I don't need him seeing some guys with his hands all over me again. I have others plans for him. I start to dance, dancing only for Elijah. I close my eyes and let my body speak for me.

When I can't take it anymore, I turn toward him, pulling off my sunglasses, and our eyes meet. Sadly, I can see the hurt and the anger in his eyes from here, and I know I need to do everything I can to fix it.

Drew appears next to us, breaking my stare down with Elijah. He greets us all with big hugs. He glances around before landing on me. "Are you ready?"

I nod and I follow him to their cabana. Here goes everything.

Elijah

I watch Gemma approach, my heart begins to race as she nears, but I gaze at her impassively through the lens of the mirrored shades I threw on. I'm not ready for this reunion, but it looks like I don't have a choice. She approaches me immediately.

"I know I'm probably the last person you want to

see, let alone speak to, but I couldn't let another day pass without seeing your face. I miss you. Can we talk?" she says as she takes my hands in hers.

I withdraw from her hold and nod at her. "I'm not here to talk. I'm here to celebrate with my friends."

She smiles softly, nodding. "Yes, I'm so proud of you. Congratulations." She stretches to kiss me, but I don't bend to meet her, so she grazes my chin.

"Thank you."

"Can I help you celebrate?"

"Nah, I'm good," I tell her before I walk away.

She snorts at my dismissal and nods. She calls out to me after a few moments, "Elijah."

I pause as I look up from my seat on the couch, quirking a brow.

"This isn't over. We're not done. Accept it now or later, but we're happening," she says before she leaves. I watch her go, drinking in the sway of her hips. She's looks fucking amazing, and I want to stop her, but I'm still too pissed.

I exhale a deep breath and look up to find my friends all staring at me like I've grown a second head.

"What?"

Drew shakes his head at me. "What's your problem? That girl just traveled across the country to see you. To fucking surprise you, and you brush her off? At the very least, you need to talk to her and tell her it's over."

I scoff but Xander cuts me off. "I'm with D for no other reason than she is hot as fuck and for some reason, she's into your ugly ass. I'm usually the 'don't bring sand to the beach guy,' but your beach is better. Get over your shit and talk to her."

I look to Ty. "Anything you want to add?"

He shrugs. "I already told you my thoughts, but you're going to do what you want to do. Just know I think you're making a mistake."

He holds his hand up to cut off my protest. "I'm done talking about this. It's time to celebrate. Let's take some shots."

Before we can grab drinks, several cocktail waitresses appear with a magnum bottle of Dom and sparklers.

Our waitress gazes at us. "Which one of you is Elijah?"

Everyone looks at me and she smiles. "This is for you from Gemma. She said congratulations on your deal, she's so proud, and she loves you."

I bite my lip to stop myself from smiling before telling the waitress, "Don't let her pay for that. Put it on our tab."

She nods before gesturing to the bottle. "Champagne?"

I duck my head. And just like that, Gemma has put a smile on my face.

Gemma

I didn't get a chance to speak to Elijah again at the pool party, although I felt his eyes on me the entire time. I'm here to have a good time. If he doesn't want to do that with me, he can watch me have fun with my friends, drinking, and dancing the day away.

After another bottle of champagne and a few shots deep, we're back to dancing on our daybed. I cackle as I fall into Sasha, and she and Mia laugh hysterically as they steady me. The song changes and we all scream and start yell singing, holding hands, and jumping around the bed.

As I step down to grab another drink, I glance up and see Elijah and Ty leaning against the railing, talking as they watch us. I sigh. I'm having a great time, but it feels hollow with Elijah so close. I can't wait until this impasse is over.

Tonight, I have another surprise for Elijah. With an assist from our partner in crime, Drew, we know when and where he will be. The guys are having a late dinner before heading to a club. No surprise here. We're absolutely going to crash their night.

The guys are dining in a private room at some fancy steakhouse, but Drew gave them my name and they immediately escort us back to them. I walk in hauling a huge array of gold and white balloons that say *Congratulations* and one that says *I Love You*. Elijah catches sight of me as I yell, "Surprise!"

Sweet Sasha also has an arrangement of balloons

for Ty. She couldn't resist when I mentioned getting them for Elijah. She didn't want him to be left out.

Elijah's eyes widen, but he schools his expression quickly. All the guys stand as we approach, hooting and hollering. I offer Elijah the balloons, I don't go in for the kiss this time, but I give him a hug that he stiffly accepts.

We join them at their table. Xander kindly moves down to offer me the seat next to Elijah. I turn to him and wink. "I'm just here for dessert. Don't try to talk to me or anything."

He actually laughs, which I take as a good sign.

He looks at Drew. "This is why you insisted on this big ass table? You guys are plotting against me."

Everyone laughs. "Yeah, we're Team Gemma this weekend."

Elijah frowns and shakes his head as the waiter returns to take our drink and dessert orders.

I gaze around the table at everyone talking and laughing, even Elijah looks like he's enjoying himself, and I'm so happy I decided to take this leap for him this weekend. Our groups of friends get along so well, and everything just feels right.

I turn and catch Elijah watching me, with an expression I can't read, and I smile sadly at him. I reach over and place my hand on his thigh and sigh when after a moment, he moves away from my touch.

Elijah

We're heading to the club, and it appears that the girls are again joining us. I shake my head as I watch Gemma walking ahead of us with her friends. Their arms are linked as they talk and laugh. I really can't believe she's here, looking sexy as hell in a white dress. White against her sun-kissed brown skin is my kryptonite.

After all the shit that happened, avoiding her was my best plan of action until I could wrap my head around what to do next. Having her here is confusing me. I watched her as she talked and ate her dessert, not caring to be discreet. She looked over at me a few times and I hate how sad she looks. When she touched my leg, I wanted to let everything go, but I just couldn't. Not yet.

Ty heads straight to the front of the line, and we're immediately led into the club. I step closer to Gemma to make sure she isn't jostled as we walk to our table, and she takes my hand. I don't pull away this time, and she pulls my hand to her lips to kiss it. She gives me her sad smile again, and my stomach turns at her expression. I miss her bright smile, that smile that lights up her beautiful face. I sigh and drop her hand as we reach our table. It is going to be a long night.

I take a look around the club. It's a pretty cool spot, with the DJ raised high above us, and aerial artists spinning and falling from the ceiling like we're at Cirque du Soleil. It's dark and moody, the decor blacks and deep purples.

I sit back and take a sip of my drink as I try and fail

to stop staring at Gemma dancing. She's winding her body in a way that reminds me that it's been too long since I was inside of her.

Xander picks that moment to bring three girls back to our table. I have to stop myself from rolling my eyes when the brunette sits next to me and practically smothers me with her tits. I try to ignore her until her hands move to my shoulder and thigh and I turn to her.

Gemma

We immediately notice the girls sitting at the guy's table. Of course, Xander couldn't help himself. I stare intently at Elijah as one of the girls practically sits on his lap with her hands roaming all over him.

Fuck this.

I'm in front of Elijah in seconds.

"May I talk to you?" asking but not really.

He looks up at me with a smirk. "Sure," but I barely wait for him to respond before I'm pulling him up by the elbow. I drag him to a dark corner before I snap.

"You could fuck up a wet dream; you know that? Do you really want to play this game with me? I came here to see you, to make things right between us, and you're talking to other girls? I did all of this to surprise you and have some time together since you're too much of a child to talk to me. I know you're upset, and I take responsibility for my actions, but you will not disrespect me." I hold up my hand when he goes to speak, cutting him off. "You are mine and I want to be yours. Talk to me or get over whatever crap that's holding you back."

Shaking my head, I turn to walk away. Shit, that was not the speech I practiced, but hopefully, I didn't just make this worse.

He catches me before I can leave. "I'm sorry. I do want to talk to you but not right now. I'm still working through my own shit. Not just about you but toward myself. Maybe I'm overreacting, but I have doubts now, where before, I didn't. It's going to take me some time to work through that."

Shit, this is so fucked up. I squeeze his hand that's holding mine. "I'm ready to talk when you are. Just know I was not seeing Dustin behind your back. He showed up that day to talk and then he kissed me without my consent. I hadn't spoken to him before that for months, and I haven't spoken to him since."

I walk away before we can hurt each other again. I knew he was angry, but I didn't know he had doubts, doubts about me, about us.

CHAPTER TWENTY-THREE

ELIJAH

*G*emma is driving me crazy, and I'm sure she knows it. I think about her sexy smile as I step in the shower. She avoided me the rest of the night after our confrontation, but she didn't seem upset. I saw her laughing and dancing with her friends. She even took a couple of shots as if nothing were wrong. I, on the other hand, couldn't stop staring at her, my mind going a million miles a minute.

She caught me staring multiple times, but I didn't care, nor did I look away. I wanted her to feel just as uncomfortable as she made me feel. I wanted her to know I'm always watching. She was a good girl, staying to herself, just dancing with her friends. She turned down guys who tried to dance with her or talk to her. I'm not sure how I would have reacted had they touched her. But each time, she'd shake her head no and point to me, always watching. I refused to feel like a creep because she is mine, even if I'm still pissed.

Last night when Gemma said Dusty kissed her without her consent, I was livid. I had regrets about losing my shit, but now I want a re-do so I can do some real damage. Violence is never the answer, usually, but I'll make a special exception for that asshole. I'm tempted to hunt him down and teach him a fucking lesson.

I step out of the shower and start getting ready for another pool party. I'm in a much better mood today. I don't want to attribute that to Gemma, but I'm ready to celebrate and let loose and party. I meet the guys in the hall, and we make our way down to the lobby. I chuckle, taking everyone in. We're all in various states of hungover, with Xander being the most obvious, but over the years, we've all learned to rally when we're on vacation. I listen to Xander and Drew recap the night before noticing Ty standing off to himself, appearing to be lost in thought.

We jump in the provided limo and head over to the hotel where the pool party will be held. It'll be a short ride, but I lean back and close my eyes. I'm going to see Gemma again today, and I think I'm finally ready to talk. Hearing her say she hadn't spoken to Dusty before or since the incident, started cracking the ice that had reformed around my heart. I want to believe her, and I just need to grow the fuck up and talk to her.

We're escorted to another cabana. This one is more impressive than the last with nice couches, fucking throw pillows, a huge flatscreen TV, and a gaming system. I immediately grab the food menu and order everything I don't usually let myself enjoy. I'm going to need it to suck up the copious amount of alcohol I'm about to inhale. I also order the usual bottles of vodka, tequila, and champagne, along with water and mixers. This, this feels like a vacation. There's some famous DJ here today and the place is a fucking zoo. I take off my shirt and walk out of the cabana to check out the insanity when I see Gemma approaching.

Fuck me, what is she wearing? I loved her in her barely there bikini yesterday, with the tiny strips of fabric exposing her delectable curves. She's not at all disappointing today. Again, she's wearing white, and I wonder if it's because she knows I love her in white, it's such a sexy contrast with her golden-brown skin. We maintain eye contact as she approaches and there it is. That zap of energy between us makes my cock twitch.

This is going to be fun.

Gemma

Elijah's gaze caressing my body heats me to my core. He holds my gaze as I step toward him, and I can see the appreciation in his eyes. Thank goodness I wore this swimsuit; I may have just broken him. I'm wearing another one of Mia's selections. This suit is white, the top so minuscule, one wrong bounce and I'm Janet Jackson at the Super Bowl. Everything is sheer besides the straps and the strategic appliques that cover my nipples, my ass, and my good girl. I knew he would like it.

After our little spat last night, I was a little wary of spending the day with Elijah, but the girls made me suck it up. Seeing his face now makes me happy I caved.

"Hi, handsome."

"Hi, lovely."

Sasha and Mia join the guys in the cabana. If they mind that we've crashed their party, they can blame Drew for inviting us.

I turn my attention back to Elijah. He's wearing black trunks that hang off his hips in that way that makes me want to lick his entire body. He obviously didn't eat everything that wasn't nailed down while we were apart. He looks leaner, more cut, and fuck me, I want to fuck him.

I look him up and down, obvious as fuck. "You've been working out? You're looking damn good in those trunks."

He looks away with a shy smile before he turns back to me. "You're still the biggest flirt I've ever met."

"If that's what you want to call it. I just call it like I see it. You, shirtless, is a treat, an absolute delight." I step a little closer and place a palm to his chest, looking up at him. "Goodness."

He starts to lean down to meet my imploring lips before he catches himself and backs away. "Let's get you a drink to cool you off." He steps away and I nearly growl; he's such a tease.

I stand there for a minute to gather my thoughts. I can feel the shift. I'm beginning to breakthrough. I just have to keep pushing and get him over whatever hump is holding him back.

I follow him inside where everyone is standing around the table making drinks. I slide my hand into his, and my heart skips when he doesn't pull away. I try to play it cool and look at everyone else. "What are we drinking?"

Our waitress appears at that moment and insists we all take the complimentary shots she has to "get the party started." I don't know what they are, but I take two. Feeling bold, I lean into Elijah pulling him from his conversation with Drew.

"I need your very talented fingers," I say, and he quirks a brow at that. I laugh as I pull him away for some privacy. "I mean, I need your hands," I tell him as I spray sunscreen across my chest and stomach and rub into my skin slowly. He watches me, his eyes darkening. "I'm not trying to threaten you with a good time, but I need you to help me with my sunscreen."

He finally tears his eyes away from my body and meets my gaze and I can see the hunger there. I squeeze my thighs together, and he absolutely notices because the heat in his eyes ratchets up a few dozen more notches.

I spray each leg from hip to ankle before holding my leg out to him, asking for help. He holds my gaze as he slowly lowers himself to one knee and starts rubbing the sunscreen into my skin. Our eyes are locked as he kneads my thigh. I don't try to stifle my moan as his hands slide lower and he massages my calf. I place my hands on his shoulders before I begin to stroke his hair. I've missed him so much. I hope he feels it too.

He finally turns and grabs the spray, spraying his hands, before he pulls me closer to him. He really is in the perfect spot for me to grind into his face. But before I can get lost in that thought, he reaches behind me and begins to rub the sunscreen into my ass. Each squeeze brings my pussy closer to his face. I have to close my eyes as memories of us in this exact position invade my mind. I sway a little as his hands trail down the back of my legs for a few glorious seconds before he slaps me on the ass, a full-on 'good game' slap to the ass. "There you go," and he stands and walks away.

Well, shit.

Elijah

After we returned to the group after that little rub down, Gemma's friends offered her a drink to cool down, and she really hasn't stopped drinking since. I watch her as our waitress brings over another bottle of champagne and she screams in delight. She's consumed champagne, shots of vodka, some fruity shit, and even though I know she hates it, tequila shots. I'm surprised she can still walk, let alone dance. She stumbles a little when she closes her eyes to take a deep drink of her champagne and I've had enough. I stride over and take the drink from her hand.

"You're done. Let's go." I might as well have been speaking French because she just laughs and throws her arms around me and starts dancing on me. I hold in my groan as she pulls me into her, practically humping my leg.

I lift her chin, forcing her to look at me. "Love, I need to get you out of here. You're wasted."

She beams at me as if I hung the moon just for her and nods. I stroke her cheek before I sit her down on one of the couches and put on her shoes before gathering her things. I turn to everyone and tell them, "I'm getting her out of here. If she keeps drinking, she'll be no good for tonight and she'll be mad she missed out." They all nod and I pull Gemma up before she can pass out of the couch. I tuck her into my side and weave us through the crowd and out to the limo. I buckle her in and cradle her to my side the entire drive. She snuggles into me, and I breathe in her scent, the one that always reminds me of sunshine and happiness. I kiss her crown of curls a few times and relish the sense of contentment I feel. Yes, I'm angry. Not at her but at myself.

I get her back to my hotel room. I practically have to carry her after she passed out on the short ride here. No one gives us a second glance as I stride through the lobby with a semi-conscious, half-naked woman in my arms. I guess people are used to seeing it. We make it to my room, and I immediately take her to the bedroom. I sit her down on the bed and grab her a bottle of water.

"Love, I need you to drink this and then get some sleep. I'll order you some food too." I'm trying to talk to her as she falls back on the bed and rolls around a little, trying to sit back up. She finally makes it up to the pillow, and she buries her face in it, inhaling deeply. "I missed your smell." I chuckle softly, watching her. Then she whispers softly, "I love you so much, Elijah, more than anything. I'm so sorry."

Fuck. She has nothing to be sorry for. I hate that she feels like she has to apologize for my crap. I know I fucked this up.

I watch her sleep for a bit. She sporadically reaches out and searches for me, sighing happily if she makes contact. I stare at her face as my mind blurs with thoughts and images. I love this woman so much, it's almost tangible. I can feel it, taste it, touch it. Deep in my heart I know she loves me too. This is just a minor setback, but that initial shock hurt all the same.

I watch as tension lines her face, and I wonder if she's dreaming. I rub my thumb back and forth across her forehead, coaxing her to relax. I feel terrible because I know I'm the reason for all her stress. "I'm sorry, baby," I whisper. "I wish you could open me up and see that all the good in me is made up of all the happiness I soak up from you. If you could see my heart, you'd know that it is full of the love I have for you. I'm sorry that my pride got in the way. You know I've got a big ego." I chuckle softly. "But I'm man enough to admit when I'm wrong. Sleep now, but know when you wake up, you're all mine, and I have plans for you. However long it takes, even if it's forever, I'll make it up to you. Please forgive me." She reaches out again, searching for me, and I give her what she wants. I pull her into my arms and kiss her head softly. I've missed my love.

Gemma

I wake sometime later at the feel of strong arms wrapped around me, holding me close. Sighing, I snuggle deeper into the heat of a hard body before my eyes shoot open, remembering where I am. I turn slowly to get a look at his face. He's sleeping behind me, his beautiful face relaxed and peaceful with just a hint of a smile. He looks as content as I feel being held by him again. I stroke his cheek softly, not wanting to wake him and lose this moment, but being unable to resist him.

I look down at myself. I'm still in my bikini, my hair is a mess, and I'm sure my makeup is smeared all over my face. I slowly slide out from under his arm, out of bed, and head straight to the bathroom to get a good look at myself. Yep, I was right. I'm an absolute mess. I jump in the shower and lather myself in all his products. I smile as I remember our last stay together in a hotel. Elijah told me he loved me, and we'd made love all night. He was so thoughtful, packing all the items he'd thought I needed. It was such a sweet, perfect moment, a memory I'll always cherish. I wash my hair quickly and braid it up into a bun before I jump back into the bed and cuddle Elijah's back. I pepper kisses across his broad shoulders and hug him tight. I've missed him. My hands roam his smooth olive skin. He's gotten some sun and it makes him even more enticing.

I squeeze just a little tighter and whisper. "Elijah, I love you. I've loved you since the moment I saw you, that very first day of our vacation. You have been and will always be the man I compare all others to, and they will always be lacking. Dusty is nothing to me. I feel horrible that you saw him kiss me, because I know I'd be wrecked if it was the other way around. I will spend the rest of my life showing you, proving to you, that you are my love, my everything. I always choose you. Take however long you need but please, choose us, choose to trust me."

I wait a beat, but he doesn't respond, so maybe he really is asleep. I sigh before kissing his back again and rolling out of bed. I throw on my coverup, grab my bag, and head to my room. It's time to get dressed for battle. This standoff ends tonight.

CHAPTER TWENTY-FOUR

GEMMA

*Y*ou know what the good thing is about getting drunk by 2 pm? You pass out for hours to sleep it off. Then you get to do it all over again later that night. The girls were still out when I texted them once I got to our room, so I had the time to think.

I'm still in shock that I woke up in Elijah's bed, in his arms, no less. I don't remember what happened after about shot number six, but it appears that Elijah can't help but step in and take care of me. That must be a good thing, right?

I'm pacing the length of our junior suite, shaking out my jittery hands, when I hear loud voices. I hear a thump against the door and raucous laughter. I check the peephole. I see Sasha and Mia holding each other up and laughing hysterically while they struggle to open the door. I hurriedly pull the door open, and they immediately crash to the floor in a flurry of limbs and hair.

"Fuck."

I look up to see Ty, but he's staring down at the heap that is my besties. "Don't worry, Ty. I've got them. Thanks for getting them here safely."

He doesn't take his eyes off them but says, "No, let me help you." He bends and picks up Sasha, who is rolling around laughing like a loon. He carries her further into the room before slowly lowering her to the couch. I turn my attention to the sweaty blond at my feet and laugh. She looks like she's more than content to sleep right here on the floor. Ty comes back, helps her stand, and walks her to the couch. He stares at them for a minute before walking back to me.

"How are things with E?"

I shrug. "Better, I think. We haven't had a chance to really talk, but that's changing tonight. I'm done with whatever this is."

He smirks and nods. "Time to put all of your cards on the table. You're going all in." I snicker at his gambling puns.

"Yes, tonight's the night. Make it or break it."

He sighs. "Well, you have my vote. He's right on the edge. I've spoken to him a few times. I think he's finally ready to move forward." He lets out a breath. "Dinner is at 9 pm. Then we're heading to the Big Whorl around 11." He looks at the drunk girls passed out on the couch, "I understand if you don't make it to dinner, but you can't miss the Big Whorl. It'll be the best opportunity to speak to him where he can't walk away so he won't be able to escape the big talk."

"Thanks, Ty."

He bends and kisses my cheek. "See you later. Get those girls some water and some carbs." He winks before he steps through the door.

I sigh. These guys are all so sweet. I wonder why Ty doesn't have a girlfriend. He and Drew, not so sure about Xander, seem like definite boyfriend material. Plus, they are all easy on the eyes.

* * *

Ty was right; we completely miss dinner. The girls passed out, and I couldn't help but join them. We finally pull it together enough to get dressed to meet them at the Big Whorl.

"Ok, here's the plan. I'm putting it all on the line with Elijah tonight. I'll need your help to distract the guys so we can talk, uninterrupted." They nod as we wait for the elevator.

"Entertain three gorgeous men. What a hardship. Being your friend is the worst." Mia laughs.

"I know, right? How dare you ask us to do such things," Sasha chimes and we all crack up.

"Ok, I get it. I need to chill, but I'm so nervous. This is make or break for us."

Sasha takes my hand as we walk through the lobby. "No, it's not. This is step one, or five, of your forever.

Don't put so much pressure on yourself. Have fun and just reconnect with him."

Mia nods. "We all know you're not walking away from him. Even though he's pretending to, he's not walking away from you. Like Sasha said, just have fun, no pressure."

I take a deep breath and nod. Have fun. I can totally do that.

Elijah

Waking up to find Gemma gone was like a hard knee to the gut. I finally got her back in my arms, and I wasted it. I held her while she slept, and I talked to her just because I missed being able to do so. Nuzzling into her body, inhaling her scent, I told her about the deal we closed and the plans I have for our future. I finally drifted off, after making a few calls, only to have a dream of her kissing me and telling me all the things I needed to hear, which made me realize I should have gotten over myself, like yesterday.

All through dinner, I anticipated her arrival, surveying the room hoping to catch a glimpse of her beautiful face, but no luck. I ordered another drink and again tried to follow the conversation around the table. The guys were talking about our after-dinner plans. I scrubbed my face. I didn't want to leave my boys hanging, but I really needed to see my girl.

Just as I'm about to excuse myself, Ty looks at me.

"Don't even think about it, fucker. I told the girls to meet us there, fucking relax."

I flip him off and happily dig back into my dinner, finally able to breathe easy. I'll see her again soon. I hurry the guys along. I need to get to my baby.

We amble over to the Big Whorl a little before our reservation. Apparently, it's one of the largest Ferris wheels in the world. What makes it cool is that you go up in an enclosed pod and you get these amazing views of the strip and, as a bonus, there's alcohol. Ty reserved a private pod just for us that will give me an uninterrupted time with Gemma. Based on how I've treated her, I'm going to need it.

We head over to the bar for a few more drinks and to wait for the girls.

"All of the girls were pretty wasted today. I hope they make it tonight," Drew throws out.

"Sasha and Mia passed out as soon as I got them back to their room. Gemma was up and appeared marginally sober compared to when she left the pool party," Ty adds and looks to me.

"We took a nap when I got her back to my room," I tell them.

All eyes fly to me. "Hold up. You had a half-naked, drunk Gemma in your bed. Did you guys make up? What the fuck happened?" Leave it to Xander to cut straight to the point.

"Nothing happened, asshole. I just took care of her until she sobered up enough to go back to her room." They nod, eyeing me suspiciously. "Stop looking at me like that," I say as I step away from the bar to make room for the group of people approaching us.

I turn away to check my phone, hoping for a message from Gemma, before I shoot off a text. I hope they make it. We only have about five minutes before our reservation. No messages. I think about calling her when someone bumps into me.

I turn to apologize when I meet the gaze of a woman, with clear interest in her eyes, smiling coyly at me. She pretends she needs to steady herself and puts her hand on my arm. Apologizing again, I try to step around her, but she stops me. "I'm so sorry. I'm such a klutz. I can't believe I bumped into you. Are you okay? Let's get you another drink."

I decline and tell her everything's fine and as I hear her ask for my name, the energy in the room shifts. I look up and see Gemma striding toward me. She's a fucking siren tonight in a beautiful red dress with an alarmingly high slit with what looks like fucking safety pins or some shit, holding it together at her smooth upper thigh. Her hair is up on top of her head, fully exposing her slender neck and beautiful face.

I see her gaze flick between me and the woman at my side, and she narrows her eyes. I remember a time when all I wanted was for her to boldly claim me. I don't know why but for some reason, in my mind, that was the ultimate sign of her love for me. But right now, all I can think is she shouldn't have to prove herself. I should make her feel so confident in what we have that she doesn't have to claim me because she knows I'm not going anywhere. Just how she makes me feel. I had a moment or two of weakness, but the moment has passed. I'm getting my love back.

Before I can say anything, Gemma steps in front of me, between me and this random woman, her back against my chest.

Oh, fuck.

Gemma

I spot Elijah as soon as I walk through the doors and of course, he has a beautiful woman draped all over him. *Look at him.* He's dressed a little more casually, but he's no less gorgeous in dark jeans, a white shirt, and a dark blazer. His shirt is unbuttoned at his throat, showing off one of my favorite places to kiss on his body.

I saw her purposely bump into him and now she can't keep her hands to herself. He looks up and freezes when he sees me. I see the appreciation in his gaze as his eyes travel up and down my body, but I'll deal with that later. I have to deal with this one over here first.

I step between them, my smile sugary sweet. "Hi, please take this as disrespectfully as it is intended. Fuck off. This one right here is mine. Go be desperate somewhere else. Have a nice night."

My saccharine smile is firmly in place. I give her a little wave as she stares at me for a moment, shocked as all hell. She looks between the two of us before she turns in a huff and walks back over to her friends. I hear a "yes, bitch" from Mia before I turn to him.

He's staring at me in shock. "What was that? *Who* was that?"

"I don't let her out often, but when I do," I shrug. He laughs and shakes his head as I fix him with a faux glare. "I can't leave you alone for a minute. Are you always going to be so much trouble?"

Before he can answer, Ty calls us over to board the pod. Fuck, the pod. The pod that's going to take us 500 feet in the air. I don't know how I forgot that I'm afraid of heights, but stepping into this thing has promptly reminded me. I go directly to the bar to avoid the 360-degree view. I can do this. This is my time to talk to Elijah. I am not plummeting to my death. I'm fine.

I order a double shot of Grey Goose and throw it back quickly, shuddering at the taste. Moments later, I feel the heat of Elijah on my back, and I want nothing more than to lean into him, but I have a few things I need to get off my chest first. I turn around, ready to go in, when we're interrupted. Everyone joins us at the bar, a round of shots is ordered, and Ty clears his throat, preparing for his toast. My eyes remain locked on Elijah. His face is unreadable, but there's a light in his eyes that I've missed. I also miss Ty's toast, too caught up in Elijah's gaze to concentrate on anything else around me.

As soon as everyone cheers and we take our shots, the desire to pull Elijah away is strong, but I hesitate, not ready for what could be. I don't want to let him go, but I can't make him stay if he's done. I shuffle over to stand next to Sasha and Mia, needing their comfort and a minute to gather myself. I don't even try to jump into their conversation. I glumly stand there and let Sasha put her arm around me as I think about what to do next. I don't have long to think about it before Elijah joins us. He doesn't say anything, but his hand trails up my body before I feel his warm palm on the back of my neck. He rubs his thumb back and forth a few times before tilting my head up to meet his gaze.

"I'm ready to talk."

I take a deep breath and nod. Mia and Sasha take that as their cue and walk away to join the others, while we just stare at each other for a full minute.

I take his hands in mine and plead, "Elijah, tell me what I need to do, and I'll do it. Please forgive me. I love you. I don't want Dusty, or anyone else. I just want *you*."

His lips crash into mine, kissing me so deeply. I can feel the yearning and adoration with each swipe of his tongue, each nip of his teeth. He pulls away and grips my face fiercely.

"Baby, I love you. I've been an ass; I know it and *I'm* sorry. You don't have to do anything, and you have nothing to be sorry for. You're perfect, from the top of your head to the bottom of your adorable little feet. It's me who needs to get my shit together and show you how much you mean to me, how much I love you. I'm so sorry, love. I was hurt and angry at the sight of you and Dusty, but I was more ashamed of myself, and I took it out on you. I'm sorry that I walked away from you, ignored you. You'll never again have to wonder about how I feel. You are perfect and so precious to me, and you deserve to be cherished. Please forgive me." He drops his forehead to mine, and I close my eyes and soak up this feeling as relief flows through me.

I wrap my arms around him and exhale the breath I didn't realize I was holding. "Babe, don't do that to me again. I forgive you, but I can't forget how you treated me. You have to talk to me when you're hurt or upset. I've been so heartbroken; I was devastated that you could walk away so easily. It wasn't something I expected from you. I was so gutted. I spiraled into tubs of ice cream and cake frosting."

I can see the anguish at my words on his face as his hands slide down and he grips my ass with a squeeze and brings me closer to his body. "I hate that I hurt you. I'll spend the rest of my life making it up to you. I will do everything in my power to never make you feel that way again...but that cake frosting is sitting real nice right here."

I slap his chest and laugh before he continues. "I know we have things to talk about. Trust me, I have so much I need to say, but this is our last night in Vegas. Let's have some fun knowing that we're ok. We're more than ok," he says as he kisses the corner of my mouth. His mouth trails along my jaw until he reaches that spot just below my ear. I shiver as he peppers light kisses along my neck and bare shoulder.

He whispers in my ear, causing goosebumps to rise

on my skin, "Have I told you how extraordinarily beautiful you look tonight? What is this dress?"

I smile to myself; the one-shoulder of this dress and the obscenely high slit are held together by silver hardware, leaving my fevered skin exposed between each piece. "Well, the white wasn't getting your attention, so I had to up my game and bring out my weapons of mass destruction."

"Love, you've had my attention all weekend. You know I love you in white, and this red is sinful." He kisses me again, sucking my tongue thoroughly and reigniting the fire in my belly.

I tilt my head, giving him better access to my mouth. I can't hold in my moan as he bites my bottom lip.

Elijah finally pulls away, kissing my nose before he looks over my shoulder. "Love, let's take a look at this view."

I groan. "Babe, I'm afraid of heights, which is being exacerbated by being in this tiny pod."

"Just one quick look, then we'll have a drink."

I sigh in acquiescence and turn toward the window and gasp.

From here, the bright lights of the Vegas strip twinkle vibrantly, but what catches my eye are pictures of me blown up on several large digital billboards. I cover my mouth as different slideshows play across the screens. Elijah directs me to the massive billboard located on the hotel, directly across from us. I recognize a few pictures I posted of myself on social media, but there are several candid shots that I don't. There's one of me with my head thrown back, laughing. Another one shows me with my arms above my head as I dance. After each picture, a word or phrase appears, and I read along with everyone.

Gemma, your beauty is evident, but it's your pure heart and joyful nature that I love most about you. I've missed waking up to your heart-stopping smile and infectious laugh. Love, you are my happiness.

The pictures then change to pictures of us. Pictures of us smiling at each other during that first brunch, hugged up while out with the crew, and sitting on his lap, his arms around me, at my brother's wedding.

Know that I'm sorry. I was wrong. This is me, on my knees, begging for you to fulfill my fantasy and forgive me. We're just getting started. I love you. Always yours, Elijah

The last picture is again of us, I'm looking at the camera with a huge smile splitting my face, and Elijah is hugging me from behind as he kisses me on the cheek. A huge heart appears around us before the slideshow starts again.

Everyone is standing near the bar, watching us, and laughing at my expression. I turn, meeting Elijah's bright eyes. "How? When did you have time to do this?" I ask, as I take a deep breath and wipe at the few tears that have escaped.

"When you were passed out today in my bed." He kisses my forehead before adding, "I love you, Gemma Davis. I know I messed everything up and I'm sorry. Take all the time you need..."

I grab the collar of his shirt, tugging him to me for a ferocious kiss. Everyone begins cheering and whistling. We slowly pull apart, laughing at the spectacle they're making. I begin to cheer right along with them. Before, my face would heat with embarrassment, but now, I don't care. This man is mine and I want everyone to know it.

Elijah pulls me in for another kiss before we join everyone at the bar.

I get a glass of champagne and Elijah grabs a vodka on the rocks.

He clears his throat before he says, "I want to make a toast. First to Gemma, my little lovely. This dazzlingly, stunning woman dropped everything and traveled here to surprise me. Thank you for your unconditional love and support. I love you." He kisses my cheek before continuing. "To my business partner, Ty, thank you for putting up with me during this hectic time. I'm proud to share this success with you. We've only just begun. And to the rest of you, thank you for supporting both Gemma and me as we lost our minds. We appreciate you more than we can say. Cheers!"

We all clink glasses and he adds, "Now, let's make Vegas our bitch."

CHAPTER TWENTY-FIVE

GEMMA

$\mathcal{W}$e make it safely back to the docking station, thank God. Having Elijah's arms around me helped keep my mind off being elevated in the air in a clear ball that could send me to my death at any moment. I'm ecstatic to have the security of the solid ground beneath my feet.

We head into the lobby and Elijah has me tucked into his hard body as we wait for everyone else. I'm tired, but this is our last night here and my first real vacation with Elijah, so I want to make the most of it. I scan our group and notice Ty escorting Sasha to the bar. At the other end of the bar, Mia is in a deep conversation with Drew and Xander.

Sasha and Ty return a few minutes later. Ty then tells us he reserved a table at a club downstairs. I bounce a little. I'm ready for a fun night out with our crew without fighting or tension with Elijah. We trek down in the elevator, and Elijah can't keep his hands to himself. He's almost restlessly caressing me as he talks to Ty. I love that he may not even know he's doing it, but he can't help but touch me. I lean into it. I've missed his touch so much.

Ty leads us to the doorman at the front of the line and we're immediately led into the cavernous club. This place is amazing. The DJ is in the center of the club, and lights are flashing along to the beat of the music. I cover my ears as loud blasts from a horn go off. I watch as the dancefloor is sprayed with faux smoke. People going wild, dancing everywhere, on just about every flat surface, and the DJ is playing the remix to a song that was hugely popular this summer. I can already see Sasha dancing. She's going to love it here. We're escorted to our table up on the balcony level, which I'm thankful for. The dance floor is too packed for my taste.

We sit down and order our usual bottles before Sasha grabs Mia and me from our seats. We head over to the balcony's railing and look down at the writhing crowd. Sasha sways to the music. "This place is insane," she yells before horns blast, lights flash, and bubbles begin to float through the air. Our waitress returns with sparklers and our bottles. I accept a glass of champagne and take a small sip. I don't want to get drunk again today, once was enough. Elijah and I have been terrors all weekend. I want to make sure everyone else has a good time tonight. Plus, I'm high just off the thought of being alone with Elijah tonight, this champagne pales in comparison to that. I've missed his body and all the ways he uses it to bring me joy.

He must've picked up on my thirstiness because he looks up, licks his lips, and shoots me a wink. I exhale. Damn, he's so fucking hot. I motion for him to come here with a crook of my finger, and he obliges. I walk him over to the balcony railing, and we begin dancing. I press into his body, my head on his shoulder, as he bends, kissing my neck and shoulder. I sigh. I've missed his kisses. I close my eyes and angle my head away to give him better access. He bites me hard then, and I give a little yelp but he's already sucking the tender spot. I moan as his hands drift down my hips. I feel his fingers caress the bare skin at the slit in my dress.

"You know I'm going to ruin this dress when we get back to our room, right? It's been too long since I've been inside of you and this dress is between me and what's mine. I can't wait to feel you wrapped around my cock, your pussy dripping with my cum. You're in for a pounding tonight." I shiver at his words. He can light the dress on fire for all I care. I swallow and nod.

His fingers continue to creep between the hardware of my dress and his long fingers stroke my thigh, searching like heat-seeking missiles. I turn my head and he takes my mouth in a hard kiss. We're panting as we finally pull away.

I turn in his arms. "I'm counting down the minutes until I get you alone again. I can't wait to sit on your dick." He bites me again and we finally separate when we're called back to the table to take shots with everyone. I try to pace myself and drink water. This bunch together equals trouble.

We drink and dance all night, basically shutting the place down. As we head outside, Elijah and I decline the offer to go to the afterhours club or strip club Xander keeps going on about. We've already decided to haul ass back to our hotel. I need my man naked *now*.

We stare at each other from opposite sides of the elevator the entire ride up to his room. The look on his face, oh, I feel the heat down to my toes. He looks like he's starving, and he's found his feast. It's been too long since we've been together, and I feel it too. I'm ready to be devoured by him. I need his hands all over me. I want to feel the weight of his hard body pressing into me, over me, making it hard for me to breathe. Yes, I'm starving too.

We crash into his room in a tangle of roaming hands and fierce kisses. I'm up against the back of the door and Elijah did not exaggerate; he ruins my dress. He goes right for the slit and pulls, tearing it free of the hardware holding it together, and ripping it up the rest of my body. Before I can register that I'm standing before him, practically naked, he's on his knees, kissing and licking me through my thong. He pulls it to the side, and the first contact of his warm tongue almost makes my knees buckle. *Fuck.* He's murmuring words that I can't quite make out, but I can feel the vibrations tickling my skin.

"Oh, god," I moan. My chest heaves as I try to catch my breath. I love him when he's like this.

He barely pauses when he throws my leg over his shoulder, and I have to grasp his head to hold steady. I take a deep breath, hoping to extend this, because I never want it to end. I buck and moan as he licks and sucks my clit. I watch him in awe as my body chases an orgasm. I thrust into his face and at that moment, I catch what he's murmuring as he ravages me, "I love you; I love you so much. I'm so sorry. I need you. I love you." His words push me over the edge, and I cry out as an orgasm is ripped from me.

He doesn't give me any time to recover before he rises to his feet, undoes his pants, and with me wrapped around his waist, impales me. I cry out at the brutal intrusion because it hurts so good. He lifts me up and down on his cock, slamming into me each time. "You deserve this pounding. Take it and know that it's with love."

And take it, I do. It feels so good, and I'm so sensitive from the orgasm he just gave me—that I feel myself already starting to quiver and tighten around him. He must feel it, too, because he slows his thrusts. He carries me through his suite and to his bedroom before he pulls out. I feel the loss of him immediately. He finally removes my thong, my destroyed dress, and shoes. I reach out to remove his shirt so I can see his beautiful, ripped body. I lick his chest, his collarbone, and up to his neck. My ardent hands seek the warmth of his body as they touch, scratch, and pinch everything they touch. His hands are the same squeezing, kneading, twisting, and I know I'm going to be marked come morning.

I push down his pants, and he kicks off his shoes and socks. By the time he is completely naked, I'm on my knees in front of him. He steps to me and traces my lips with his cock, and I feel the wetness it leaves behind. He does that a few more times, evading my open mouth, and just as I'm about to protest, he thrusts in. I accept him, ready to give him all the pleasure he's given me. I'm sloppy in my excitement, but I know he loves it. The sloppier, the better. I look up at him, his eyes hooded, as he squeezes my face with one hand and cups the back of my head with the other. I swallow around him, and he hisses and pulls out of my mouth.

He pulls me to my feet, into a kiss, and I moan when I taste myself on his tongue. I suck his tongue and nip his lips as he lifts me and carries me to the bed. He's gentle again as he lays me down and covers my body with his. Yes, I need to feel the weight of him on top of me. It feels like nothing else. I whimper as he kisses down my body, sucking and biting my nipples. I almost jump off the bed as he pushes two fingers inside of me. I suck his tongue as he strokes me slow and deep. I start to grind into his hand, but he pulls away and withdraws his fingers, bringing them to my lips. I open my mouth, knowing what he wants. He pushes them into my mouth and bends and kisses me as I suck and lick his fingers. "Please," I whisper as he runs his nose along my jawline before kissing and sucking my neck. "Please," I say again, and I raise my hips to his.

"Since you asked nicely," he grunts as he slides into me again. I gasp and he licks my open mouth. 'I love you, baby. It feels so good to be inside you, to be home."

"I love you."

He rocks into me slowly, continuing to pepper my lips, cheeks, nose, forehead with kisses. I love it when he's like this. The mix of the sweet and dirty. He hikes one of my legs over his shoulder, and he starts to hit that spot that makes my eyes cross. "Yes, ohmygod."

He raises my other leg, cupping my ass and holding me right where he wants me. I close my eyes to block out the sight of him in full sex god mode. I want this to last, but I feel the tightening in my body. I'm going to explode any second. He licks my sweaty leg and picks up his pace. He knows I'm close and he's chasing me.

"Look at me." He reaches down, massaging my clit, and it only takes three swipes before my body detonates around him. I clench hard, my orgasm stealing my breath and my eyesight for a moment, but I feel him fighting through the tightness of my walls as his orgasm builds, his thrust long and hard. He throbs and explodes, and the force of his orgasm strengthens mine and prolongs my aftershocks.

He lowers my legs but continues to thrust into me like he doesn't want it to end either. He finally brings us chest to chest, and I bite his chin and lick his sweaty neck.

I smile up at him. "You know what? I might just keep you."

He laughs. "As if you had a choice."

I pull his face down to mine, "This is our new beginning. Our life together starts now."

He shakes his head. "Our life together started forever ago."

I'm awoken by the heat of the sun on my face and sweet kisses trailing along my neck and shoulder. Humming, I press my body back into the hardness pressed against me.

"Wake up, lovely. We have to get going soon." I hear in my ear.

I pout. "No, I need five more minutes."

"You know I can't say no to you when you give me a pouty face. I'll give you a few more minutes. Love you."

He kisses me once more and I feel him climb out of bed before I drift off again.

The smell of bacon pulls me from a deep sleep. I jump out of bed, grab a robe, and follow the smell. I squeal as I take in the breakfast spread on the dining room table. My man pats his lap and I happily oblige.

"Good morning, lovely. I have all your favorites."

I scan the table. Eggs, bacon, sausage, chicken, waffles, and hash browns. Yes, this man knows the way to my heart. I throw my arms around his neck, inhaling his scent. "Don't we have to check out soon?"

He kisses the side of my head. "Nah, I got us a late check out. After last night, I think we all need an extra hour to pull it together."

He fixes me a plate, and I happily dig in. We're both quiet as he strokes my hair as I munch on all the yummy food. After I've had my fill, I push my plate away and grab the juice he's poured me. I've missed this. Missed us. Especially how well he takes care of me. I may just be a little spoiled. I hum as he continues to kiss and stroke my hair. We need this, some time alone to reconnect. I know I still have some residual anger and hurt to work through. He pulls me in close and kisses my head again.

We head back to Chicago today. What a whirlwind trip. I came here on a mission to get my man back, and I'm returning home a victor. We have a few minutes before we need to leave for the airport and we're all meeting in the lobby soon. The guys chartered a plane, and fortunately, it has enough room for all of us. If not, I would have flown back with my girls.

We're in the casino, and I'm going to place my last bet of the trip. I'm not much of a gambler, but I usually play twenty dollars upon arrival and another twenty at departure. I'm looking for my game when Elijah clears his throat.

"I have a new fantasy for you to fulfill, Ms. Mission Promiscuous."

"Ok, what's your fantasy, handsome?"

He stops at a roulette table. "Let's place a bet. Winner takes all. On the next spin, red, you move in with me. Black, I move in with you."

I gawk at him. "You would give up your place? For me? You put so much work into it. I can't ask you to give that up for me."

"You don't have to ask. Plus, I never lose. What do you say?"

"I'm all in. Let's do this."

We turn and step up to the table to place our bets. I play my twenty dollars because I'm feeling extra lucky.

"No more bets." The roulette dealer drops the ball and time stands still as we watch it bounce around.

"Winner..."

EPILOGUE

GEMMA - THREE MONTHS LATER

I walk into our home, locking the door behind me. I moved into Elijah's two weeks after we got back from Vegas. I guess the strategy of always betting on black worked either way. He wanted me here immediately, so I was lucky to get those two weeks to get everything sorted out, and I haven't regretted it once.

We've grown so much closer, and our families couldn't be happier. I was concerned they would think we were moving too fast, but they have all been so supportive. I smile thinking about the weekends spent with each of our families.

My parents, Grey, and Brooke, all came to visit us here in Chicago. It was just like our previous trip, the boys got to reconnect, and everyone got along great. Elijah was his typically swoony self, and my entire family appreciated how well he takes care of me. They know me well enough to know I'm blissfully happy.

Then we went to visit Elijah's family in Wisconsin. His parents welcomed me with open arms, and my apprehension faded away immediately. Elijah's dad, David, is still a handsome man, with just a few wrinkles around his eyes when he smiles. I know immediately where Elijah gets his charm from and those vivid blue eyes. But it's obvious he gets everything else from his mom, Sylvia. Sylvia is gorgeous and curvy, with the same olive skin, thick, inky hair, and a welcoming energy.

Sylvia took my hand and led me through the house where she had the old photo albums we'd talked about ready for me to look through. As I sat with them and they regaled me with stories about Elijah's accomplishments and baby milestones, I felt so content. I watched him blush and duck his head as I looked at a baby picture of him in a diaper with his face covered in food. My heart flutters at his sweet face, and I know I'm meant to be here, in this moment, with him.

I was flipping through another album while everyone is talking around me, and I gasp. Everyone stops and looks at me. I look up and turn the album around to show them the pictures. Pictures of that vacation where we met. I take in his sculpted teenage body, brushing my fingers across his gorgeous face. There are two pictures of him and Grey together on the beach. I remember how much they hung out that week, how closely they bonded. But in the background of one of the pictures, I recognize my younger self sitting nearby. I'm on a lounger with my cloud of hair billowing around me, smiling big as I watched the boys, watched him.

Now it's my turn to duck my head in embarrassment, caught on camera ogling him. He takes the album from me and looks at the picture for a long moment before he brings his eyes up to mine. Reverence is so clearly written across my face in that picture, and it matches the expression I'm sporting right now. I feel exposed, but not in a bad way. Just in the way that makes me want to cry because maybe now he'll know how much I love him. How much I've always loved him. How he's been my perfect man since that week when my obsession began all those years ago.

He must see all those things in my eyes because he places the album on the table and takes my face in his hands, in front of his parents, and says, "Aw, Lovely," and he kisses me softly, "I love you, too."

His mom picked the album up and excitedly talked about how we could use this picture in our wedding slideshow. I feel my face heat, but she's made comments like this before, she says it's because Elijah's never brought a girl home, so I must be it for him. I look to Elijah, hoping he's not upset, but he just nods. "Sure, mom."

Elijah gave me a tour of the rest of the house, and of course, we ended up in his childhood bedroom. His parents were getting things together for an early dinner, so we took the time to wander around. I noted pictures of him and Ty throughout the years, mostly in different sports uniforms. He had trophies and medals from all his sporting and academic achievements displayed. I look at the posters on his walls and the books on his old desk.

I turned to him. "I wish I'd known this Elijah too."

He smiled and pulled me against him and whispered, "Thanks for coming over to help me with my homework, Gemma. How can I ever repay you?"

I quirked a brow, a little role play action?

He led me to his bed and pushed me down before dropping to his knees and lifting my dress. "My parents are downstairs, so we have to be quiet."

I snap out of the memory, shaking my head. I still can't believe he did that with his parents right downstairs. Thankfully, they never found out, and I have a great relationship with them. The holidays are right around the corner, and both our families will be spending them here with us, in our five-bedroom home. I told him this place was meant to be filled with family, especially for the holidays.

Elijah is amazing. He's given me complete control of everything. This is my favorite time of year and Elijah is on board with me going all out and getting me everything I want. He's already hired a caterer and a party planner to make my every wish come true. The decorators have done an amazing job with the house. We have multiple trees up and mistletoe throughout the house. Wreaths and lights are aplenty. I hated not decorating myself, but we've both been swamped with work and Elijah was sweet enough to surprise me.

I take a quick shower, throw on my silky pajamas, and curl up with a good book. Winters in Chicago are brutal, it's already dark outside, and it's not even 6 pm yet. Elijah should be home soon, and he said he's cooking dinner, but I can't wait to cuddle him in front of the fireplace.

Warm lips wake me sometime later. I hum, and I inhale Elijah's sexy sandalwood scent mixed with the faint scent of tomato sauce. "Dinner's ready, sleepyhead." I let him carry me downstairs, where there's soft music playing, the lights are low, and a gift bag sits on the coffee table.

"What's this?"

"Open it and find out." I drop to the floor to do just that, and he moves to grab his remote for the surround sound. As I'm unwrapping my gift, I murmur, "Something smells good."

"I decided to treat you to my world-famous lasagna tonight."

I smile softly. I do love his lasagna. Pulling back the tissue paper, I find a beautiful white negligee. "Babe, this is beautiful." I caress the silky fabric and soft lace.

"Yeah, I have plans for you tonight that involve me putting more than just my lasagna in your guts."

I make a face and burst out laughing, "Eww."

He takes my hand and pulls me to my feet. "Do you remember that game we played the first night I stayed the night at your apartment? Where we played songs that brought back an awesome memory. I want to do that again tonight. Dance with me."

I happily oblige and I walk willingly into his arms. He picks the first song, and I recognize it immediately, Rihanna's *Diamonds*.

"Babe, this is the first song we ever danced to." I smile up at him.

He smiles back softly. "I remember. It's forever on my favorite songs list. We also danced to this at Grey's wedding, the night I first told you I love you."

I pull him closer, swaying to the music. That was a magical night. A perfect night.

"Love, tonight I wanted to recreate some of our firsts, the firsts that stick out in my mind, in our love story. The first gift I ever bought you was lingerie." I smile, remembering the thong he got me after our first date. "The first time you came to my house, I cooked you lasagna. Even though we didn't get a chance to eat it." We both laugh at that. Yeah, we were pretty busy that night living out our fantasies. "Our first dance, and again that perfect night we had after the wedding. This song brings all those perfect memories to mind. Every time I hear it, my heart beats just a little bit faster for you. And tonight, I want to add yet another perfect memory to that list, and every time we hear this song, we'll be inundated with all the wonderful memories that we share." He takes a deep breath before he continues, and I feel my heart start to race out of control.

"Gemma, you are everything that is pure and sweet in this world, perfectly precious. Your spirit, your smile, shine brighter than all the diamonds or stars in the sky. My goal in life is for you to never lose it, for that smile to never leave your face. You're such a beautiful person, as much on the inside as the outside. I never knew I could feel like this, love this much, love you this hard, but you make it so easy. You make me feel like I'm 10 feet tall and I want to be the man you make me feel like forever. You make me better, stronger, kinder. Life before you was drab. My world was black and white. And you burst into it and suddenly everything was in technicolor, and *polka dots,* and I realized that was because of you. You are my happiness, my home. My life."

"I remember you said you wanted to get married one day and be happily in love and in lust with your husband, be his everything. And that love would then culminate in two, *or four,* children. I've thought about this incessantly, and I know I'm that man and the father of your children. Baby, you're already the center of my world, the center of my universe, and I choose you today, tomorrow, and forever. I was your first love. Please let me your last." He drops down to his knee and pulls out a red ring box. "I'm asking you, Gemma Cornelia Davis, will you give me the honor and the privilege of being your husband? Let me love you forever and always. Fulfill my fantasy. Marry me, baby."

He opens the ring box, but my eyes are too full of

tears to see the sparkler clearly. I drop down to my knees and take his face in my hands, "Yes! Yes, Elijah Matthew Adler, I will marry you!"

THE END

OPERATION I DO?

Sasha

Three Months Ago... Vegas

I love elephants, they are one of my favorite animals, but the one sitting on my head telling me I had too much fun last night is such a jerk. Rubbing my face, I groan as I'm hit with that drunk guilt. You know, when you wake up, and you can only remember bits and pieces of all the asshole things you did, or the embarrassing social media posts you shared. I feel instant regret at how many drinks it took to get me here because I don't remember anything and I'm just thankful I made it home safely.

Vegas does it again.

Snuggling into the delicious warmth at my back, I say a silent prayer for the comfiest bed I've ever slept in, and I just want to luxuriate in the feeling and let it soothe me back to sleep. Note to self – self, check the label, we totally need one of these.

Since I can already feel the sun against my skin as it streams through the floor-to-ceiling windows, I decide I should probably get myself together for our upcoming flight back to Chicago. Slowly opening my eyes, I squint, peering around the room, ready to beg one of my besties to close the curtains. Drunk us must have forgotten to close them last night.

My mouth shuts as my gaze wanders. This isn't my room. It's similar enough that I know I'm in the right hotel, though. Same patterned carpet and curtains, colored throws, the same neutral couch, and bright wall art, but this room is bigger, and it only has one bed. Also, this room is clean. We tore out of our room earlier, ready to hit the pool, and it looked like a tornado with shoes and clothes tossed about.

My brain finally catches up to my building panic as I scan the room again for answers. Spotting my shoes, and that's my purse over there, I breathe a little easier. Lifting the blanket, I look myself over, and I'm still in my dress from last night, even though it's up around my waist. I have a moment of panic. *Am I still wearing panties?* Groping around, I sigh in relief. *Oh, thank God.*

Wait, what is that? I rub my eyes a little, as if that will help, as I raise my hand to my face. A simple gold band adorns my ring finger on my left hand. A gold band on *that* finger.

A deep groan sounds behind me, and the sound shoots electricity through my body and goosebumps along my prickled skin. Before I can turn to look at the person with the heavenly groan, a hand lands on my thigh, lightly caressing my hip. On that hand, I spot a similar gold band on *that* finger.

Oh, fuck!

Taking a deep breath, I count to three, before turning over slowly, hoping not to wake up the giant with the huge hand with long graceful fingers. A hand I recognize, a hand that belongs to the sexiest man on the planet. A hand that is wearing a gold band that matches mine.

My eyes are squeezed shut as I turn, and when I finally work up the courage to look, gorgeous green eyes stare back at me.

"Good morning, wifey."

Wifey? Holy fuck balls.

Grab your copy on Amazon: mybook.to/OperationIDo

ALSO BY LALA MONTGOMERY

FOR KEEPS SERIES

Operation I Do?

mybook.to/OperationIDo

WILD BLOOMS SERIES

Lotus and Longing

mybook.to/LotusAndLonging

ACKNOWLEDGMENTS

Who knew writing a book would be such hard work?!
Don't answer that.

Thankfully, I had such amazing people in my
corner.

First and foremost, I want to thank my amazing
husband, Mr. Montgomery, for putting up with me.
We quickly learned I could take any conversation and
lead it back to my book. Gemma and Elijah lived rent
free in our house. Honey, you are cutest. Thank you for
spoiling me and supporting all my dreams.

Huge thanks to my number one alpha reader, my
mom, Mimi. I know those first drafts were *rough*. You
were probably too kind about how good they were.
Thanks for helping me sort through it all. I tell people
all the time that I'm probably the most confident
person in the world because you've told me my entire
life how wonderful, smart, and amazing I am. You and
dad told me I could do anything, and I believe you.
Thank you!

To the authors and book lovers that read all the
drafts of Mission Promiscuous along the way -
THANK YOU!

JJ, thank you for reading my first draft. Your

enthusiasm for this story and your supportive words helped me finish this book. I fell in love with Elijah and Gemma all over again through you.

To Beth, Hope, Kristin, Nola, Savanna, Sionna, and Vicki, thank you for taking the time to read this book. I so appreciate your guidance and feedback. Your thoughts and advice were immensely helpful and prompted me to look at this story from all the different angles. Sharing this story with you pushed me out of my comfort zone. It was stressful AF at first, but you made the entire ordeal worth it.

TL Swan, you inspired me to begin this journey. I've appreciated all of your support. THANK YOU!!

Kisses to my furbabies, Bubbies, Hendrix, and Pixy. I love you and your unconditional love, wet kisses, and cuddles.

To you, the reader, I appreciate you. Huge thank you for taking a chance on this baby author!

Lastly, I love you, dad. Thanks for not reading this!

ABOUT THE AUTHOR

Lala Montgomery was born and raised in the Midwest where basketball is life and fizzy drinks are indeed called pop.

Lala enjoys spending time with her husband and cuddling with her pups. While she is obviously a lover of reading, reality TV, and podcasts about reality TV, Lala considers herself a vodka enthusiast, a wannabe wine connoisseur, and a caftan fashion icon. Writing has always been a dream of hers, and Mission Promiscuous, her first book, is a dream come true.

Lala is sincerely thankful to everyone taking a chance on this new author.

Like my books?
https://bit.ly/LMAuthorNewsletter

Follow Me!
Facebook: @AuthorLalaMontgomery
Facebook Reader Group: bit.ly/LMFBReaderGroup
Instagram: @Author.Lala.Montgomery
TikTok: @LalaMontgomeryAuthor

Made in the USA
Monee, IL
21 June 2023